# WE ARE
# HOLDING THE
# PRESIDENT
# HOSTAGE

BOOKS BY WARREN ADLER

Twilight Child
Random Hearts
The War of the Roses
Natural Enemies
Blood Ties
The Casanova Embrace
Trans-Siberian Express
The Henderson Equation
Banquet Before Dawn
Options

*MYSTERIES*

American Quartet
American Sextet

*SHORT STORIES*

The Sunset Gang

# WE ARE HOLDING THE PRESIDENT HOSTAGE

## Warren Adler

★ ★ ★

MACMILLAN PUBLISHING COMPANY

*New York*

Macmillan Publishing Company
866 Third Avenue, New York, N.Y. 10022
Collier Macmillan Canada, Inc.

Library of Congress Cataloging-in-Publication Data
Adler, Warren.
We are holding the president hostage.
I. Title.
PS3551.D64W4 1986      813'.54      86-12616
ISBN 0-02-500390-9

Printed in the United States of America

*For Ike Pappas*

*John Dean*

"This is the sort of thing the Mafia can do. . . ."


*The President*

"That's right."


FROM THE WATERGATE TAPES

## ✯ 1 ✯

EVEN HERE, MARIA THOUGHT, A PEBBLE'S THROW FROM THE GRIMY once-ornate facade of the Egyptian Museum, the fetid stew of Cairo in July hung in the air, noxious and unhealthy. From the car she could see shimmering thermal patterns, like ghostly dervishes, whirling through the late-afternoon *falluca* traffic on the river.

Joey's rubber ball made pocking sounds against the rear deck of the Mercedes. It printed smudges in the dusty surface but left no damage, and she let him amuse himself. Her gaze drifted toward the hodgepodge of vehicles thrashing forward in the streets: ramshackle buses choked with people, trucks belching dark exhausts, cars of every vintage, donkeys pulling flatbed carts, a slow-moving river of molasses. She contemplated the impending Friday run to Alexandria. It would be a gut-wrenching punishment.

One more time she looked at her watch. Robert had told her that the schedule called for the delegation to be finished with the museum tour by four, which meant five or thereabouts, acknowledging the Egyptian penchant for defying punctuality. It was now fifteen minutes past five.

"Can't duck this one," Robert had apologized at breakfast, offering his mock-exasperated smile, mischievous under his shock of sandy hair, which made him appear so deceptively yielding and innocent. How misleading, she thought, warmed, once again, by the image. After all, hadn't he defied the vaunted all-powerful Padre? She allowed herself a private grin as a momentary picture of her father, like a bit of flotsam on the slate gray of the Nile, passed briefly on the flow of memory. Padre! Her voice could never say it, although it resonated often in her mind. He is daddy, she protested, yet again, whispering the word.

"What?" Joey asked, coming to the open window.

"Nothing, sweets."

"We'll be late, Mommy."

"Late for what?" she asked patiently.

"For a swim." Joey pouted. "You promised."

"Then I'll keep it. Even if it's dark."

"But I'm afraid of the dark, Mommy."

She was disturbed that her irritation had made her say that. Impatience and the heat, she rationalized.

"We'll make it, sweets. You'll see," she said gently, putting out her hand, ruffling his hair. He smiled and went back to the rear of the car, resuming his game.

The Assistant Secretary was a classmate from Princeton, Robert had explained with his usual bias, one of the foot soldiers who ventured into the muck of irreversible entropy, which was, specifically, modern Egypt and the Arab world in general. Robert, ever the antiquarian, often vented his contempt for the modern world using the Arab example. The visit of the Assistant Secretary had set him off that morning.

"Their entire culture is dominated by a mentality that will not rest until it gets the upper hand, which is impossible, like immortality. Yet they continue to haggle away like traders in the marketplace. They have a sweetness in them that is very attractive, but they cannot compromise."

"Are you saying we shouldn't deal with them?" Maria asked gently. She had heard the monologue before.

"Not shouldn't. Can't"

"That goes nowhere."

"Why must there always be a somewhere?" Robert asked.

"For an archaeologist, you are remarkably cynical," she said, an old refrain.

"For the daughter of the Mafia don, you are remarkably hopeful."

"I just don't believe in the sins of the fathers falling on the heads of the children. Look at me. Living proof." She had bent over and kissed his cool forehead. Painful issues, once grating and divisive, had finally reduced themselves to domestic banter, for which she was grateful.

"Someday," he replied, "somebody like me will be poking around in our rubble."

"And what will they find?"

"Artifacts and a lesson too late to learn."

It was obligatory for Americans, especially in the case of first-timers like Robert's Princeton friend, whose name was Bigelow, to view the geegaws of antiquity in the musty museum. American voluntary contributions attempted to hold back further decay, but they were sufficient only to provide for figurative sandbags to top the barricades.

Maria's husband was an exchange professor of Egyptian antiquities from Amherst doing research under a government grant. He was, therefore, frequently asked to shepherd official visitors through the museum. Normally, especially in the stifling summers, he had begged off on Fridays. Unfortunately, his Princeton connection made his attendance obligatory.

"But where is Daddy?" Joey whined, exhibiting his five-year-old petulance. He suddenly lost the rhythm of the ball, which bounced out of range and rolled along the macadam of the parking lot. The ball came to rest under a car.

"Now look what you've done," Maria said, sliding out of the driver's side and following her son to the car. Six men sat in the car's interior, which surprised her mildly since the windows were pulled up and the temperature was nearly one hundred. She tapped on the window.

"My son's ball," she said in pidgin Arabic, offering an accompaniment of miming gestures. She assumed, from the men's rough appearance, that they did not speak English. The men scowled back at her, her intrusion an obvious annoyance. Hoping that her phony smile was ingratiating, she stumbled through another awkward explanation, using her hands to illustrate the location of the ball.

The men looked at her with frigid indifference, which was baffling. Even her persistent tapping against the drawn window could not stir them. Her attention was suddenly diverted by Joey's attempt to crawl beneath the car to get at the ball. She pulled at his legs, dragging him to safety.

"Are you crazy?" she said, waving a finger in front of his nose. "They could suddenly start to move." Wouldn't put it past these hard cases, she thought.

Tamping down the momentary panic, she tapped the window again with her knuckles.

"Just move the damned car," she said, this time in English, feeling the anger rise as she mumbled to herself. "You indifferent bastards." She had absolutely no doubt that they understood her request.

The driver lifted heavy-hooded eyes and dismissed her with a wave of his hand. He was a young man with a black scraggly beard and an expression of unsmiling menace. Still, she would not be intimidated. Not the daughter of the Padre. Again she tapped on the window with her knuckles, angling them to use her wedding ring to increase the noise level.

One of the men in the back seat waved his finger at her and snarled. Another tried to wave her away. She tapped again. Arab machismo, she decided with contempt. To these stubborn asses, a woman was nothing. It stirred her rage, reinforced her female consciousness, and stiffened her resolve. She continued to tap insistently against the window.

They apparently got the message. She saw the man sitting to the right of the driver move his lips, muttering some words to the others which she could not hear. Without rolling down the window, the driver gunned the motor and moved forward by half a car's length, just enough for Joey to scoop up the ball. She waved her hand, resisting the temptation to raise her middle finger, and mimed a sarcastic thank-you to the men. She wished she could emulate her father's expression at such moments, that look which telescoped the message of harnessed hate which could strike consummate fear in those who received it.

But the men barely glanced her way. After the ball had been removed, the car was driven back into its original position.

"Hope you bastards fry," she mumbled as she grabbed Joey's hand and led him back to their car. Her anger triggered her curiosity. Why would six grown men sit in a locked car in the parking lot of the Egyptian Museum on a steaming Friday afternoon? It jogged a shard of memory. Men in cars. The image subliminally absorbed in childhood suggested that six grown men sitting in a locked automobile, watchful and waiting, ignoring heat and discomfort, were about to perform something momentous and probably violent.

In memory, she heard her father's voice admonishing her gently but firmly, "Go do your school." Or was it "Help Mama" or "Go play with your dollies"? A signal for her disappearance, an absolute order for her obedience. It meant "none of your business."

She recalled cars filled with adult men with gruff voices and odd names. Even now, the smell of them was vivid, odors of masculinity, winey, garlicky, thick with the pall of cigar smoke and masking peppermints. Always with the memory came the feel of her father's gentle hands stroking her thighs as she sat on his lap scrunched against his chest. Occasionally his lips would brush against her cheek and his breath would sing past her ear. Daddy's little girl.

The guilt of survival bubbled up inside of her. Total containment inevitably failed. Without warning, it attacked her like a sudden volcanic eruption blowing the head off her control. The men in the car had set it off, starting the endless chain of recall, the curse of memory. She railed against her brothers for stupidly making her the last sibling. Yet it was pointless to admonish two dead brothers. She was the dregs at the bottom of the pot, the only survivor of the three Padronelli children. Which put the onus on Joey, the grandson, the worshiped one, whose wiry little body throbbed with the beat of Padronelli blood.

The mystique of the blood. One would think it had been pumped directly from the veins of St. Peter himself instead of that product of a Naples slum that had been the American Padronelli, the dynastic beginning. Often she had suspected that the name itself, Padronelli, with its obvious diminutive, was his synthetic concoction, a private joke. Later, visiting Naples, she had found two columns of Padronellis in the telephone directory, which considerably dampened her suspicions.

It didn't matter, however. By then the myth was irrevocably cut into the stone of history. He was her father's father, the patrone of patrones. He had died, as befits the invulnerable, in bed, twenty years before her birth. By then the blood-encrusted mace had been passed to her own father, who embellished the throne from his Greenwich Village castle and consolidated the Kingdom, the mythical land of Mafiosa bounded by the East River, the Atlantic, the Hudson, and mysterious other liquid points in the universe.

To his everlasting credit, Robert had stood before the Padre and fought for her as if she were the lady locked in the castle turret. A lousy no-money professor with the temerity to court and win the heart of awesome daddy's little girl. "We want no part of your scummy life," he had shouted, flinging down the gauntlet in the face of the Padre's loyal pistolas.

Secretly, of course, she knew that the old bastard was delighted to have her safely ensconced in the embrace of this handsome young WASP from Boston. "Some of the boys checked the family out," the Padre had told her.

There were always some of the boys to check things out. And worse. Their house was always filled with them. No one, not herself or her mother or her brothers Gino and Mario, ever ventured into the mean streets without some of the boys within sight or earshot.

Of course they were not boys, but men like those in the locked car—malevolent, humorless, dark-eyed, and menacing, their Draconian energy held in check by the mythical power of the charismatic Padre and the mumbo-jumbo code of honor that underpinned the myth. What acts these men performed, even then, seemed outside the pale of what ordinary mortals did to survive. Doing business, the Padre called it. She was never certain what that meant, only that it was violent and rapacious.

Whatever all that Gothic energy was supposed to produce, it couldn't have been money alone. The Padronellis had lived modestly in a two-story brick house in that corner of Greenwich Village known as Little Italy.

Yet the enterprise had claimed her two older brothers and, one might speculate, her mother as well. A grieving heart also kills, she had discovered. Suddenly she shook her head, hoping the movement would dislodge the memories.

She resented the six men for having induced them, looking their way suddenly, catching the metallic glint of sunbeam on metal, another familiar image engraved in memory. Not that. Was her imagination running away with her? Go play with your dolly, she ordered herself, reaching out to once again ruffle Joey's thick sandy hair.

But the image had induced a sense of discomfort. The men in the car and all her resultant memories had taken the patience out of the exercise. She now resented her husband's reluctance to meet their time frame. Friend or no friend, his obligation was still to his family first, one of the few inherited values she had preserved.

She looked toward the museum entrance. The official caravan of three shiny Mercedes limousines with little Egyptian flags perched on their fenders waited as chauffeurs watched the entrance for emerging signs of their VIP guest. Maria assumed that the usual security types would be inside protecting their charge as he poked around the mummies and sculptures of animal-faced deities of the old Egyptian dynasties.

There was no escaping the signs of tightening security and paranoia that had gripped the government. It was no secret that the fanatic Islamic Brotherhood made life difficult for the moderate posture of the Egyptian President.

Signs of the Islamic fundamentalist tide were everywhere in the city. One could see frightening anti-Western graffiti slogans on walls and in handbills scattered on the city streets like confetti. From the American press, she read occasional stories of murders, kidnappings, and student riots, echoes of which filtered through the walls of their comfortable apartment in Cairo and their rented villa in Alexandria.

No cause for anxiety, Robert had soothed. This was Egypt not Lebanon. Americans were not being plucked off the streets or murdered in airplanes.

For her part, she managed to blithely eschew most information that contained reports of violence and bloodshed. One does not grow up as the daughter of a Mafia boss without acquiring certain protective characteristics. Think it's easy, she had asked herself ad infinitum, to be perpetually balanced on the razor's edge between pride and loathing, between profound love and dark uneasy guilt?

Robert also had the wisdom to accept the fact of the fierce mutual love between father and daughter. Maria and her father spoke frequently on the phone, an achievement in itself, considering the reliability of the Egyptian telephone system. If Joey was out on some school project, she would have to catalog his routine and the events of his young life. The Padre doted on every word. A baby tooth gone. An "A" on a test. A clever retort. Apparently the stuff of grandfatherly ecstasy.

"Mommy. When is Daddy coming?" Joey whined. His tone mirrored her own thoughts.

"Soon."

But soon didn't seem early enough and her voice lacked conviction. Joey shrugged, shook his head, and pouted. Again she looked toward the museum's entrance. Not far from the limousines, a young boy in striped pajamas squatted next to a ramshackle ice-cream cart. The boy sat staring into space, his eyes transfixed in an attitude that the Egyptians called *kayf*, staring into nothingness. She felt Joey's tug on her arm.

"Absolutely not," she said without looking at the boy. No explanation was required. Eating ice cream purchased from a street vendor was like playing Russian roulette with one's stomach.

"I have to go peepee," Joey said.

She looked down at his sweaty little face and smiled. He could, of course, have tinkled against the car's tire, a favorite habit in this part of the world. Not the grandson of the great Padre, she told herself with a pursed smile, as she grasped Joey's hand and started moving toward the museum's entrance.

# ✫ 2 ✫

AHMED FELT THE TWITCHING BEGIN IN THE LEFT SIDE OF HIS JAW. IT was a sign of extreme tension and it annoyed him to know that he could not control the visible throbbing. It gave him away, telescoped to others his anxiety, exposed his nakedness. He sat in the front seat beside the driver, sweat pouring down his cheeks and back, his eyes, behind dark glasses, alert to everything that moved near the entrance of the museum. His moist muscular thighs gripped the AK47, like a giant phallus.

At thirty-five he had become a veteran of urban warfare, skilled in hostage-taking and violent harassment. As he evolved into a professional, the need for his services had grown considerably in this long winter of discontent.

Indeed, he had never known any other season. Born in southern Lebanon of a poor Shiite family, he was barely able to read before he found himself in a PLO training camp learning the rudiments of killing. He had joined a tiny Shiite militia recruited by the PLO as an ally against Israeli attempts to control southern Lebanon. In those days, he believed the political rhetoric. He could be stirred by the rousing call of Jihad, Holy War. The lure of paradise was tantalizing.

Then the Shiites in Lebanon, buoyed by the remarkable revolution of the Ayatollah Khomeini, switched gears and the political logic was recalibrated. Paranoid over any kind of domination and authority, they began to fight the PLO. Survival considerably enhanced Ahmed's professional credentials. Soon he was fighting the hated Christians, then the Druse, then recalcitrant Shiites, depending on the ebb and flow of politics, clashing egos among the leadership, and the latest betrayal and double double cross.

Because of these spinning changes and floating alliances, Ahmed, like many others before him, concluded that the only sure loyalty was to himself. The Jihad, the driving force of Holy War, had become a matter of dubious fervor. The prospect of paradise was now seen more as a lure for young chickens than a possibility for an old fox like himself. He had discovered profit in terror.

But killing and kidnapping for profit alone, given the absence of ideology, possessed the stigma of shame. Ahmed was a man who needed the anchor of honorable intentions. He had obeyed earlier familial injunctions, had taken a wife and fathered a child. He was eighteen then and had not yet come to grips with the true nature of his sexuality. The child, who had nearly died at birth, was afflicted with a congenital heart disorder.

It was only a short journey for Ahmed to reorient his commitments. He had a new justification. Something to kill for. He had purchased the boy and his wife a villa in Jordan, with servants and the best medical care available. He did not visit him more than once or twice a year. Often, he assured himself, the boy was the only thing he truly loved. Such thoughts left him cleansed and justified.

Three scrawny men, their beards replicas of Arafat's, sat tense in the back seat of the Mercedes. The metal of their AK47's glistened with their sweat. Ahmed sat between the driver and the clean-shaven Jaber. He turned in his seat, patted his head, and gave him a reassuring wink. Sweet Jaber. A tingle in his crotch reminded him of the boy's ivory smooth body. Another easy conquest made possible by the knowledge of Arafat's predilections. A pederast, the man remained, whatever the whim of the moment, the enduring role model for disenfranchised Arab youth.

He would not, of course, have picked Jaber to be with them if he had not been absolutely assured of both his skill and his commitment. It could be said that he had handpicked the five of them primarily for their blindness, their absolute faith in the joys of martyrdom.

For this mission, the planning had been impeccable. Bigelow was an Assistant Secretary of State for the American Government, a troubleshooter on the Middle East, an emissary of the American President. The purpose of the mission, Ahmed knew, was to embarrass the Egyptian Government and its so-called moderate lackeys and illustrate its unreliability to the Americans, to move the prisoner to Lebanon and parade him in front of the cameras with all the hoopla of the usual media circus.

There was no sign of movement among the chauffeurs chatting together outside the three official limousines. The boy squatted by his ice-cream cart, looking lost in *kayf*. Ahmed knew that he was tense and alert. He would have only a minisecond to place the bomb under the rear fender of the lead car and less than that to duck away, an impossibility that had been carefully calculated. The boy's ticket to paradise was all but assured, Ahmed reflected.

The woman's annoying persistence had very nearly triggered a compulsive reaction in the men. They were also edgy with heat and expectation, their inner springs taut, which was only natural prior to an operation.

"Hide those weapons," Ahmed had snapped in time to inhibit their movement.

"Bitch," one of the men had mumbled.

"Don't open the window," Ahmed had warned.

But the woman, obviously an American, had been tenacious. Her tapping on the window had made a racket. One of the chauffeurs had squinted curiously in their direction. As Ahmed had determined by careful rehearsal, the sun's reflection on the automobile's windshield rendered them invisible from the chauffeurs' vantage. But he had not reckoned on sound.

"The ball is under your car," the woman had said, pointing. A small boy stood beside her, peering into the car.

"Better move it," Ahmed finally had ordered. The car rolled forward. The ball retrieved, the woman and her son moved back to what was undoubtedly her own car at the edge of the parking lot.

"You think she saw something?" the young man behind the wheel asked.

"We'll know soon enough," Ahmed said, looking at his watch.

"Why are they this late?" Jaber whispered. Ahmed felt his sweet breath sail past his ear.

"Maybe he is making love to a mummy," Ahmed said, deliberately facetious. These young men reveled in facetiousness. It was reassuring to them. Ahmed was getting edgy too.

He turned and looked behind him. No sign of anything amiss in the parking lot. Only the woman and her boy. Holding the boy's hand, she had begun to move toward the museum's entrance.

"What is it?" Jaber asked. "I see nothing."

Following his lead, the others had uncovered their weapons. He heard the familiar click of the AK47's safety mechanism, the prelude to death. It was now a matter of experienced judgment. Would the woman accost the chauffeurs, point to their car? He followed her with his gaze, finger on the trigger of his weapon.

She and the boy passed the chauffeurs without a word and walked quickly up the front steps. But he was not relieved. It was unusual for him to doubt his instincts, which were now giving him mixed signals.

To chase the idea of the woman from his mind, he went over the details once again. Bigelow in a phalanx of security men would proceed down the steps of the museum. As he reached the midway point, the boy would set his fuse and roll the bomb under the lead limousine. At the same time, the driver would move forward. Jaber and the others would step out of the car and spray everyone but Bigelow, who would have ducked to the ground. Then Jaber and one of the men would pick him up, throw him in the rear of their car while the other two continued to fire away. They would disable the remaining limousines and dash back into the car, which would already have begun to move. In rehearsal they could do it in twenty seconds.

In a narrow, seldom-used alley one block from the museum, behind an abandoned half-finished building, another car would be waiting. Bigelow would be transferred to the other car along with Ahmed, Jaber, and the driver. Their present car would be abandoned under the half-finished building and the others would disappear in the maze of Cairo street traffic. Quick, simple, and thorough.

At that moment the ornate doors of the museum opened. Adrenaline shot through him. But it was only the woman and the boy emerging. They started down the stairs. She was holding the boy's hand and he was jumping beside her one step at a time, a laborious process in which she indulged him with motherly patience.

Suddenly Ahmed realized that she had waylaid his attention. His concentration had strayed. Precious seconds had been lost. The phalanx had come out of the museum and was already moving swiftly down the stairs. But the boy beside his ice-cream cart had been alert. The bomb was placed.

"Now," Ahmed cried, punching the driver's upper arm. In mini-seconds the car moved forward, the rear doors opened, and the AK47's were sending their lethal message simultaneously with the blast. The lead car of the limousine caravan rose like a feather in the wind, bursting into flames.

Unfortunately, their split second of hesitation pushed the schedule awry. As expected, Bigelow was flung to the ground in a reflex action by one of his guards. But unexpectedly, he had the presence of mind to roll toward the site of the blast instead of away from it, causing the two men who were to pick him up and throw him into the rear of their car to hesitate another split second. This was just enough time for one of the dying guards to get off a round of his automatic pistol. It caught Jaber's companion in the head, spilling his brains on Jaber's shirt.

Jaber struggled for a moment trying to get a good grip on Bigelow, but Bigelow was not cooperating. And with good reason. He had been caught in the cross fire. Another man stepped forward to help Jaber, but he, too, was cut down by the guns of a surviving guard. When the last man attempted to grab Bigelow, he was blown away.

A botch, Ahmed knew almost from the first. He looked at Jaber, still struggling to bring Bigelow into their car. Suddenly the boy looked up. It was futile. Briefly their eyes met. Ahmed saw the panic and knew what it meant. Jaber, if he was not killed, would break under interrogation. Ahmed lifted the muzzle of his automatic pistol and raked the boy across the chest.

"Go," he shouted to his driver, jabbing the pistol muzzle in his ribs. The driver jammed his foot on the accelerator and the car shot forward. Then it stalled. The driver reached for the ignition key, turned it. The motor coughed hesitantly, sputtered, but did not catch. It was in that interval that Ahmed once again saw the woman and the boy. The stalled car had apparently cut off their flight to another part of the parking lot. They stood, apparently rooted to the ground by fear.

"Hello, my lovelies," Ahmed said calmly as he jumped out of the car. At that moment the sweating driver started the motor. Ahmed grabbed the woman and the boy and pulled them into the rear seat. Then calmly, as if this exhibition of his courage was necessary, he stepped slowly into the seat beside the driver. As the car disappeared around the corner, he turned to the woman and shrugged.

"An American is an American," he said.

The woman looked at him coldly. She had, he noted, recovered her arrogance.

"You won't get away with this," the woman hissed as her arm shot out. Her fist glanced off the side of his head. Calmly, he directed the pistol toward the boy's crotch.

"He'd be such a pretty little soprano," Ahmed said, watching the woman as the blood drained from her face. After a moment, she expelled a word. It sounded very much like "Daddy."

"Daddy," he said with a chuckle. "No Daddy can help you now."

# ☆ 3 ☆

AS HE HAD DONE WITH RELIGIOUS PUNCTUALITY FOR MORE THAN A quarter of a century, Salvatore Padronelli, the Padre as he was called, planted his black Thom McAn shoes beneath the table of the private back room of Luigi's Trattoria on Mulberry Street. It was located one block from his modest two-story house in which he had resided for forty years. As always, the table was covered with a crisp checkered tablecloth. On it was the usual basketed bottle of Chianti, a container of standing breadsticks, and a half dozen small tumblers. The table was round. It could seat six comfortably.

The Padre always sat with his elbows on the table, and when he was not drinking or eating, he clasped gnarled stubby fingers. His face was thin, but he was not hollow-cheeked and he did not shave more than three times a week. It was not uncommon to see his chin stubbled with spiky gray hairs. His head was bald except for wisps of fine hair that lay helter-skelter on his pate. He wore dress shirts, old white-on-white designs, the cuffs frayed, button closed to the neck, but no tie. For some reason, he rarely wore jackets that matched his pants, much to the despair of his housekeeper, Mrs. Santos.

Rosa, his late wife, had kept him neater, well-shaven and well-groomed. Yet no amount of carelessness or lack of grooming could detract from the alertness of his green eyes, penetrating and predatory. The Padre was sixty-nine years old.

Another man sat at the table with the Padre. Angelo Petinno, a narrow, small-boned man with a thin mustache and a head of thick silvery hair. He had the look of a man who eschewed sunshine and fresh air. His skin was dead white. In bygone days he would have been referred to as the Consigliari, but the Padre had decreed that such nomenclature should be avoided wherever possible. This was America. The Padre was American-born. The time had come for the organization to disassociate itself from media clichés.

As leader, a kind of chairman of the board, the Padre, of course, demanded respect, but he drew the line on reverence. He knew that his power and his ability to delegate it were essential to the organization's health. He felt uncomfortable and distrusting when people treated him like some sainted Godfather of movie legend.

Angelo Petinno, his companion at the back-room table, was known as "the Pencil." He was called that not because of his mustache but because he was always making notes in pencil on little scraps of paper. The notes were indecipherable to anyone but himself and they reflected the various decisions and decrees handed down by the Padre.

These decisions were always scrupulously carried out by the Pencil through a network of underlings. The Pencil was an organizational genius. When he wrote something down on the Padre's orders, the Padre always considered it done.

No telephone calls were ever taken in the back room of Luigi's, although there was a pay phone for private use, but only in extreme emergencies. When someone called the Padre on the pay phone, its very ring constituted a four-alarm alert. All "business" was conducted by the Pencil in a small building two blocks away on which was posted a battered sign. It read "Import-Export." The phones there were swept three times a day for government taps, which meant a constant switching of lines.

Near the back door, which Luigi had had installed on the Padre's instructions, rested a little square table. When the Padre held court, two leathery-faced men of uncertain age sat at the little table. One was Vinnie Barboza. Only behind his back did they call him "the Prune" because of the peculiarity of his facial wrinkles, especially when angered.

Seated with him was Carmine Giancana, "the Canary," a nickname based upon his resemblance to the Italian fighter Primo Canero, for those who remembered. Often he was forced to dispel

· 13 ·

the confusion about the origin of his nickname, since Canary had other connotations.

Beneath their somber suits both men carried an enforcing mechanism known as the Magnum. For nearly a decade they had had little use for them, although the weapons were always kept carefully cleaned and oiled just in case.

At a table in the main room of Luigi's sat two other men. One was Rocco Mondavano, known as "the Talker" for his penchant for silence. The Talker talked only when absolutely necessary. He was the keeper of the gate. No one could speak to the Padre without the Talker consulting first with the Padre. He was the intermediary, a good choice, since it was the economy of language that particularly endeared him to the Padre. That and his swift expertise with the razor.

The other man was Benjy Mustoni, known since he was barely thirty as "the Kid." He was the second son of Padre's lifetime friend Angelo Mustoni, deceased now for a dozen years.

The Padre had made his friend a deathbed promise, a contract of binding significance, to take Benjy under his wing. He had obeyed the promise warily. He used Benjy to deal with the new blood, usually sons and nephews of the old faithful who were scrambling to become "made" in the organization. Unfortunately for these younger men, the Padre never fully trusted anyone more than ten years younger than himself, which meant that the men close to him grew considerably grayer as time progressed.

This distrust of younger men had heightened after the death of his sons, Gino and Mario. They had been his blood heirs and they had died unnecessarily of the most potentially lethal of all terminal ailments—ambition. They had confused age with weakness, the old ways with stubbornness, the ancient methods with ignorance. Not that the Padre was an enemy of new ways of doing business.

His father had warned him that he must move with the times. This did not mean that to fulfill the terms of modernization he had to move out of his small house in Little Italy and live like a king in a palace on Park Avenue. The old neighborhood was a protected watershed where strangers came at their peril. These days he rarely went beyond its boundaries.

Perhaps the outside world had simply grown too big to understand. Perhaps men felt a need to belong to something they could touch and feel in their hearts. Perhaps such things as honor, loyalty, adventure, rebellion, and danger were more important than mere survival and safety.

The Padre's love and respect for his father had been intense. Not a day went by, even now, thirty years after the old man had died, when he did not measure his decisions against his father's. The man was, it was true, old country, his English poor, his dress sloppy, but his knowledge of men, his ability to lead and inspire were uncanny. To betray his father was inconceivable. Where had he gone wrong with his own sons?

He had warned them about dealing with heroin. It destroyed a human being's chance to survive, to fight back. Trafficking in these types of drugs went beyond the pale of legitimate plunder. His father had made that choice years before. He had reinforced these points to his sons again and again.

They had been murdered through a contract put out jointly by the black gangs of Harlem, and he had been obliged, as a solemn duty, to extract his revenge. It had been a bloody business, necessary, preordained. Step on my foot and I will cut off your head. Cut off my head and I will cut off ten of yours. It was the lesson of punishment learned at his father's knee.

He drank the first drink of the day and felt the sweet and gentle Chianti warm against his palate. The Pencil did not drink anything stronger than iced tea. Luigi waddled in from the kitchen, as he had done for twenty-five years, perspiring, wiping his chapped chunky hands on his apron.

"And how many today, my Padre?" was his invariable query.

Habit, Padre knew, was essential to firm rule. It encouraged the ritual of obedience. At that moment the Talker rose and moved into the room.

"The Chinee," he said.

The Padre nodded. Actually the Chinee, as he was called, was Japanese. The Padre quickly remembered his last name. Mr. Akito. He addressed all representatives of groups outside the family by either their formal title or mister.

A tiny, polite little man who served as the agent for their little dumping operation, the Chinee arranged with his cohorts in Japan to dump electronic equipment on American shores through the good offices of the Padre and his organization. The goods were actually shipped out of Japan for less than a quarter of their value, transshipped in mid-ocean, then moved through the organization onto the organization-controlled docks and into the so-called free marketplace.

It was enormously complex and profitable, the kind of business that the Padre favored. He enjoyed duping governments and their bureaucratic and corrupt minions. Also, he liked the Chinee, liked his solemn little rituals.

"Ah, linguini with the white," Luigi said as he rushed back to the kitchen. As the Padre's caterer, Luigi's role was never to forget a guest's favorite dish or beverage.

In the doorway stood the Chinee, bowing with exquisite grace and politeness. The Padre and the Pencil stood up, although neither returned the bow, nor was it expected. The Padre directed the Chinee to sit on a chair beside him.

"With great respect, my friend," the Chinee said, executing another smaller bow as he sat down. The Padre poured him a drink. He lifted his glass, lowered his eyes, and sipped. The Chinee's precise textbook English amused the Padre and he felt himself obliged to emulate it.

"To you as well, Mr. Akito."

"And your daughter and grandson. I wish them great bounty and good health." The Chinee emptied his glass and the Padre refilled it.

"And likewise to your wife and children."

The best wishes continued, covering their colleagues and finally themselves.

Luigi brought their food. The Padre's lunch rarely varied. Broiled fish and buttered pasta. For the Chinee, he served the linguini with white clam sauce.

It amazed the Padre to see the anomaly of this Oriental eating pasta with such skill, never a strand unraveled. After a few mouthfuls, the Chinee put down his spoon and fork and delicately wiped his lips. The Padre, who had been eating sparingly more for form's sake than from lack of appetite, soundlessly put down his knife and fork.

"We have a troublesome problem, my friend," the Chinee began. His smile never left his face.

"Troublesome?"

"Three hijackings last week," the Chinee said, still smiling, his hands serenely clasped at the edge of the table. "They have knowledge beforehand of our movements."

"Someone on the inside?"

The Chinee nodded but did not move his hands.

"You think it is at our end?" the Padre asked. This was the first consideration. The crime of betrayal was one of the first magnitude.

"I am afraid this is true."

The Padre felt his stomach congeal; the bit of fish that he had ingested seemed to expand into a hard ball. Betrayal, unfortunately, was endemic to organizations such as his. Try as he might, there was no stopping it beforehand. One could only gamble on a man's character. Only in performance, the Padre knew, within parameters that required absolute obedience to the principle of loyalty, could a man be truly tested and judged.

"Have you any ideas?" the Padre asked.

"I do."

Both knew that the Chinee would not have come to the Padre if he did not have information on the culprits. Only the Padre was allowed to make decisions on enforcement. The Chinee drew a piece of paper from his pocket. On it was written the name of the perpetrator. The act of recording the name was not merely an allegation or even an indictment. It was a guilty verdict. He passed the paper to the Padre, who, in turn, passed it to the Pencil, who recorded it on another slip of paper. Then he burned the Chinee's piece of paper in an ashtray.

Dominic Tameleo was the name of the accused. The man's dark face sprang into the Padre's mind. A friend of Benjy. With great effort he forced his features to remain serene. Another second-generation member, he sighed, hoping it did not signify that the organization was at risk. It was one of his principal fears.

The Chinee resumed eating his pasta. The Padre continued to pick at his food. But his mind was already devising a plan. Enforcement did not always mean death. Indeed, elimination sometimes was less effective than a living example.

After a long silence, the Chinee emptied his plate and cleared his palate with the Chianti. Once again the Padre filled their glasses and they toasted the health of their respective families. Nothing more needed to be said on the issue between them. Someone in the Padre's organization had breached the code of honor, the contract. This must now be dealt with.

The transaction between the Padre and the Chinee was now officially over. The moment appropriate to departure had come. They stood up. The Chinee bowed, took two steps backward, bowed again, and departed.

When he was gone, the Talker appeared once again.

"Benjy," the Padre said. The Talker nodded, his eyes closing at the same time.

The young man came in from the other room. He was handsome, slender, and wore an expensive pin-striped suit cut in an Ivy League style, a button-down white shirt with a yellow tie that picked up the flecks of yellow in his hazel eyes. He was, the Padre knew, a ladies' man, a dangerous hobby in their line of work. Nevertheless, he had promised the boy's father, and to date the boy was a "made" member. He had killed on demand with his own hands. Such an act assumed a solemn entitlement.

"Tameleo," the Padre whispered.

"Him?" Benjy said, his lip curling, his Adam's apple jumping in his throat. "No way."

"Mark him, Benjy," the Padre said.

"But I . . ." Benjy's words suggested the kind of protest that had to be dealt with quickly.

"Mark him," the Padre whispered, narrowing his green eyes, focusing on the younger man. "I want everyone who sees his face to know." Benjy flushed, accepting the assessment.

"Hell, Tameleo should be wasted and dumped. The bastard."

It was Benjy who had sponsored him. The Padre studied him. Was his indignation genuine?

"Then go down the chain and finish it," the Padre said.

This meant that everyone who touched the goods would be eliminated. Purely business, the Padre sighed. Tameleo's facial scars would mark him forever. They would be deep and ugly, but they would send the message that would cause him to live in fear for the rest of his life. His legacy, to become a living example.

Luigi came in and took away the Padre's uneaten food. He also brought him another bottle of Chianti, a peeled peach in ice water, and a knife. It was approaching late afternoon. There were still many other people to see.

As he sliced his peach, the Talker came in followed by a large rough-looking man. He was about forty, with old-fashioned stained jeans and an oil-specked khaki shirt, a size or two too small, which showed off both his enormous biceps and a hard, pooching beer gut.

"Mozak," the Talker said.

The big man stood hovering over the table, looking down at the Padre, who searched him carefully for any signs of potential violence. The two men at the table behind them also tensed. The Padre saw Mozak take in the situation. He seemed to seethe with repressed anger.

"I got no choice. That's why I come here," he said. He had one of those flat Slavic faces, with deep eyes set wide apart.

"You must sit down, Mr. Mozak," the Padre said expansively, waving toward a seat. "Have some wine."

"I stand," the big man said. "One of your guinea boys come to my place and tell me I gotta shut down my trucks 'cause I got no permission to make my airport runs. I say shit to that. I work hard, buy five trucks, and I run where I want. There's enough business at the airport for everybody."

"Come sit down," the Padre said soothingly. "No problem that cannot be worked out."

The Padre's conciliatory attitude must have taken him by surprise. He stepped forward, then stopped abruptly, as if his legs had to be suddenly commanded to cease all movement.

"Look," the Padre said. "We're talking business. Like gentlemen."

The display of camaraderie seemed to placate the man for a moment. With caution, he moved to the table and sat. He looked at the Chianti bottle, which the Padre had just lifted, and sneered.

"I don't drink that piss," he said.

The Padre put the bottle down and called for Luigi. The man ordered double whiskeys.

"Just 'cause I drink your fucking whiskey don't mean I'm gonna take orders from anyone."

"I think you misunderstood our people," the Padre said, after Luigi had swiftly brought the man his drinks. "And maybe they were a little too, you know, pushy. They meant to say they wanted to buy out your business at a handsome profit."

"Why should I sell to you? I don't need no shit from bosses," the man grunted.

The Padre, from behind his tranquil smile, assessed the man. An immigrant. Ignorant. A hard case. But even the most brutish man was entitled to his say.

"The offer wasn't good enough?" the Padre asked politely.

"I don't remember no numbers," the man muttered.

The Padre looked toward the Pencil.

"More than he would make in five years," the Pencil said.

"That's a wonderful offer," the Padre said. "You want to work your ass off? You could start something elsewhere and still have some bread in your pocket."

"Shit," Mozak sneered. He slammed the shot glass on the table as if to emphasize his defiance.

The effort to ingratiate abruptly terminated. Why were people so opposed to reality, the Padre wondered. Airport cargo was the organization's franchise at Kennedy and La Guardia. Everybody knew that.

"You got a family?" the Padre asked. The change of tone confused Mozak.

"Yeah, I gotta family."

"You're not doing right by them."

The man stood up, his heavy bovine face flushed, his hands balled into fists. Behind the Padre the two men stood up, opening their jackets, displaying their Magnums.

"I ain't afraid," Mozak said, but his courage had waned.

At that moment the pay phone rang. It was such an uncommon

happening that the Padre turned to it as if it were something human that had just made an insulting remark. But the ring was persistent. The men in the room froze, waiting for the Padre to react. He looked at the Pencil and signaled with his eyes. The Pencil rose and walked to the phone, lifting the receiver.

"Yeah," the Pencil said.

The Padre watched him.

"Who?"

"What about me?" Mozak snapped.

"I can't hear you too good," the Pencil shouted.

"I ain't afraid of you guys," Mozak said with bravado, trying to stare down the two men who had stood up. The Padre ignored him, watching the Pencil at the pay phone.

"Robert . . ." The Pencil was confused. He scratched his head. Then it dawned on him. "Robert!" He looked toward the Padre, whose heartbeat had already accelerated. The Padre stood up abruptly, rattling the table. Drops of Chianti fell on the white tablecloth.

"So what about me?" Mozak shouted.

"You?" the Padre said, shaking his head as he moved toward the outstretched receiver. "We'll fix it tomorrow," he said. "You go home."

You're finished, he thought. By tomorrow he would have no trucks left. He looked at the two men standing by the table. Without a movement of his features, the message passed between him and them. Mozak's eyes searched the faces of the men in the room, then he shrugged and stormed out, muttering under his breath.

With trepidation, the Padre took the earpiece from the Pencil. Sweat had already broken out on his back.

"Robert? This is your father-in-law," the Padre said, hearing the familiar whoosh of international long-distance.

"I didn't want you to hear it first from anyone but me," Robert began.

# ☆ 4 ☆

BIRDS. FROM WHERE SHE LAY, ONE LEG STRUNG OUT ALONG PAUL'S
bare thigh, the other at an angle that dangled one foot over the
edge of the king-sized bed, Amy Bernard saw birds. Most of them
flew, glided, or dove helter-skelter over the white hand-painted
Chinese wallpaper that her predecessor had installed in the bedroom. Some merely primped and exhibited themselves. One that
looked suspiciously like a lowly barnyard rooster pecked at the
ground near the hand-carved marble mantel. There were sound
effects, too, birdsongs from the live chorus of winged creatures
that occupied the magnolia that Andrew Jackson himself had
planted just outside their windows.

After more than three years of sleeping in this place, the painted
birds and the background songs had become reassuring, validating
as she awoke each morning, that she had, indeed, spent yet another night under the roof of the most powerful house in the land.
She raised her head and squinted at the ornate gold clock on the
mantel, more out of habit than purpose. She never could see the
numbers clearly. But the clock looked so good on the mantel. Must
be six or thereabouts, she thought. They rarely slept past six-thirty.

She raised herself on one elbow and looked at her husband. She
watched his face in repose, the features relaxed, the skin taut
against his skull.

More than three decades slipped away. He looked that much
younger when he slept, a reminder of the eager young student she
had first met at the University of Minnesota, the gangling, blond,
blue-eyed, intensely motivated competitor who she had seen for
the first time when he beat the bejesus out of all comers on the
debating team from the University of Iowa. Of all memories, this
first-time image persisted.

His eyes fluttered. He was dreaming. She frequently wondered
what his dreams were like. When she asked, he could not remember. With her finger barely touching, she traced his lips,
pursed slightly, as if he were smiling at his good fortune.

Often he told her, "I am the luckiest bastard in the world."

Her response was to tap her forehead. "Brains, too."

Also those, she told herself, drawing an imaginary line down to
his crotch, which set off erotic signals. Her arm crept around his
bare middle, fingers fluttering, brushing delicately like birds' wings
along the thatch of hair that surrounded the presidential phallus.
Just thinking that way made her giggle. Considering their life in

· 21 ·

the goldfish bowl, it was delicious to be wickedly uninhibited in private.

Paul stirred, grunted, his conscious mind still tucked away in some mysterious fog. But other parts were reacting. Certain of her own as well. The giggle flattened inside of her. It was this morning moment she cherished the most, as it always came before the giant tide of "responsibility" that would carry them off to the fantasy world of the presidential stage.

What good was power as an aphrodisiac if you never had time to harvest its rewards? she thought, sensing the feathery tickle of sensuality. This moment was the only special private unscheduled frame of time in the waking day. Or was it scheduled? Had some aide penciled in "Six to six forty-five. The President and the First Lady engage in recreational copulation." Perhaps there was a code name for it. Like Jellyroll.

Her nightgown was rolled to her waist and she slowly undulated against him, her hand growing bolder, her upper leg cradling his thigh.

"Stop faking," she whispered. "You're up."

She caressed him with growing eagerness, her sensual motions accelerating. He turned toward her and in the half-light she could see his smile and the moist glistening of the white space in his opened eyes. He snuggled against her, his hands busy, his head moving to her bosom. Her arms embraced his head, held them to her breasts as his tongue rolled over a nipple, sending thrills of expectation through her body.

So precious, she thought. There was no other way to describe this stolen moment. They rolled slightly in the big bed as she positioned herself under him in the missionary way. Middle-of-the-road in every way, she happily thought as she concentrated on the serious business of giving and taking pleasure.

"Fuck me, Mr. President," she whispered, biting his earlobe, lightly, playfully.

With her hands she directed the course of his movements, each obeying private signals that three decades of marriage had taught. Like most marriages, there wasn't a jackpot in it every time, but the act itself and its frequency gave the lie to those who said that political marriages were rocky in the sack.

Not mine. Not now. She felt it begin, somewhere deep, as if a centipede were crawling over exposed nerves. Her mind stopped looking for its source as she lifted her legs and raised her hips to meet his, concentrating on the foamy curl of the breaking wave. Then it began. For him, too.

But somewhere in the tangle of impressions a faraway sound intruded, rhythmical, urgent, the nightmare tapping of the inevitable spoiler. She removed her hands from his buttocks and put them against the sides of his head, pinning his ears, hiding the sound. Not yet, she cried, bringing his lips down to hers, waiting for the waves of primary pleasure to subside. A victory of sorts, she decided, recognizing the persistent knuckling on the bedroom door. She had beat the bastards to the punch.

"They really flew this time," she said in his ear, eyes opening to the flocks on the wallpaper.

"I heard the flapping," he said, lifting his head to focus on her face. "But you had the better view."

"Just an old-fashioned couple."

The knocking continued.

"Mr. President," a voice said.

"Go away," she whispered in his ear. "You're robbing me of afterplay."

"Meet you same time, same place tomorrow."

"A date."

"I better go," he said, disengaging from the tangle of extremities. He gave her a smacking kiss and bounded out of bed, hustling into his paisley robe. She pulled the covers up to her neck and watched him pad across the room in his bare feet and unlock the door.

She heard urgent whispers, recognized them as those of the redoubtable Bob Nickels, Paul's Chief of Staff. Then the voices moved in the direction of the office that adjoined the bedroom.

She flung away the covers, slipped out of her nightgown, and moved naked across the room. She peered into the mirror over the mantel and fluffed up her short-cropped blond hair. Not bad for two and a half score, she assured herself, patting the underside of her chin, which was still, miraculously, firm and tight.

She heard the door close. After a while, it opened again. Paul was alone. In the mirror, she saw him frown and shake his head.

"Crazies," he said, striding across the room to the windows. He drew the draperies and looked out onto the lawn. Sunlight streamed into the room, but it apparently did not brighten his mood. "Look at those godforsaken things."

She knew he meant the ugly cement globs that blocked the gates. Of all the things that annoyed him, the cement barricades were the most irritating, the ultimate symbols of the siege mentality. He continued to look out of the window, shaking his head.

"They got two more. A mother and son. Picked them off in

Cairo. Badly wounded an Assistant Secretary of State. At least they got four of the bastards. Damned cowards. Too good for them. A woman and a child, for chrissakes."

She knew the count, of course. That made twenty-four in all, an even two dozen Americans. Now the media could say "dozens." No more groping for euphemisms of exaggeration. It wasn't just the numbers. It was the paralysis, the inability to act.

"Who is it this time?"

"Everyone and no one. Islamic Jihad, a cover for every nut case in the Middle East. They got pros on the payroll now. You never know who's who and what's what." He shook his head. "Egypt is supposed to be a buddy of ours. Where the hell is their intelligence?"

"And ours?" she asked, which wasn't entirely fair, since he had told her that the CIA had it pretty well sorted out.

She had read the memos. Maybe it wasn't entirely legal, but they had resolved that problem early on. No secrets, baby. No fun sharing the triumphs if she couldn't share the frustrations and defeats. Maybe she didn't know quite everything he knew, but she did get a charge out of reading Jack Harkins' clever little memos where the real challenge came in spotting the signposts of sly manipulation.

The CIA Director's prose was impeccably subtle. But it did inform, and there were issues, terrorism and hostage-taking, among an array of thorny problems, that she was determined to be informed about. An ignorant wife, especially in her position, could be downright dangerous.

"Makes me look so damned helpless. You saw that cartoon in the *Post*. Me tied up like Gulliver while all those Lilliputians wearing khafis and sporting AK47's were climbing all over me."

"Very clever idea," Amy said. Sometimes a wisecrack might cajole him into a good humor. This time he ignored her, and she knew he was heading swiftly into a black funk.

"It's either bomb the bastards . . ." He blew air through his teeth. "Not like that Libyan tea party Reagan ordered. I mean really bomb them. Never mind where they go. Or send in the coverts. That's Harkins' broken record. Him and his damned computers."

She understood the reference. The CIA Director boasted of the best covert operation in the world, all computerized. It frightened her to think about it. And worried Paul. Once he stepped across that line, he had little control over it. She tried to deflect his thoughts from going down that path.

"A five-year-old kid. That's a new wrinkle."

"A woman, too. That's also new. To them, women aren't supposed to be worth the trouble." She sensed an element of sarcasm in her tone. She wondered if it had occurred to him.

"Don't get the female consciousness all fired up. Taking hostages supersedes gender."

"Just an indication that they're broadening the attack," she said defensively.

By the time she had retreated, his thoughts seemed to have drifted elsewhere.

Mustn't, she berated herself. Be a good First Lady, helpmate, soulmate, bedmate. It was her only job now. After three years, she was still prone to forget. She watched him as he began to dress. Unlike past Presidents, he eschewed valets, trusting to her judgment on how he should present himself to the world.

"I'll tell you what I'd like to do about it," he muttered as he paced the room, thrusting his shirt in his pants.

"I don't want to hear it," Amy said.

"It's going to come. Encourage them by doing nothing, they'll rub our noses in it."

"I suppose that's the prevailing theory."

"One of many," Paul said. He pulled a tie from the rack and showed it to her.

"Not that one," she said. He pulled another and held it up.

"The Wedgwood blue with the olive stripes."

He looked for it, found it, and began to tie it.

"Better," she said.

He put on his jacket, then turned and kissed her on the forehead, always a signal for their little good-bye ritual.

"Off to the salt mines," he said.

"Wouldn't have your job for all the tea in China."

He winked, patted her naked butt, and left the room.

When Paul had gone, she put on her robe and pressed the bedside button. In a few moments, Farmer, the family butler, would arrive with coffee and rolls. She sat down at the desk and put on her half-glasses and looked over the neatly typed sheet that outlined her chores for the day. One of them read "Preparation for the state dinner for the King of Spain."

Well, that was something, she thought with amusement. Something pleasant to look forward to. It was nearly a month away, but the planning had to be long-term and scrupulous.

The gloomy hostage business moved further from her consciousness. Entertaining royalty would be fun, all that pomp. We must do something special for the King. She had already begun to draw up a list of names when the coffee and rolls arrived.

# ★ 5 ★

THE PADRE SAT SLUMPED IN HIS CHAIR IN THE DARKENED FRONT parlor of his house. He had watched the shadows lengthen and disappear along the much-worn oriental rug, his wife's, Rosa's, favorite. He had changed nothing in the house since her death, had not removed the family pictures. Not even those of his sons who had betrayed him. Nothing ever changed the fact of family. They had died before they had married and their seed had dried out in their coffins.

"Damn," he muttered, raising his eyes to the ceiling. He poked a finger into the darkness. "You want an eye for eye. You got it."

Robert's voice on the telephone was a hammer blow. The Padre's feet became weights, as if all the blood of his body had drained downward. He had to lean against the wall for support and, for a brief moment, he was certain he had fainted, sustained upright only by the fear of showing weakness to his men.

Despite the whooshing sound in the telephone line, the Padre heard Robert's words distinctly. His first reaction, he remembered now with shame, was to direct his wrath at his son-in-law.

"Bastard. I trusted you to take care of them," he cried. "You take them to this foreign place and then you let this happen. I cut your heart out. . . ."

Then he had slammed his fist into the wall. Alarmed, Rocco and Benjy came rushing in from the main dining room.

Luigi ran in from the kitchen, wiping his hands on his apron. He was waved away by Vinnie, who had, as a misguided gesture of protection, drawn his Magnum, his face a mass of prunelike wrinkles. The Canary, imitating his colleague, had also drawn his gun in the face of this intangible enemy. But the Padre's misplaced anger quickly dissipated.

"Maria told me this did not happen in Egypt," the Padre said, trying desperately to calm himself.

"I know how you feel, Salvatore," Robert said with a sob in his throat. "I love them. They are my life."

The Padre searched himself for some lever of control. The pain seeped into his gut. The long training of reacting to crisis forced his voice to respond. Was it because of me? he thought. The organization? In Egypt? Impossible, he concluded.

"Who are these people?"

"No one knows. They say Islamic Jihad. Someone called a television station. It's madness. Maria and Joey. They've done nothing."

"They gave no reason?"

"They wanted someone else, an Assistant Secretary of State. She was waiting for me in front of the museum." His voice faltered. "They want their people released."

"What people?"

"Their own. Their brothers."

"For Maria and Joey?"

"I know, Salvatore. It makes no sense at all. It has to do with hating America."

"My Maria." The Padre swallowed hard, keeping the pain on the inside. "My grandson."

"Oh, Salvatore. I'm so sorry," Robert said.

The Padre held back his own grief.

"What can we do?" he asked hoarsely.

"There are others." Again Robert's voice faltered. "Some have been killed. Few have been released. Most of them rot. It's very cruel, Salvatore."

"If they touch one hair on her head," the Padre said. "If they put one finger on my grandson." Rage smoldered. Then an idea occurred to him. "We make a deal. Buy her out. Any money they want."

"I would do that in a minute, Salvatore. Unfortunately, it's a political thing. Our own government takes the position . . ."

Helplessness was besieging the Padre now. He felt his anger shifting to the old familiar target—governments, authority.

"Our own government. Like a helpless giant." He could hear the persistent choking in his son-in-law's voice. Then the long, statical silence as Robert fought for control. His own tears were flowing like a river of burning oil, inside himself.

"They came to me," Robert continued. "The ambassador himself. They said they would do everything possible."

"Bullshit," the Padre said. He spat on the floor, an old-country gesture of his fathers. He had not done that for many years.

"I just don't know what to say, Salvatore. I feel so helpless. I have no idea what to do next."

"Do they know where they are?"

"They say no. We must do something, Salvatore."

"We will think of something, Robert."

"I'll keep calling," Robert said. "Can I call you at home?"

"You call me anywhere."

"We'll find a way, won't we, Salvatore?"

"If there's a way to get them, we'll get them."

"Please, Salvatore."

His son-in-law's words continued to echo in his ears. He paid little attention to the darkness descending in the room. The present was too painful to accept. It was more comforting to deal with memories. They were filled with both joy and pain. But the real incurable pain was in confronting the reality of his own loneliness.

Yet all around him loyal people fawned and scraped and depended upon him. No. It was not the same. What he wanted near him, to touch, was Maria, his little girl, his grandson, Joey, Rosa, his boys.

Finally he stood up and shook himself like an old dog. When the knock came, he knew he had recovered, although the aching pain remained inside him. Mrs. Santos opened the door quietly. Even in the darkness he could imagine her sour, perpetually frowning dark face. Their relationship was based on sarcasm, mutual disdain, and absolute fealty to each other's welfare.

"You can't starve, you old goat," she croaked. Her skin was wrinkled, her body bowed. But her eyes were clear, her look fierce. Bent and wiry, she was as tough as aged leather.

"Put the light on."

She flicked the switch. Suddenly the room was bathed in light.

"The boys?" he asked.

She made a movement with her head.

"You bring me food and tell them to come in."

He waited as they filed in, filling the small room. With the exception of Benjy, they were an aging, gray, bulky-looking group. In this atmosphere, pushed close together on the couch and chairs, they looked like overripe fruit that had rolled out of its sack and rearranged itself helter-skelter in the room.

"We saw it on the television," Vinnie said, his voice gruff and rasping. "A statement from the President. He said they better stop pushin' us, that they better release our people. All of them."

"Same old shit," Benjy said. "We should go in an nuke 'em all. Crazy shits."

"They showed pictures," Angelo said, as always his pencil and pad at the ready. "Maria and the boy."

He was glad he hadn't seen them. What he needed most now was to contain his emotions.

"Did they say she was my daughter?" the Padre asked.

The men looked at each other, as if they were not quite certain what answer would please him. Finally it was Rocco who spoke.

"Nothing. We would remember."

The Padre was not sure whether the knowledge of their relationship would make Maria and Joey's situation better or worse.

Robert and Maria had gone to great pains to keep Maria's identity hidden. He had, of course, secretly disapproved. But he understood. It wouldn't have helped Robert's career if the university people knew he was married to the daughter of a so-called Mafiosa boss. It crossed his mind that, had their captors known who he was, they might have thought twice about kidnapping Maria and Joey.

"We got something in Egypt?" the Padre asked Angelo.

"They got gambling there. And junk. Girls. Not too organized. Too many cooks, too much religious shit. Lot of rackets but heavy stuff. Arms. Things like that. Lotta Sicilian connections."

"We take some of theirs, we get them back. Right, Padre?" Carmine, the Canary, said, the deep creases in his bovine face showing his concern.

"Like who?" the Padre asked gently.

"Everybody got somebody."

"We need the horses," the Padre said.

"Then we'll get 'em," Vinnie snapped.

He knew they all shared his frustration and it made him feel better to hear their talk, their bravado. Naturally, he would send word to the other American families. All would be eager to help, to return his many favors. Perhaps someone would even have an idea, a connection, the ability to make a deal. He would pay any price, of course. What were worldly goods compared to the life of his daughter and grandson?

The men stayed with him half the night, for which he was grateful. Although he had first sought seclusion, he now dreaded it. But his mind had finally begun to operate and he had ordered the Pencil to send emissaries to the families, mostly to learn about connections in the Arab world. He also ordered a sweep of all their inside contacts on the federal level. From long experience he knew that before anything could be done, information was needed. Information always came before action.

He stayed near the phone in his house, afraid he might miss a call on his way between the house and Luigi's. And, of course, he continued to make decisions for the organization. Above all, the organization must continue to operate. Any hint of faltering leadership or weakness was dangerous. Anyone taking advantage of his situation would receive swift punishment.

Stories about Maria and Joey's kidnapping appeared on television and in the papers for three days, then faded as regular fare. It surprised him that no one had, as yet, revealed their relationship to him. Maria had covered her tracks well.

Only years later did he learn that she had used another name, Panelli, when she worked as a buyer for Bloomingdale's before she was married. She had even had her own apartment on the East Side in those days. With pride, he remembered her stubbornness.

Not that she had defied him. She simply stuck to her guns.

"I am an independent woman, Daddy. Which does not mean I will ever stop loving you."

There was no way to stem the flood of memories. My little girl. He also could not stop the burning tears that flowed inside him.

Robert called with little to report. He was standing by in Cairo. The officials in Egypt, he told the Padre, were becoming increasingly annoyed by his aggressive inquiries.

"Can't even get them on the phone now," Robert said, his voice heavy with despair. "It's pretty rough, Salvatore. I go back to our apartment, see their things. God it's awful."

"I know," the Padre responded. But it was faint comfort for them both.

The Padre watched the television news, saw the President's handsome, smiling face. Once he was pictured at a dinner, his pretty wife beside him. He was telling a joke. While his daughter and grandson were locked away in some terrible hole. He had wanted to kick out the screen.

Occasionally, one of the relatives of the hostages would make a public query to the government and a spokesman from the State Department would respond that the government was doing everything it could to free the hostages. Unfortunately, the Padre had learned, everything meant nothing.

Two weeks after Maria and Joey had been taken, Robert appeared at the Padre's door looking pale and exhausted. His house in Princeton was rented and he had no desire to stay with friends.

It had been years since he had been to the Padre's home, although Maria and Joey had been frequent visitors. He did not seem too happy to be there now. Yet, inexplicably, he had brought his suitcase and the Padre understood. Maria, they both knew, would have wanted them to be together.

"The President has agreed to a meeting with all the hostage families the day after tomorrow," he announced, as if that bit of information made it all right in his own mind to be with the father-in-law he had avoided all of his married life.

"You want me to go with you?" the Padre asked, but only as a formality, since he knew the answer in advance. Robert's response was surprisingly gentle.

"I think you're entitled to go, Salvatore. I've thought about it a great deal. But I think your presence might complicate matters, maybe raise the stakes for her and Joey. No need to add a new dimension."

The Padre was not sure he agreed totally, but nodded consent. Mrs. Santos gave Robert Maria's old room upstairs and made them both dinner. They sat in the dining room saying little as they picked at their food.

"No gas in the tank. No gas in the head," Mrs. Santos said, tapping her skull, but it made little difference. Neither of them had any appetite. After dinner they sat in the front parlor. Despite their common problem, the awkwardness between them remained.

"So damned unfair," Robert said suddenly.

"He'll say nothing of value," the Padre said.

"Smile and fob us off."

The Padre shook his head in agreement.

"I could write tomorrow's script," Robert said. "He'll explain, once again, ad infinitum, the government policy of never negotiating with terrorists, never giving in to their demands. And it's going to sound perfectly logical. Except to our little group."

Robert sighed and was silent for a long time. "And how can the rest of the country dispute the logic that if you give in to terrorists you give them a blank check to take hostages again and again? He's probably right about that. I might do the same thing if I was him. But it's not his loved ones that are being victimized."

Robert banged a fist into the palm of the other hand. "But the worst part is the inability to do something. To act."

He looked toward the Padre, who shook his head. But the look began to linger, extend itself, fasten onto the Padre's face. The Padre turned to meet his gaze. It confused him at first, until he realized that the look carried a fervent appeal.

"I've not been idle, Robert."

"Do you think it's possible?"

The Padre shrugged.

"There is no knowing who to deal with. And our connections in Egypt are not good. But I'm waiting. Maybe someone will have an idea."

"You people are supposed to be more powerful than governments," Robert blurted. He checked himself, as if he had overstepped. "I know what I'm saying, Salvatore."

His voice faltered and he cleared his throat. "I just want them back, Salvatore. That's all I want. And I don't care how it's done."

He stood up and moved toward his father-in-law. "If anyone can figure out a way, it's you, Salvatore. Please. She and Joey are all we have." He knelt beside the older man and reached out a hand. The Padre took it.

"I can't make miracles, Robert," he whispered.

"Yes you can, Padre. Yes you can."

# ⋆ 6 ⋆

THE PRESIDENT AND HARKINS LEANED BACK AGAINST THE WOODEN
slatted bench. They toweled the sweat from their faces. The President liked playing tennis in the heat, despite the warnings of his doctor. He caught the eye of one of the Secret Service people who stood watching them and smiling through the grating of the metal fence. He winked acknowledgment. He had just beaten the pants off his CIA Director.

"You were lean and mean today, Mr. President," Harkins said.

"As always, you were a worthy opponent."

Amy, with her infallible instincts, had once said that his secret weapon was his passion to win and, yet, to appear indifferent. Only she knew how defeat twisted his guts inside. She had dubbed him a much better actor than Reagan. He would always be the one who got the girl.

Jack Harkins, too, loved to win, which made their matches memorable. His game revealed a great deal about the man. He had a kind of feinting junk shot. His arm would arc back for a long-angled swing, then he would cut it short, abruptly reduce its power, and send a soft floater that barely cleared the net.

Devious bastard, the President knew. But a good man to have on your side, he supposed, especially in this job. Hadn't he wanted an aggressive CIA Director? He had gotten more then he had bargained for. The intelligence boys were always tempted to make policy.

"Maybe the win will get you up for that meeting later," Harkins said.

"Trying to say you took a fall," the President responded with a touch of mock sarcasm. But the mention of the meeting took the edge off the satisfaction.

"What the hell am I going to tell those poor bastards?"

"You've got the pictures. And the letters."

Through his sources Harkins had managed to acquire photographs of some of the hostages taken in captivity and a handful of letters. Of course the letters had been carefully screened and resealed. The President hadn't liked the idea, but it was better than going in empty-handed.

"Shows that we're in touch with them," Harkins had argued.

"How the hell do I explain how I got them?"

"Say it will harm them if you revealed the source."

"Will it?"

"No more than they're already harmed."

"And do I say the others were shy and had writer's cramp?"

"Tell them it wasn't easy getting these," Harkins said.

Harkins' earlier explanation on how he had acquired the letters and photographs was, as always, laced with the copious use of the term "assets," the ultimate code word for his covert operation.

"The point is, Mr. President, that it suits their purpose to get these pictures and letters out. Keeps the pot boiling."

"Why don't they just pop them into the nearest mailbox?" the President asked.

"Because they know that by doing it this way, making you the mailman, gives them the biggest echo in the media."

"That again."

"Name of the game," Harkins said, pausing. As always, the President knew, the man would wait for just the right moment to bring up his covert solution.

"Nothing wrong with dispensing hope, I suppose," the President sighed.

To make this latest decision on meeting with the families of the hostages, he had assembled his secretaries of Defense and State, Ned Foreman, his National Security Advisor, Harkins, and two of his closest old friends and loyalists, Lou Shore, a counselor, and Bob Nickels, his Chief of Staff, along with Steve Potter, his press secretary.

It was, the President had known from the beginning, a deliberate exercise in futility. He had listened patiently to their various points of view. They were all good men, intelligent with the right instincts. An adequate military response was impossible. Above all, it could not be small. It had to be massive, specific, devastating. The Secretary of Defense had outlined the option.

But on whom would this devastation be directed? The concept of a surgical strike had pretty well been discredited a few years back by the Reagan-ordered bombing of Libya. It hadn't really helped stop the problem and it had killed an unacceptable number of civilians. The press secretary had suggested giving in to their demands by some subterfuge. Foreman got his dander up over that one. Can't do that, his National Security Advisor had interjected. Not even surreptitiously. Buckling under only encouraged more of the same. The old story. Round and round.

Harkins, as usual, got in his pitch for covert action, eliciting the usual rebuttals. No guarantees. Too vulnerable to legalities and moral strictures. And, of course, the dreaded Congressional Oversight Committee.

"We blow it, they'll be the first to scream foul," Foreman had said. Harkins had retreated. Only temporarily, the President knew.

"What about the Egyptians?" the President had asked the group. "Have they any leads as yet on the bastards that took the woman and her child?"

"They're working on it," Foreman had responded. "I wouldn't rule that out." Foreman had come from academia and his comments always seemed to come out in a superior, world-weary tone. He also looked the part, brown hair, spiky and dry, partless, his skin pallid, his eyes squinty with tension above satchel bags of fatigue.

"I would," Harkins had countered, his words clipped and cocksure. They were always biting at each other. As always, his pale blue eyes were clear behind his thin horn-rims. His face was all sharp planes, his steel-gray hair side-parted with perfect symmetry, as if it had been done with a T-square.

"We giving them support?" the President asked.

"Some," Harkins had replied. "Unfortunately, they've got a pride problem." He had paused and looked at the men's faces around the room. "And you know what pride goeth before."

Eventually they got around to the public relations aspects of the situation. Just thinking about it sometimes made the President want to puke.

"You've got to look upbeat and appear to be doing something about this," Bob Nickels had said. His Chief of Staff was a former PR man from Minneapolis. It was then that someone had come up with the mailman ploy.

"Better than ignoring it," Potter had pointed out. "Besides, some of the relatives are beginning to make odd noises in the press."

"Can you blame them?"

"That's not the issue, Mr. President."

"Then what is?"

"Four years or eight," Nickels had reminded him. On that note the meeting had broken up.

Cooled down, he and Harkins got up from the bench and headed across the White House lawn to the south entrance.

"God, I dread that meeting," the President said.

"Might be better to tell them the truth and be done with it," Harkins said. The President stopped and faced him.

"What does that mean?"

"That there's not a damned thing we can do for them."

## ★ 7 ★

AMY BERNARD TAPPED HER TEETH WITH THE EARPIECE OF HER HALF-glasses. She was mulling over the neatly typed memo that the caterers had presented to her suggesting the menu for the state dinner for the King and Queen of Spain. Her social secretary, Millicent Hartford, stood behind her, looking over her shoulder.

"*Vol-au-vent* Maryland, *gigot d'agneau aux flageolet, épinard à la crème, mousse aux concombre,*" Amy read aloud. "But it's for the King of Spain, my dear." For obvious reasons, Miss Hartford inspired in her these little antique pirouettes of language.

"The King adores French food," Miss Hartford said. "And the Queen's favorite color is yellow." Which explained the choice of yellow roses, yellow tablecloths and napkins, and the use of the dinnerware with the yellow trim.

"Will she wear a yellow ribbon?" Amy asked, knowing she would not get a smile from the impassive Miss Hartford, the quintessential snob, which was exactly why she hired her when Paul was elected. And she had bagged the real thing. Miss Hartford had, as they say, impeccable breeding. Even Amy's smart-ass needling had no apparent effect on Miss Hartford. The woman was impervious, also extremely knowledgeable and efficient, shouldering a burden that had devastated many of her predecessors.

Earlier, Amy had suggested a main dish of chicken à la king as appropriate thematically. Miss Hartford had ignored her remark completely. She made a mental note to convey the story of her suggestion to Paul, complete with Miss Hartford's grand duchess expression.

Even after three years, Amy dreaded preparations for a state dinner. The pomp and formality were just too incompatible with her Middle West pass-the-plate, meat-and-potatoes upbringing.

"And here is the seating list," Miss Hartford said, providing a white board with eighteen tables of ten simulating their placement in the State Dining Room and including a five-table spillover into the Red Room. It was Amy, over Miss Hartford's and the White House chef's objections, who had insisted that more than the usual 128 be invited. When neither of them would back down, she simply ordered all state dinners to be prepared by an outside caterer.

She knew the significance of symbols to a politician. An additional forty at a state dinner meant, somehow, that the Bernards were more open and democratic. Indeed, the very act of insistence gave her a rare sense of victory over Miss Hartford's obnoxious surety. As for the White House chef, he was quickly replaced.

From each of the circles indicating tables, rays of penciled names emanated. Amy contemplated the names, impeccably placed by Miss Hartford with an eye for protocol and a commonality of interest. Having won the the main issue, she felt she could surrender with dignity to all the others and she demurred to the superior social knowledge of Miss Hartford. In her heart, she knew, it was a Pyrrhic victory. Miss Hartford was invariably correct.

The guests, despite the claim that they came from all walks of life, were, unquestionably, the elite superachievers of America, most of whom knew their manners, which seemed to matter most to Miss Hartford.

"You seem to have thought of everything, Miss Hartford," Amy said, mentally going through her closets, waiting for the last detail to be "suggested" by her nibs.

"I do believe the white dress with the yellow sash would go well with the flower arrangements, which will have white accents."

"The one with the open back?"

"That one."

Although it did not exactly plunge, it showed just enough flesh to expose her to the judgment of that brooding man whose eyes would peer down at her from over the mantel in the State Dining Room. How could she explain to anyone, especially Miss Hartford, that Mr. Lincoln's somber gaze made her uncomfortable? She heard a sound, wondering if it was her own groan of concern.

"Yes?" Miss Hartford asked.

"Why can't . . ." she began, groping for a thought that had been nagging at her. "Why can't we throw open the doors like old Andy Jackson and greet anyone who wants to come, give them a hunk of cheese and be done with it?" She was certain she had said this many times before, the kind of statement that becomes a tradition.

Miss Hartford offered a tight smile, tilting her head as if she wore a pince-nez and was sniffing at something in the ceiling.

"Yes," she said, "President Jackson and the cheese."

Another bit of one-upmanship, Amy thought, with more amusement than contempt. Of course Miss Hartford was an expert on White House lore. Old Hickory had been given a giant wheel of cheese, which he offered to all who wished to have a chunk. Crowds arrived at the White House en masse and tore the cheese apart. It took days to scrape it off the rugs, floors, and woodwork. At times, Amy believed, if you sniffed around, you could actually still pick up the residue. Comes of living with ghosts, she had decided, and catching them doing their number was a form of private entertainment.

She and Miss Hartford were working in a little office just down the hall from her bedroom. She heard noises outside in the corridor and recognized the footfalls. She terminated the conference with Miss Hartford and went into her husband's dressing room. He was emerging from the shower.

"Win?"

"Beat his ass."

She looked at him archly. He did not reflect the win.

"So why so grim?"

"Damn meeting with those relatives," he muttered. The hostage problem was becoming a constant irritation, but he was managing it as he dealt with most problems. He had the ability to tuck things away in compartments, close their doors. Only this door refused to stay shut.

"Just be a good soldier," she said.

"That's the problem. A soldier fights." He slipped into a T-shirt and pulled it over his chest with an angry gesture. Then he slid into his pants and pulled his belt tight around his waist.

"They're looking for it," he said. "Maybe Harkins is right after all. Hell, he brags about his covert assets. Why not go in and secretly wack 'em. Nice clean surgery." He stepped into his shoes. "All this crap about violence begetting violence. Morality bullshit."

"Hate to think of what you might dub immorality," she said with a lilt, hoping to calm him.

"Point is, we let them get away with it, no one's safe. Especially us." He turned to study her face. "You think we're really safe and snug in this place with all those Secret Service guys climbing in our soup?" He waved his arms. "And those cement barricades and walk-through detectors. A determined bastard would find a way."

Alluding to that possibility genuinely alarmed her. She turned from his gaze, deliberately hiding her fear from him. Under the circumstances, she had tried to follow a routine as normal as possible. But the idea of danger was never far from her thoughts.

When Paul was a senator and they lived on Capitol Hill, he had bought her a little silver-plated .22-caliber pistol, which she had kept in a drawer next to her bed. She was alone a great deal and, although she detested the idea of it, she had not removed the gun from the house. Just in case, he had said. God forbid, she had thought. But she had kept it in its place. Worse, she had brought the pistol with her to the White House, where it had remained in the drawer next to her side of the bed, hardly a weapon to match the Secret Service battery of Uzi machine guns that surrounded them.

"Times like this you almost wish you could be a dictator," Paul said as he pulled up the knot of his tie. She knew he was trying to prepare himself mentally.

"So what would you do differently?" she asked.

"I'd blast the hell out of everyone that aids and abets these bastards. Governments, clans, financial supporters, families. Everyone."

She remained silent, letting him vent himself.

"Nixon wasn't so dumb," he mumbled.

"Nixon?"

"Remember the Watergate tapes. He used to wish he were like the Mafia. They know how to get things done."

He kissed her perfunctorily on the forehead and stormed out of the room.

# ★ 8 ★

THE PRESIDENT STOPPED BY THE OVAL OFFICE TO PICK UP THE MAIL that was to be delivered to the relatives and to review the statement he would make. He looked at his watch. Nearly three. The relatives, he knew, were already gathered in the East Room. The television cameras were set up, all the geegaws of a presidential appearance in place.

His immortal words would go out to the four corners of the world. America is a wimp, he thought, mocking himself. Sorry, folks, we've lost our cojones. Go on. Take a piece of our ass. It's up for grabs.

The Secret Service contingent was ready and waiting outside the corridor. He knew the routine, the pacing, the right moves. They wore their little lapel buttons and earpieces that plugged them in to the great orchestration known as "protecting the President."

He supposed he had upset Amy with his talk about danger. Subconsciously deliberate, he decided, regretting it. But it was easy to dispense advice about violence and morality when you were safe and snug. Or thought so.

The fact was that danger existed every second of every day. Indeed, he had been continually reminded of this situation by the head of the Secret Service contingent, Ike Fellows. No system was perfect. To press the point home, he had been shown notes, letters, transcripts of conversations, all threatening, in one way or another, to eliminate him. Whenever he exhibited the slightest bit of bravado or machismo, the material was trotted out for his perusal.

"You make them up," he had told Fellows. "Just to scare the hell out of me."

"I'm not asking you to be a believer. Just to remind you of four things." It was his standard reply and the President knew his response.

"And what are those?"

"Lincoln, McKinley, Garfield, and Kennedy."

"And Roosevelt and Reagan. The two that got away."

The reminder would invariably find its mark.

Nevertheless, he had offered a pro forma objection to the placement of cement barriers around the White House entrances and the use of walk-through security devices to check all incoming personnel, visitors, and guests.

"It's demeaning," he had protested to Fellows.

"Yes, it is," Fellows had agreed. "But less demeaning than lying on the floor showing the world the presidential innards."

Fellows knew all the stock answers and was savvy enough to spare him the "My job is to keep you alive" crap. Mostly, the President worried about Amy and the kids. Their children were both grown. They had their own lives; Tad, a stockbroker in New York, Barbara married to a doctor in Connecticut. They, too, were protected by the Secret Service. But there was some comfort in the historical fact that no presidential wife or child had ever fallen victim to either an assassin's bullet or a kidnapping.

As instructed, he moved through the corridor from the Oval Office in the direction of the East Room. Nickels met him at the corridor's entrance.

"Ready?" Nickels asked.

"Like a pig being introduced to a python." The President smirked.

"Which one are you?"

The President looked at his Chief of Staff and snorted.

"Where's Potter?" he asked, looking around for his press secretary.

"He just called, Mr. President," Nickels said. "He asked us to wait."

"Wait? I'm the President."

The little self-effacing wisecrack seemed to fall flat.

"Got a good house?" the President asked.

"Unfortunately."

"Want to switch jobs for the rest of the afternoon?"

"I would if I could, Mr. President."

And so you would, the President thought. Nickels was a good man, loyal and tough on the troops. Just the way he wanted it. They waited for a minute or so. The President began to get impatient. Then he saw him, coming across the corridor from his own office. He was walking slowly, as if the unhurrying gait was a deliberate attempt to advertise an oncoming sense of doom. He was obviously not carrying happy baggage.

"What's with you, Steve?" the President asked. For some reason, he had the impression that Potter's burden was of a personal nature.

"Jesus, Mr. President," his press secretary replied. His voice seemed to hang in his throat. The President reached out and put a hand on his shoulder.

"They've executed three of them," he whispered.

"Three. My God."

"Ruthless bastards," Nickels said.

The President leaned against the wall and shook his head.

"How can I face them?"

"They won't know until after it's over," Potter said without conviction.

"But I know," the President whispered. "Can we call it off?"

"Probably be worse," Nickels said.

"But they'll know I knew," the President said.

"Who'll tell?" Nickels replied. He turned to the Secret Service man standing a few feet from the President, just out of earshot. "No one in or out of that room until after the President is finished. All doors closed." The Secret Service man nodded and whispered hurriedly into the microphone on the inside of his wrist.

Subterfuge, the President thought with disgust. How he hated that part of it.

"We better hurry," Nickels said.

The President straightened, breathed deeply, determined to compose himself. There was no alternative but to go through with the charade, no time to debate a course of action. He strode toward the room, holding the file of letters in a manila envelope. His hands were sweating.

It did not occur to him until he reached the podium that he might be carrying letters from the dead.

# ⭐ 9 ⭐

THE PADRE SAW IT ALL ON TELEVISION. THERE WAS THE PRESIDENT handing out letters, assuring them that the government was doing everything it could, appealing for their patience, implying that negotiations were going on at this very moment. It was sickening, especially since this performance followed the disgusting exhibition of three Americans being executed by smiling masked men. The Padre stood up, furious. Something had to be done. Anything.

"This man is a fool," Vinnie said, his creased face mirroring his reaction.

"Only one way for these people," the Canary said, patting his Magnum.

But the voices were distractions. The Padre motioned for them to leave the room. When they were gone he shut off the television set and moved about, fingering the various objects that Rosa had collected over the years, a glass vase, a carved wooden figure of the Holy Mother, a Wedgwood ashtray, a miniature tea set that Maria had played with as a child. Maria! Had she or Joey been hurt? He felt impotent. He did not like the feeling.

He put a fist in his mouth and bit down hard, although not hard enough to break the skin. Sooner or later, when it suited their captors, they would kill them too. He could not stand by and let them die.

He paced the room like a caged animal. His mind was turning over at lightning speed. What would you do, Father? Had he said the words aloud? He found himself waiting for an answer. None came. All he could hear was the pounding in his head.

His head was still pounding when Robert returned.

"It was beyond belief," his son-in-law said, throwing himself into a chair.

"I saw it on television," the Padre said.

"It was definitely not a good day for the President. We got the news just as we walked out the door. An army of the press surrounded us. I felt so bad for those relatives who had to learn the truth that way. They said the President hadn't heard until after the meeting."

"Bullshit," the Padre hissed.

"Who the hell can you believe?" Robert said.

"No one. Never the authorities. They always lie."

"What does it matter?" Robert sighed. His head rolled over onto his chest, as if it was too heavy a burden for him to carry. He was silent for a long time. Then suddenly he looked up. "Salvatore. Why doesn't he meet their demands?"

"Because as soon as he agrees they will ask for more."

"How can you be sure?"

"We are dealing with people who do not know how to compromise."

He seemed suddenly vague and distracted.

"Salvatore, what would you do if you were him?"

"You would not agree with my solution."

It was more than enough of an answer to a man who did not approve of his way of life. Maria, bless her wisdom, had never forced him to justify himself in front of her husband. Maria had never needed such justification. She was a Padronelli.

Of course the Padre understood the real intent of the question. Deliberately he had let it hang in the air. But behind the facade of silence, the Padre's thoughts whirled along a spiraled track of memory. Kidnapping had once been a favorite weapon of organizations that vied for turf in the early days of the century, before a sensible method had been worked out to divide territories fairly. Men were picked up in the streets, held in obscure cellars, guarded around the clock while demands were negotiated. He remembered how his father had railed against the tactic. He had called it cowardly.

But his father had found a way to put a stop to it. His theory: Tear out the root and the limbs will fall away. The next time a man was taken, he did not negotiate with the perpetrators. He punished those who had ordered the act. And he did not stop there. He punished their families, their friends, their sympathizers. He also punished their property and their possessions. Homes were blown up, businesses burned and robbed. He was indiscriminate, ruthless, swift, and sure. Blood ran in the streets. The innocent along with the guilty. And it stopped kidnapping as a tactic against the Padronelli family.

How could Salvatore Padronelli possibly explain such actions to his son-in-law? More than once, in his courtship days, Robert had arrogantly pointed out to the Padre that acts of murder for revenge or coercion were characteristics of the jungle. The Padre had not argued, although to him it was a total confusion of attributes. In the jungle, revenge was unknown and animals murdered only for nourishment, rarely for ascendancy. Compared to humans, the jungle beast was benign.

After a long silence, Robert again asked:

"So what would you do, Salvatore?"

"I would use my power," the Padre said, hoping that all the suggested implications of this comment would suffice.

"How?"

He studied his son-in-law, who met his gaze. His eyes seemed feverish, intense.

"Power is no good unless it is used," the Padre said. "I would go against all who made this action possible."

"Then why doesn't he do that?"

"You ask me that? You of all people."

Robert was becoming more agitated. He stood up and banged a fist into his palm. "He must know who they are, who finances them, what countries give them sanctuary. He has information."

"Of course."

"Then why doesn't he do something?"

The Padre shrugged. In his mind, he had already put himself in the President's place, assuming the characteristics of leadership and the various options that might be available to such a powerful man. Like him, the President was a leader. He had men who obeyed him. Why had he not used them? The question rolled through his mind like thunder.

"Surely, someone at the meeting must have asked him?"

"One person did. An old man whose son was one of the hostages. The President answered him." He had grown thoughtful. "If you're a civilized country, the President said, then you can't become as ruthless and uncivilized as your adversaries."

"And did this answer satisfy you?"

He shook his head vigorously in the negative.

"It satisfied none of us."

"You want justice," the Padre said.

"I want my wife and child."

"With this President we will never get them back."

Robert looked at his father-in-law with horror.

The Padre watched his son-in-law. He empathized with his pain. He lifted his hand, palm upward, making a five-pronged claw out of his fingers. The gesture, he knew, would appear obscene to his son-in-law.

"Only if we put his cojones in here." He moved his fingers together and slowly brought them together.

Robert's eyes narrowed as they focused on his father-in-law's closed fist.

"Whose?"

"The President's."

"And just how would you get them there?" Robert asked.

"There is always a way," the Padre said.

# ✫ 10 ✫

FROM WHERE SHE SAT ON A LITTLE WOODEN STOOL CHAINED TO A
radiator, Maria could see Joey. A chain had been attached around
his waist with the lead attached to another radiator at the other
end of the room. Beside her was a pail, which both she and Joey
used as a toilet. It was awful, dehumanizing. And it stank.

They were in a room with high ceilings and windows that looked
out on what must have been a garden. It was now totally over-
grown with high weeds, which concealed almost all of the view. But
Maria could tell the time of day by the degree of light that managed to seep through the foliage.

Her resilience amazed her, although she worried about Joey,
who had grown morose by his confinement. Yet she had derived
strength from trying to keep up his spirits. Mostly, she made up
long stories from her memory. She was, in effect, reliving her life,
creating entertainment for her son from the events of her past.

Maria was surprised at the interest it engendered in her son and
the degree to which it kept her revitalized and able to cope with
the physical discomforts of this cruel confinement. It struck her as
a miracle that she had alighted on this idea. We humans are resourceful little suckers, she told herself now, although she had
been paralyzed with fright when the man had first fastened her to
the radiator.

"Not the boy. Please," she had begged.

He had smiled and chucked her under the chin.

"Nothing to it." He had looked around the room. "We will feed
you well." With a thick hand, on which tufts of thick black hair
grew along the ridges of his fingers, he tousled the boy's hair.

"You want to play, little boy?" the man said with surprising gen-
tleness. Joey shrank from the man, cowering against the wall.

"I want my daddy," Joey whispered.

"But you have your mommy," the man smirked.

"Leave my child alone! Can't you see he's upset?" Maria shouted.

She had an urge to spit in the man's face, kick him in the testi-
cles. He had blindfolded them both, covered them with canvas and
made them lie on the floor of the rear seat. They had driven for
what seemed like days, although, after the blindfolds had been
removed, she had noted that only three hours had elapsed since
they had been kidnapped.

She heard voices of other men in the house, which seemed large
and smelled musty and old. Her nostrils picked up the fetid smell

of moisture and she decided that they were somewhere close to the Nile. Unfortunately, her Arabic was spotty and she was not able to understand some of the words that, at times, could be heard clearly.

It took Maria some time to make an intelligent assessment of the rhythm of life that went on around them. Meals came at regular intervals, giving her a time frame to adhere to. They were brought by a fat woman wearing a galabia. She also wore a veil and smelled putrid, like rotting fish.

"I hate this food, Mommy," Joey said as he spat it back into his plate.

"You must eat it, sweets."

He would try again. Sometimes he gagged and retched. Finally, he began to keep it down.

"That's a good boy," she said with encouragement.

"I want to go home."

"I know, sweets. Soon. I promise."

In a few days, she got somewhat used to the rhythm. They gave them both sleeping bags, which they spread out on the floor near the radiators. The most pressing problem was being able to sleep with the chain, but soon that, too, was compensated for by some mysterious inner mechanism. It was this same mechanism that goaded her senses, awakening in her an alertness that she had never known.

The worst part was not being able to touch her son. Even when they both stretched as far as they could, there was still a man's length between them.

"Make believe we're touching, Joey. Close your eyes and imagine that our fingers are entwining. Do that."

She watched him close his eyes and stretch his small arm as far as he could reach.

"Do you feel my hand?"

"Yes, Mommy."

"Is it warm or cool?"

"It is cool."

"Shall I tell you a story?"

"Tell me about when you were a little girl."

It was essential to keep the mind going. She was proud of her son.

"I love you, Joey," she said often.

"And I love you, Mommy."

In the middle of the day it grew very hot in the room. Occasionally the man who had kidnapped them, the one with the ridges of black hairs on his fingers, would come in and squat down near them, but just out of reach. Sometimes he smoked a fat cigar, blowing the smoke out of his nostrils and spitting great wads of brown saliva on the floor beside him.

"Why are you doing this to us?" she would ask.

"Because you are a great prize," he would say.

She wondered if he knew the identity of her father, but she declined to tell him. In the back of her mind, her father represented the ultimate hope. To him the concept of family was far more important than the concept of God. Even at her most desperate, this was the primary thought that kept her spirits up.

"Why?" she had asked cautiously.

"Americans are sentimental about women and children," he said. "It turns out that this little accident may be what you call the straw that broke the camel's back. Your President is against the wall. He will have to negotiate."

"Never," she said.

It seemed a reflex. Negotiate what, she wondered. But she would not give him the satisfaction of her ignorance. As she sat there, she memorized him. She did not want his face to escape her mind. A day would come when she would exact her revenge. I am my father's daughter, she told herself. Robert is wrong. His morality is an illusion. There is only one law, one rule, one unalterable fact of life. Survival.

"The least you could do is release the boy. It is terrible to make war on children," Maria scolded him.

"Children always suffer most in a war," he replied coolly.

"It is not necessary. I beg of you."

"At least you are together," he interrupted. "I could easily separate you." His words found their mark, and she felt the paralyzing effect of her fear.

After about a week, the fat woman came in carrying a bucket of warm soapy water and a scrap of towel. Maria stripped down and began to wash herself. The fat woman stripped the boy and began to wash him. As they bathed, the man with the hairy fingers came in and watched.

"What I like most about this place is the privacy," she said. With an effort of will, she tried to ignore his gaze, washing herself as if she were alone in the shower. Whatever is done to me, she vowed, I will show him my dignity. She continued to bathe, ignoring his presence. She forced herself to remember her feelings, to record its awfulness in her mind.

The smell of vengeance, she assured herself, is pungent, like smelling salts. It will keep me from flagging. She made resolutions to herself, folding them inside her memory. Her father would do that. She wondered if she could reach him through a massive effort of will, across oceans and vast spaces. Daddy, your little girl is holding on. And your grandson is showing much courage.

As she washed, she stared at her tormentor. Let's see who blinks first. She washed her womanly parts, deliberately, minutely. You do not exist, her eyes told him. His gaze drifted from her to the boy. She wondered if he was deliberately showing her his contempt. Then he sent the fat woman away and knelt before the boy.

"He is a good-looking young man," he said. He kneeled down and smiled at Joey.

"Would you like me to wash you, little fellow?"

He took the bit of towel and slowly moved it along the boy's skin, pausing just below his midsection.

Joey threw his mother a frightened glance.

"Leave him alone, you bastard," she cried.

He looked at her and shook his head in mock sadness.

"He is such a juicy little morsel."

She knew that the perverse demonstration of his aberration was to show his power over her, to diminish her will. There was no question about its effect. It was exactly the right button to push, worse than a knife brandished across the boy's throat. At least, in that gesture, there was some dignity. When he threw down the piece of towel and left the room, she was relieved, but he had shown his mastery, illustrated his contempt. The woman returned and dressed the boy.

Later, after she had told her son a story, she urged him to sleep.

"Imagine I am kissing you, my darling."

"I am, Mommy."

"Are my lips cool?"

"Very cool and very soft."

"I love you, Joey."

"I love you, Mommy."

She must have drifted just beneath the surface of consciousness. A wave of thunder seemed to engulf her. She heard heavy footsteps on cement, then smelled sour breath as she was man-handled. Someone was unchaining her. She heard the metal clink heavily as it fell to a hard surface.

"Joey," she screamed.

A voice she recognized as the man with the hairy fingers de-manded silence. A hand pinched her arm as she was jolted forward.

"Mommy."

She heard her son's panicked voice and somewhere in the distance a coughing motor. The pitch darkness confused her sense of time and place.

"Quickly," the man's voice said, an urgent whisper.

She felt herself pulled forward as if someone wanted to tear her arms out of their sockets. The pain jolted her. Daddy, she cried in her heart.

Save us.

## ★ 11 ★

THE PRESIDENT PUT HIS FEET UP ON THE DESK AND LEANED BACK TO the full extent of the swivel so that his eyes could see how cleverly the low relief of the presidential seal had been worked into the white ceiling with its trim of dental work. Was this the power and the glory?

It was a question he asked himself often. From the very moment when he knew that the presidency belonged to him, his elation had deflated. Suddenly he was frightened. It had taken him all of that election night to understand the sensation. He and Amy had clung to each other in their own bed back home, as if the touch of mutual flesh was necessary to validate reality.

Just suppose when he got there on top of the mountain, sitting behind his desk in the Oval Office, finger on the trigger of a holocaust, responsible for the preservation of the living world, protector of the concept of human rights, of a free people, of representative government, of the Judeo-Christian value system, that he suddenly discovered that he was ineffective, unsure, unwise, inadequate.

"No way."

It was a chorus of protest, echoing and reechoing in his mind. In that chorus were the raised voices of his cheerleaders. His parents, his grandparents, his wife, his children, his teachers, his teammates, his friends. It was his secret assumption that, long ago, perhaps at the moment of his conception, he had been marked and registered for high purpose. It was even embarrassing sometimes to hear the echo of such a presumption in his own mind.

And yet the evidence was inescapable. Paul Bernard was, indeed, chosen, anointed. Then why the hell was it getting harder and harder to hear the chorus of voices? Where the hell had all the cheerleaders gone?

Suddenly he sat bolt upright in his chair and looked across the room to the portrait of George Washington in his full-dress uniform. It had been painted by Charles Wilson Peale and was said to be the only full-sized portrait done of Washington from life. The father of our country. Had someone left it there to mock him?

"What would you do, wise guy?" he said aloud, actually waiting for an answer. "Avoid foreign entanglements, you say? Good advice, George. Send Martha my best."

He hadn't seen his secretary, Barbara Higgins, come in. Looking up, he blushed. His gaze moved to the tall clock. In fact, the hands on the clock had dominated his life all day. He had signed three important bills, taken the usual picture with the congressional leadership, given away the usual quota of pens, had a long meeting with the Secretary of Defense, posed with the poster girl for Juvenile Diabetes, made a round robin of calls to senators pushing his export bill, had a cheese sandwich and a Coke at his desk, both of which were sending back reminders. But it was that damned clock, that relentless tick-tock. Harkins had assured him that he would hear by two at the latest. Well, it was after two.

"Mr. Harkins and Mr. Foreman are waiting in the outer room, Mr. President."

"Well then . . ." He made a waving motion and his secretary scurried out.

He rose to move to one of the wing chairs in front of the mantel while the CIA Director and Foreman sat down together on opposite couches. He read the news in their faces.

"Damn," the President muttered.

"They had the house staked out," Harkins said. "They were dead sure. So we let them have it all. They were bitching about our interference. You remember what happened that last time when we offered to go in with them in Malta. Hell, it was a simple house assault. Nothing more."

The President tapped his fingers on the arm of a chair. The damned thing was bedeviling him. He felt a stab of pain in his midsection and popped an antacid in his mouth. The recovery of the woman and her child would have bought him a temporary reprieve. He had even discussed it at length with the Egyptian President, that frightened fool. They were sinking billions into the Egyptian pit. What the hell were they getting for their money?

"So let's have it straight," the President said.

"They went in on schedule," Harkins said. "Object was to move in, get the woman and her kid, and, if possible, get the hostage-takers alive, parade them in front of the cameras. A real glory scene. They had all the backup needed. Helicopters. The works. Only when they got there, the bastards had flown the coop."

"How come?"

"Must have been an inside tip," the CIA Director said.

"They've got a massive search going," his National Security Advisor said lamely.

"The Egyptians couldn't find an elephant in a hog pond," the President said. The antacid hadn't started to work and the pain was now getting him just below the heart. It occurred to him suddenly that maybe he was having a heart attack. Then he belched and the pain disappeared. No such luck, he told himself.

"Their people assure me—" Foreman began.

"Their people are full of shit."

"Unfortunately, they're also stupid. They were so sure, they invited media," Harkins said. "Then they tried to put a cap on it, which only made the media more determined to get a story out. Any story. With them, they love failure better than success. By evening it will be spread over the tube."

"Another needle in Uncle's rump," the President said. He stood up suddenly, as if he felt the physical pain in exactly that part of his own anatomy. Then he began to walk aimlessly around the office, skirting the couches, over the pale gold oval rug. He secretly avoided stepping on the turquoise rosettes, as if they were cow pats, like a superstitious child. Except that disaster had already struck. He looked out at the Rose Garden through the high windows, a peaceful scene, tranquil. It did not calm his agitation.

"With friends like that . . ." he began, then swallowed the cliché.

"It's not fatal, Mr. President," Foreman said. "It's not our blunder."

"What's the truth got to do with it," the President said. "Name of the game is perception. Guilt by association. Only one Teflon President a century."

He turned away from the window and looked down at the forest of family pictures on the little table behind his desk. Amy and the kids. His mother and dad, long dead. Mom, he thought, then shrugged away the image, suddenly remembering himself as a small boy hiding his head in her apron, her sweet dough-smelling starchy apron.

"Is it a good time to bring it up?" Harkins asked.

"Oh Jesus," the President said. He turned away from the window and slipped into the chair behind his desk.

"It's not exactly another Iran," Foreman said. "Don't let it get out of proportion."

He rifled through his desk drawer and pulled out a sheaf of papers. Lifting it, he waved it at the two men.

"Polls, gentlemen." He slapped them on his desk. "If the vote was today, I wouldn't be elected dogcatcher. Imagine what it will be tomorrow." Again he stood up. With the tips of his fingers, he balanced himself on the surface of his desk.

"Listen. We've got one helluva prosperous country out there. We're rolling in dough. Incomes are up. Unemployment is down. We're fat and happy."

He sucked in a deep breath in an effort to slow down his accelerating agitation. "All that mean anything? Hell no. The box score shows an indecisive, cowardly man chasing phantoms. We're talking about only twenty-one American hostages. But it's not the numbers. It's that this yo-yo who runs the most powerful country on earth can't come up with a way to stop our people from getting hijacked and free them when they do. It's the pimple on your ass that always hurts the most." He stopped in mid-sentence, spent.

It was futile, he knew, to berate the wind. Simple explanation, he decided. His luck was running out.

"Well then, why not let me excise that pimple?" Harkins asked.

The telephone rang at his desk. He looked at his watch. He was scheduled for a meeting with his Chief of Staff and his domestic affairs counselor. He picked up the phone, turning his eyes away from Harkins' hopeful gaze. No. Not now, he told himself. Never.

"In a minute," he said, thankful that he could get on to another subject. Oddly, the men on the couches did not move. They exchanged troubled glances. There was something more, the President speculated, something that neither of them wanted to talk about.

"Why don't you toss a coin?" the President asked.

"We already did," Harkins said. "I won. I got to tell you the good news."

"Well?"

"The mother and her boy are both well," Harkins replied.

"So where's the punch line?" the President asked.

"They're in Lebanon," Foreman said.

# ✴ 12 ✴

EVEN WHEN HE STOOD UP AND STRETCHED HIS ARM, GIUSEPPE CAR-
lotti's shaking fingers could not touch every point of the White
House floor plan that required illustration. He was a small round
man with a short narrow mustache, slick black hair, and tiny mouse
eyes that blinked continuously, a condition that was obviously
greatly aggravated by his present state of extreme nervousness. It
was quite obvious that this was not his choice of an ideal situation.

"The pantry is here," he said, pointing to the plan. "But the food
comes up from the floor below. What we do there is assemble, then
we move it to the pantry, then we bring it through the door and
serve. It is not an efficient way. Even so, everything must be timed
precisely."

The Padre studied the plan silently. The others waited for his
reaction. Robert seemed to concentrate on the plan so intently that
his eyeglasses fogged. He took them off and wiped them with a bit
of tissue.

The Padre nodded and stroked his chin. Like a magnifying glass
that gathers the rays of the sun and focuses down to a single
pinprick of intense heat, the Padre had thought of nothing else for
the past week. The idea had germinated, bloomed, and flowered.

Events had transformed a once preposterous idea into a possibility. Everyone and everything was vulnerable. This was the axiom of his life. Nothing could be foreclosed if one's purpose was
single-minded. And anxiety was a forceful stimulant.

The killing of the three hostages, the unsuccessful storming of
the villa by the Egyptians, the announcement that Maria and Joey
were in Lebanon, all events that had hastened his decision, made
action essential. Of all things, the pain of inaction was unbearable.
He felt like a conspirator in his daughter and grandson's agony.

"There is no choice, Robert," he had told his son-in-law. Nor had
he asked for his approval.

"I won't presume to tell you your business, Salvatore," Robert
had said.

Certain decisions, once made, were irrevocable. This one would
take every drop of his concentration, his friendships, alliances, and
experience. Above all, he had complete faith in the reliability and
efficiency of the network of families and their various and diverse
interlocking relationships.

Tongue to tongue, mind to mind, the system radiated outward,
a giant eye fixing on selective targets stashed in crevices every-

where. The vast extended family, knit by blood, obligation, fear, and, above all, honor, would spit out the needed ingredients from its great maw. This, in his mind, would be the ultimate test for the organization. Like the blood of his father, he knew it could not fail him.

Giuseppe Carlotti was an old marker, like all the others, waiting to be called. He was a cousin of Bernotti, brother of Connie, who had married an uncle of Vincent Moroni, son of his father's trusted capo Leonardo, whose family had been supported after Leonardo had been gunned down in a West Side alley.

Old family markers were better than gold, currency waiting willingly for the moment when the debt would be called. They were irrevocable. New generations had to assume payment. Long lists of such obligations were committed to memory, handed down from father to son, uncle to nephew, brother to brother, down through the generations on the river of blood. No questions asked. To renege was a high crime, demanding a punishment that was equal in retribution for that meted out by betrayal. It was simply a matter of honor.

The technical aspects of getting into the White House became moot the more the Padre explored them. He believed, as a matter of principle, that all security precautions created by the authorities could be breached by flaws both human and mechanical.

Inquiries among people who made a living out of foiling such technology had come up with an easy method of getting weapons through the technological barrier. The weapon would be liquid explosives carried as a kind of clothes lining in flat plastic containers that followed the body contours.

Metal detectors simply could not pick up liquid explosives, of which there were a number of common compounds. The most reliable consisted of that old standby, pure nitroglycerin, which could be exploded on impact.

Of course the carrier of these weapons would also be demolished, but that was a mere technicality. In the context of the White House, and specifically the President, the actual use of any weapon by an interloper meant automatic death. In this case, if the liquid explosives chosen by the Padre for this job were detonated, everyone within a radius of twenty feet would be also killed.

Such a possibility had to be the ultimate nightmare for anyone in the business of protecting life and limb. Naturally, the plan's effectiveness as a persuader depended on the perception of the protectors. The Padre had to be able to convince the Secret Service that he and his men were willing to die in order to save the lives of the Padre's daughter and grandson.

The Padre had absolutely no doubts about the men he had chosen to accompany him.

"Not you, Robert," he had told his son-in-law.

"But I must," he had responded. "She is my wife. Joey is my child."

"And if we die?"

"Am I not worthy to risk my life for my loved ones?" Robert asked.

"That's ridiculous."

"Then you don't trust me."

"That is not the question," the old man replied. "She will need someone to be here when she comes home."

"But she would never forgive herself if you died because of her. The others as well."

"And would she forgive you if you died there? Would Joey forgive you?"

Robert did not respond, although the Padre knew he had not provided the last word.

There was an even more important question: How can four men get inside the White House and come within the required lethal proximity to the President of the United States?

Giuseppe Carlotti, his fear at war with his reluctance, was telling them how. They were sitting around the table in the back room of Luigi's restaurant. If Giuseppe suspected the real motives behind the rapt attention he was shown by his audience, he did not offer a clue. In fact, his avoidance of the subject was palpable.

"I'm just a caterer," he told them repeatedly.

"And we are just students of architecture," the Padre said, if only to lighten the somber mood. It was understandable. There had to be something fatalistic about the atmosphere. It was not simply a matter of danger or courage. What the Padre had proposed would try the logic of even the most loyal and committed. One had to suspend the traditional judgments just to consider the possibility.

Nor was he afraid to broach the unthinkable. Which was that this idea could turn out to be a suicide mission of epic proportions. But life, the Padre knew, was a suicide mission.

Of all things, death itself could never be cheated. He saw himself in a race, trying to catch up with the man with the scythe who was chasing his daughter and grandson. The President's present course could result only in the death of his daughter and grandson. Moreover, the Padre knew these terrorists were criminals and that the criminal mind would respond only to a stimuli outside the President's experience and inclination.

"I don't want to know from nothing," Carlotti was saying, determined, despite the information he was providing, to prove his neutrality. "I only know how we serve the meals."

The Padre nodded, an obvious gesture of absolution designed to soothe the agitated little man. It didn't.

"All I do is cater. I work hard. I build a good business. My partner and me, we do all the good parties in Washington. They know that when you call Carlotti and Mills, they have the best. What you do here is your business. So I lose the account. That's okay. It's a showpiece business. No big money in it. Prestige. That's all I get."

He seemed like a butterfly struggling to disimpale himself from a pin, not quite understanding that all his flapping was useless.

"Where does the President sit?" the Padre asked.

Carlotti frowned, glancing sharply at the Padre. If he was inclined to protest, it was for the briefest moment.

"Usually here. In the table directly in front of the mantel. Under the Lincoln picture. With his back to it. He'll have the Queen on his right." He pointed a stubby finger at the plan.

"And the First Lady?"

"At the next table. She sits facing the President. The King of Spain will be on her right. They are the only two tables of eight."

The Padre concentrated on the plans. He noted two small elevators and a staircase. He pointed to an elevator next to a staircase. "Does this go to the second floor?" The Padre removed the first-floor plan. Under it was the second-floor plan. The problem was that there was no vouching for the accuracy of these plans. There could be hidden corridors, dead ends.

"I don't know." Carlotti shrugged.

"You've never been upstairs? To where they live?"

"Never."

Somehow the Padre was not convinced.

"Just to the First Lady's office," Carlotti added finally.

"And where is that?"

The caterer pointed to a room on the second floor.

"None of the others?" The Padre had pointed to the rooms on the west side of the house, the living quarters. There, he had decided. Carlotti shook his head.

"You went up on the elevator or the stairs?"

"The front stairs." He pointed. "Up this circular staircase."

"But these back stairs go up too."

Carlotti looked around helplessly.

"I was there only that one time I was in her office. This area I know." He pointed to the State Dining Room and the pantry area. "And the kitchen below."

The Padre looked directly at him. He hesitated and replaced the top plan. They had been enlarged from a book on the White House taken out of the public library.

"How many men does it take to serve the meal?" the Padre asked gently.

Carlotti brushed away droplets of sweat that had gathered on his upper lip. Some rolled onto his mustache.

"In the front, eighteen waiters, one to a table. And remember, there are four tables in the Red Room. So four more makes twenty-two. And three bartenders at three stations." He pointed. "Here. Here and here. They come off the receiving line and get a drink. At dinner we serve the wine. Three kinds. White, red, and champagne for the toasts. Everything is served French style."

"And the Secret Service men? Where are they?"

"Everywhere?"

"Like where?"

"In the corners, I think. I don't watch them."

"Are they in the dining rooms during the meal?"

"Yes."

"How many?"

Carlotti thought for a moment. Above all, he seemed to know that he must not appear evasive.

"Six, maybe. But they are also in the other rooms."

"All told then?"

"A dozen, maybe. I don't count. They are very clever in the way they do this. They are all connected with these things in their ears and microphones that come out of their cuffs. You can barely see them."

"And they are armed?"

"Of course." Carlotti seemed to betray a more than casual curiosity about this point. "Uzis under their jackets. They are also clever in the way they are concealed." Suddenly Carlotti showed some hopefulness. "There are all sorts of secret things they have."

"Like what?"

"I'm not sure. I heard."

The Padre rubbed his chin. He knew he would not get much more information from this man. To work, his plan must depend primarily on persuading the Secret Service that he and his men were walking bombs. If the Secret Service failed to believe this, then the plan would collapse. It must appear fatal for the President to resist. And the attack must come as a complete surprise.

"Giuseppe," the Padre asked, offering a smile. "This food you serve. It is good?"

"The best."

"And the service, the waiters?"

He paused and seemed to puff up with pride, as if he were pitching a prospective client. "My waiters are all Europe-trained. No finer in the city. White gloves. Immaculate. The works. I resisted all their efforts to have me use the staff butlers. The White House people are cheap as hell. But they want the best and I give it to them. So I lose money. It's a calling card. I know my business."

The Padre nodded and offered a wan smile.

"Now tell me, Giuseppe, how does the help get in?"

"Get in?" Despite all the energy spent on denying the unthinkable, Carlotti could not contain his obvious wonder at the immensity of the idea. "My God." For a moment he seemed to be struck dumb. The Padre had to prod him to answer.

"How do they do it?" he snapped. No smiles now.

Carlotti shook his head with a kind of shivery jerk.

"We give their social security numbers, they investigate, and they get clearance. When they come through they show IDs to the guards. Then they pass through the security machines." He looked about him suddenly, as if a new idea had miraculously emerged to save him. "They're very very strict about this. They look into backgrounds."

When that information did not move the Padre, he tried another tack, suddenly lowering his voice. "I'm not supposed to say, but they got tasters too."

"Tasters?" Benjy asked.

"Filipino mess men. They make sure the food isn't poisoned."

Quite obviously, Carlotti was trying to build up the concept of White House invincibility, as if to further illustrate the madness of the idea, yet without letting on that he suspected what all this conversation meant.

"No shit," the Canary said.

"Like for kings," Vinnie pointed out.

The exchange broke the tension in the room. But the Padre's thoughts were elsewhere.

"You must make room for four in your crew," the Padre said without raising his eyes from the plan. His tone was emphatic. The blood drained from Carlotti's face. The inevitable had finally struck. He looked as if he might faint. The Padre waited for him to recover.

"But the clearances."

"You do your business. We do ours."

There were ways, the Padre thought. Other men would be investigated, cleared, given permission. Angelo would know what to do.

"I got family, Padre . . . I . . ." Carlotti began, his words swallowed in fear.

"Surely you will be considered innocent," Robert suddenly blurted. His face had gone ashen. The Padre shot him a glance of reproach, shaking his head. Keep out of this. Robert nodded, catching his meaning. But it did not restore his color.

Carlotti's face represented a kaleidoscope of conflicting expressions. A cowardly man, the Padre decided, but too fearful to betray them in advance. Later he would be the first to protest his innocence. On his knees, swearing on the life of his mother, he would tell them that the Padre had put a gun to his head. Poor little Giuseppe, the Padre sighed. I forgive you in advance.

The Padre said, "All you know is that you must hire four outside men. Waiters. Bartenders."

"But are they experienced?" the little man asked, as if it were still another straw to grasp. The Padre suppressed a desire to smile.

"They will learn," the Padre said.

"How can you serve a meal in the White House without experienced men? This takes training. This is French service. One hand pickups with a fork and spoon. They wear white gloves."

"You got to go to college to learn this?" Benjy said. It was an idea that added to the unreality of the scene. Carlotti shrugged.

"They'll get wise," he said. "You can't fool them. There's this woman—"

"This is our business," the Padre said, putting an end to the discussion. There was no way Carlotti could keep this account. "We'll take care of all the other details, social security cards, IDs." He looked at the Pencil, who made his inevitable notes.

"This is the White House, Padre," Carlotti said, his little mouse eyes darting from face to face. He seemed to want to say more, to argue, to protest. The Padre reached out and patted his arm.

"It's all right. You know nothing," the Padre said, as if it were an incantation. Carlotti nodded. But there were tears in his eyes. He no longer bothered to wipe the droplets of sweat that gravity forced over his moustache onto his lips and chin. As he turned, he seemed to stagger. But the Canary was quick, grasping him about the arms as he led him out the back door.

"So who knows about waiting tables and being a bartender?" the Padre asked when the Canary returned. They all raised a hand.

"You are all liars," he said, but he was greatly pleased at their reaction.

"Actually," Robert said, "I waited on tables for three years when I was in college. Good restaurants. I was excellent. I'd be perfect casting."

"No way," the Padre said.

"I'd be more credible than these people," Robert insisted.

"We must end this, Robert," the Padre said. "It wouldn't work."

"Why?"

The Padre looked at him and smiled benignly.

"In the first place," he said, "you're not Italian."

Benjy let out a high-pitched laugh. The others joined in.

"That's absurd," Robert snapped, "and you know it. I have every right."

The Padre nodded, reached out and grasped Robert's upper arm.

"It is your personal life, Robert. I know that. I know how much Maria and Joey mean to you. But we are dealing here with what is not your business."

"It is my—" Robert said.

The Padre shot him a stern glance that quieted him in mid-sentence.

"It is not your professional business," the Padre explained gently. "Besides"—he paused and sucked in a deep breath—"Maria and Joey will need you."

"Surely there is something useful I can do."

The Padre contemplated the request.

"You will stay with Angelo at Mrs. Santorelli's, Luigi's sister." He turned toward Angelo. "She is a good cook, yes?"

Angelo kissed his fingers in confirmation. More important, the Padre knew, her apartment, just two blocks from Luigi's Trattoria, was one of the organization's many absolutely safe places in the neighborhood. A good churchgoing woman, Luigi's sister was part of the early-warning network long established by the organization. Her husband, Giovanni, had been a made member until he had been gunned down by a rival family in less tranquil times. Aside from the Church, her loyalty was to the Padre and the organization.

"I still say—" Robert began.

"Enough," the Padre said. It was a dismissal. The Padre turned to the others.

"You, Rocco, must stay outside too."

Rocco nodded.

The Padre would need both these men, Angelo to facilitate what was necessary and Rocco to keep the organization going in his absence, which could be forever. In any event, Rocco could be the only one to succeed him. And yet he could not simply put his mantle on him. Rocco would have to demonstrate his authority, as the Padre had demonstrated his ability to command after his father's death.

"Now someone call Luigi to teach us how to be good waiters," the Padre said.

## ✳ 13 ✳

AMY PUT THE STUDS IN HER HUSBAND'S SHIRT AND LAID IT NEATLY across the bed. He sat in his shorts on one of the rose chairs, legs crossed, going over his prepared toast.

"Clichéd pap," he muttered. Even though he would not read the toast word for word, it would reflect the usual flattery and innocuousness that characterized the tradition.

"The King's supposed to be a really nice guy," Amy said, hoping to get her husband in a festive mood. Lately it had been impossible to jolt him out of a deep funk. The hostage thing was getting to him. He wasn't sleeping. Last night she had awakened suddenly and found him gone. She was alarmed at first. Then the Secret Service man on all-night duty in the upstairs corridor informed her that the President was resting on the Truman balcony on the floor above.

When she found him, he was seated on a straight-backed chair, with his feet on the railing, looking out toward the Potomac. It was a surprisingly clear summer night. At Camp David it wasn't unusual for them to sit quietly on the porch of the main cabin, holding hands and staring into the dark shapes of the forest and listening to the crickets.

They were both descendants of Midwestern porch people and knew the value of the soothing nature of quiet watchfulness. But it troubled her that he had not awakened her. She moved another chair, placed it beside him, and sat down, angling her legs on the railing so that her toes rested on his shins.

"Generally speaking, it's a beautiful planet," he had whispered, touching her arm, but without taking his eyes off the night view. "Except for the people."

"Not all."

"Taking hostages is such an ugly business." It was clear now where his mind was. More and more the awful reality absorbed his thoughts.

He shook his head. "I really feel for those people and their families." In the long silence, she turned and watched his profile silhouetted against a white portico. "They're gonna die, Amy, and there's no way in the world I can stop it from happening."

"Except to give in," she said. She had deliberately posed the idea as an oblique comment, gentle and noninsistent. It had nothing to do with strategy or affairs of state. It was simply a wifely response. He was being devastated by the situation. It affected everything, permeated all other issues, political and personal. It exacted a fearful toll.

"All day long I've been on the phone kissing the asses of those tinhorns who run those lousy countries. The Syrian is a polite little bastard. I get reassurances, sympathy. But no action. The Saudis? Masters of evasiveness. Talking to those people is like talking into a soft cloud. The Israelis love all this angst. I'll give them this. They're tough. They'll take it all the way. A counterpunch is an acceptable state action, no matter who or how many get hurt. Not us. Couldn't do it and get away with it. Not up front. And I'm afraid to do it covertly. If it backfires, we're finished. Had my way, I'd send everyone connected with those terrorist bastards a letter bomb airmail special delivery. Maybe even one of those small A jobs."

"Very funny," she said. Considering that her husband was always shadowed by someone carrying that horrid little briefcase, she failed to respond to what he had intended as black humor. Only way you can preserve your sanity, he had argued, was to joke about "it." He had never convinced her.

"And this is only the third or fourth generation. Just wait until we get into the fifth or sixth."

"The fifth or sixth what?"

"Generation of terrorism." He turned to look at her, his eyes intense and liquid as they gathered the reflected light. He shivered. She waited, then seemed to catch his chill in the otherwise warm night. "That's going to be nuclear blackmail. Guy will come in with a nuke on his back. Blow us all away unless we give in to whatever bullshit he has in his head. It's coming. In fact, could be done right now. It's a goddamned miracle it hasn't happened yet. I pity the President who has to deal with that mess."

"So if you look at the bright side, your little problem isn't so bad."

"I said I'd pity the guy," the President said. "But now nobody pities me. Damned if I do, damned if I don't. Problem is it's a spectator sport. Everyone can be an armchair general."

"Except the general on the firing line."

"Nobody understands. Especially if it's one of yours taken hostage."

"Well, I'm glad it's not one of mine," she said, thinking of her own children, Tad and Barbara.

He patted her arm and was silent for a long time.

"I can hack everything," he said. "All the political crap, the endless rituals and ceremonies, the staff ego wars, all the tugging and pulling, dealing with those stubborn bastards in the Soviet Union and the pigheaded self-destructive fools of the third world. Even with the idea of the awesome power of that box in the briefcase. No sweat." He paused, sighed, sucked in a breath through clenched teeth. "It's the crazies with these wacko burning causes, the ones who think they have 'the answer.' " He was silent for a long time.

She shrugged and rubbed her toe against his shin.

"On my desk," he said, "I have these option papers. We got these highly trained shoot-em-up hit teams. They go in, tear the place apart, bring home the people dead or alive. One option is to send them in. We know approximately where most of the hostages are being kept. Might get between twenty and thirty percent out alive. The Defense and Intelligence boys are big on risk analysis, kill ratios, stuff like that. Then there's the political boys. They say thirty percent is too low. Got to be at least double that, ideally ninety percent. They want both a victory parade and a funeral. Joy and sorrow. Stir the emotions."

"That's disgusting," Amy said, removing her feet from the railing.

"Then there's Harkins' way. Sneak in and kick ass."

"Whose?"

"Anybody around. Take hostages. Ten to one if necessary. Then kill them. Afterwards, deny it all with a wink."

"When mad enough, kick the dog," Amy said.

"Maybe so. But you know what I've been doing out here?" He turned and watched her, expecting no response. "I'm actually considering it, the Harkins way."

She turned, looked at him archly, then reached out with her hand, stopping just short of his head.

"Don't know if I could live with a man who orders things like that." She wondered, in the final analysis, if her objections would really matter.

"Things keep up this way, I may have to. Preempt, like the Israelis."

He looked out over the railing. From where they sat they could see the exquisitely lit Mall, the Washington Monument, the Capitol dome, the tinsel ripple of the Potomac. Following his gaze, she noted that a number of cars slowly meandered in the street behind the rear gate and she could make out dark human figures on foot, some stationary, some moving.

"I like this house," he said softly. "And I'd like to renew the lease." He swung his legs back to the deck and stood up, pressing his body against the railing.

"Mr. President . . ."

It was the voice of the Secret Service man who had been standing just inside the door. The edge of the Truman balcony had become a security hole. Standing up so close to the railing presented his body to a would-be assassin. He moved back into the shadows.

"Well, that's one compensation," the President said.

"What is that?" Amy asked.

"We're safe in here."

# ✸ 14 ✸

THEY HAD COCKTAILS BROUGHT TO THE YELLOW OVAL ROOM. NOT wishing to crease her gown, she stood by the marble mantel and sipped a white wine while her husband fingered the bronze jousting knights on the gold-inlaid table.

Miss Hartford arrived at the door. She wore a simple black gown with straps. As always, it was perfect for her role as social secretary.

"They'll arrive in exactly five minutes."

The President nodded. Amy stood in front of him, inspecting.

"Last-minute check," she said, patting an errant lock of his hair and kissing him lightly on the cheek. "Come on now," she whispered. "Buck up. You're Paul Bernard starring in *State Dinner* and featuring the King and Queen of Spain."

"Let the cameras roll," he said, flashing his best politician's smile. He bent slightly, offering his arm. She took it. Moving out of the Oval Room to the center hall, they were joined by the Secret Service men who surreptitiously fell into position.

They walked past the octagonal partners' desk, the antique lamps, tables, and chairs, and the lovely painting of the woman and her two children by Mary Cassatt. A young boy and girl. She loved that picture. It reminded her of herself and her two children when they were young. She wondered whether she would look back on this White House experience as a happy time. The question irritated her and she put it out of her mind. Silly, she told herself. Isn't this, after all, the top of the mountain?

They walked slowly down the red-carpeted steps, hands sliding along the gold banisters. At the landing they continued through the marbled foyer, past the gauntlet of resplendent young Marines in full-dress uniforms.

Amy glanced at her husband. He was wearing his public smile now, the one that reflected unbounded joy, showing off his handsome angled face. They came out of the front entrance into the glare of the light and descended the steps, covered by the red ceremonial carpet. The cameras flashed. The King and Queen drove up in a spit-polished limousine and the Chief of Protocol darted out of the front seat. He waited until the King and Queen were clear and the door to the car had slammed shut.

"May I present His Majesty Don Carlos and Her Majesty the Queen, Mr. President."

The President put out his hand. Cameras flashed and the two couples exchanged pleasantries. They walked in together and took their places on the receiving line.

"I've been looking forward to this visit for a long time," the King said.

"I hope we won't disappoint you, Your Highness," Amy responded.

# ★ 15 ★

ABOVE ALL, THE PADRE KNEW, HOWEVER CAREFULLY ONE PLANNED, one could always expect an unforeseen problem. Carmine's uniform had presented a formidable obstacle. It had been intended that the four men would carry the liquid explosives on their bodies in long plastic flaps. Because of the extreme sensitivity of the liquid, it could be detonated by impact. They had tested exactly how hard this impact might be by dropping a tiny bag of it from a height of six feet. It had exploded with a surprising thunderclap. It could also be exploded by a sharp blow from a metal hammer.

The Pencil had found the best boom-boom man on the East Coast, a safecracker who was a fanatic on the subject and who eagerly lectured them on "the exciting new advances in explosive technology." He was tall, with long hair. He wore little round glasses and affected what seemed like a slight lisping British accent.

"It's the latest trend," the man told them. "In my business, you have to keep up."

"And you are certain it will pass through all known detectors?" the Padre inquired.

"Like your own skin. But every new idea spawns an evasive action and the technology to detect it is coming fast. At the moment it's clear sailing. Me, I prefer the plastic for my line of work. Not as unstable. But you can't disguise it like the liquid. And some of the new detectors can pick up the plastic explosives. Then there's the detonators. No matter how small they are, there is always the risk of detection. But not the liquid. That's why I will never fly again. Some asshole will carry it on board disguised as cough syrup or booze."

They had actually sent someone through the airport detectors to test his assertion and it was confirmed.

"The only problem," the man began, "is convincing other people that this stuff is really dangerous. Not too many people know what it can really do. Looks innocent. Like water. But it can do a nasty job on flesh and bones."

""How much force would be required to set it off?" the Padre had asked.

"Depends on how the substance is contained," the boom-boom man said authoritatively. "The less air, the less evaporation. And, of course, the greater the density, the less impact required."

"What would happen if it were carried in plastic bags?"

The boom-boom man thought for a moment. According to the Pencil, he had an uncanny record of cracking safes, although he had spent a decade of his life in various prisons on two continents.

"Plastic bags?" The man rubbed his chin, and the Padre studied him as he thought. "Soft?"

"Yes."

The man's eyes narrowed behind his round glasses, although he tactfully avoided any special study of the Padre's face. He had gotten the message.

"Like a fall?"

"Depends on how high and how hard. Also on the surface." The man sucked in a deep breath. "And the density. How thick?"

"You tell me," the Padre said. It was a command and the man knew it.

"About as high as the seat of a chair from a standing position to a hard uncarpeted floor with a two-inch density. Change the variables and you got a different result." He scratched his head. "Man wants to make a weapon out of himself, this is it." He looked at the floor. "Never thought of it like that," he said innocently. "Thing is, though, if the bag leaks, or is sliced open, you get nothing but wet pants." He laughed.

The Pencil had paid the man and had urged him to take a long ocean cruise.

The uniform Carlotti had provided for the Canary was too small to be worn over the flaps of explosive. By then it was too late for changes. Carmine would have to go in without it.

Luigi had given them a cram course in basic table service. It was, of course, less than adequate, since Luigi's knowledge of fancy service was sparse. It had come mostly from working as a busboy on four crossings of the old *Queen Mary*.

They had taken turns in being the server and the served. The Padre had never realized how clumsy he was, how little he had noticed when other people served him. Luckily, Benjy had some experience in bartending. He was also the only one who looked presentable in his uniform.

They had driven down from Manhattan and checked into a motel on the Virginia side of the Potomac, where Carlotti met them. He brought with him plates, silverware, large serving trays, and implements, even chunks of food as props for further instruction. Understandably, the man was nervous. His hands shook when he demonstrated how the food was scooped and served.

The Canary, with his big clumsy fingers, proved the worst. The Padre and Vinnie were barely passable. For a moment he was almost tempted to call Robert, who had protested to the last. But the Padre had been adamant.

"We will stay in touch through Angelo," the Padre had assured him.

But the matter of Carmine's clumsiness nagged at him.

"We'll put him in the Red Room," Carlotti suggested. He was still fantasizing about his professional standards. The Padre did not tell him it was highly unlikely that the meal would reach the main course.

Carlotti informed them they would be serving trays of drinks and hors d'oeuvres during the cocktail hour while the President and his party stood on the receiving line. It was, the Padre knew, a crucial time. If they blew it then, the entire enterprise could fail.

They arrived, as Carlotti had instructed, at the East Gate of the White House at precisely 6 P.M. along with others among the serving help, many of whom eyed them curiously.

The Padre had reluctantly shaved and carefully groomed his hair. He hoped that no one would recognize him. Actually, he had not been photographed for years, and the only pictures ever taken of him showed him with a three-day growth of beard and mussed-up hair. Above all, he had taken great pains never to look like a greaseball. Looking in the mirror now, he felt, for the first time in his life, that he resembled one. Good, he decided. An excellent disguise.

"You work this place before?" a man asked the Padre as they stood on line waiting to get through the first checkpoint, manned by the White House police.

"First time," the Padre muttered.

"What happened to Harry and Joe?" the man persisted.

"Other commitments," the Padre answered patiently.

Carlotti had, a week earlier, given their new social security numbers to the security people along with the dates of birth of the cardholders. They were guaranteed numbers with matching IDs, Maryland licenses, and credit cards. The names were authentic and fresh, of bona fide living men, all of them clean under scrutiny, guaranteed to pass muster except under the most scrupulous investigation. Best of all, they were carefully matched.

Later, the men who were being impersonated would be shocked by the allegation, although they would be cleared as genuinely innocent, which they were. The organization understood the reliance of investigative agencies on computers and had adapted to the new technology with a few tricks of their own. Yet, no matter how advanced the technology, all of it was people-dependent. And people represented the vulnerable soft underbelly of all technology. People had flaws, made mistakes, could be compromised.

As they moved forward the man who had asked the questions frowned and shook his head.

"Just surprised to see so many new faces," he said.

"A job's a job," the Padre responded. Beads of sweat had already sprouted on his forehead. The flaps of explosives were heavy under his uniform.

Benjy was ahead of him on the line. The Padre watched as the man in uniform looked at his ID, then checked his list on a clipboard and waved him through. They had memorized their new names and birth dates. The Padre was pleased. He had no anxiety about the numbers. Providing IDs was a highly efficient operation of the organization.

Ahead, he could see the frame of the metal detector. It was manned by three uniformed men, with two others in civilian clothes observing. From the little buttons in their ears, the Padre could tell that they were Secret Service.

He came through the first checkpoint without incident and watched as Benjy moved through the detector. The uniformed men were intense about their job. They watched the monitor with deep concentration, and the Secret Service men's eyes seemed to bore through everyone as they passed through. The Padre could not deny his anxiety. Suppose he was stopped and searched? The flaps were hanging from a harness that hung from his shoulders and reached down front and back. He was literally encased in it. Even the most cursory hand pat would detect them.

It surprised him to move through the detector so easily. He was also, inexplicably, annoyed. They were supposed to be protecting the President of the United States, for chrissakes. The uniformed men smiled at him and he returned the pleasantry. Even the Secret Service men seemed less grim. He patted his side pocket where he had put the typewritten note. Four copies had been made. Each man carried one.

Would they be convinced? The Padre hoped so, although he knew that none of them looked either suicidal or fanatic. He would settle for determined. Why then would they have put themselves in this position? If the others were bothered by the prospect, they did not voice any objections. None of them had families. The organization was their whole life. Loyalty was fundamental to their character.

After passing through the machine, the Padre lingered in the corridor, pretending interest in the pictures displayed there, photographs of earlier days in the White House. From the corner of his eye he watched Vinnie move through without incident. He was concerned about the Canary. It hadn't occurred to him, perhaps because he was so used to the man's heavy features and bulky body, that Carmine was so different-looking, so bovine, so suspect.

Now he glanced at him as he towered above the others on the line. The man was slavishly devoted, loyal beyond the shadow of a doubt. He would fall on a grenade if it endangered the Padre's life. Indeed, the Padre's well-being and safety were his only reasons for living. It would be unthinkable to be parted from Carmine. At that moment he wished he had not brought him.

He could tell the Secret Service men were eyeing him with more than cursory curiosity. He passed through the first checkpoint without incident, but as he moved through the detector the Padre noted that one of the Secret Service men nodded. A White House policeman then whispered something to the Canary. The Padre watched as the policeman and Carmine, who towered above him, moved aside.

Benjy and Vinnie had already disappeared beyond the corner of the corridor. They would proceed along the lower hall to the downstairs kitchen. There they would get their last-minute instructions and move up to the State Dining Room, where they would set out the beginning course. It would be waiting for the diners when they arrived.

The Padre moved toward another picture display where he could get a better view of Carmine and the policeman. He watched as the Canary unbuttoned his uniform jacket. No way to save him, the Padre thought, until he realized that the Canary was not carrying any explosives. With clumsy fingers, Carmine was opening his shirt. He reached through the opening to draw out a huge St. Christopher medal, which obviously had been picked up by the sensitive detector. He saw the policeman smile and lift the medal for the Secret Service man to see. The Secret Service man nodded and turned his gaze back to those men still coming through the detector.

Then the Padre proceeded along the corridor, waiting for Carmine to catch up with him.

"It works. He was looking out for me," Carmine said.

"Who?"

"St. Christopher."

The Padre smiled and patted the Canary's arm.

In the kitchen, Carlotti scurried about giving last-minute instructions. He was obviously ignoring what had occurred, carrying on as if it were business as usual.

"You, the new men," he cried imperiously. This was his turf and he was not going to give the impression that he was under anyone's domination. The Padre admired his courage. Good, he thought, confirming his view that Carlotti would not bend until the end. Then he would surrender completely.

He assigned tables to the men, pointing to a large diagram on the wall. The Padre would be two tables from the President. Benjy would remain in the pantry mixing drinks. Vinnie was assigned to the table nearest the door and Carmine to the comparative Siberia of the Red Room.

Then Carlotti led the serving crew up a staircase, through the pantry, where he stopped briefly to explain how the food would arrive in the large serving elevator. He warned them it must be dispensed with split-second efficiency. After the explanation, the crew filed out to the State Dining Room.

The Padre was struck first with the profusion of roses—reds, pinks, yellows. There were two huge vases filled with them on the mantelpiece below the picture of Abraham Lincoln. In the center of the mantelpiece was another huge bouquet, which was replicated in a smaller version on each yellow tablecloth. The candle-shaped bulbs on the large gold-plated chandelier were lit as well as the sconces that hung between white, fluted bas-relief pillars. Lights were reflected on every piece of crystal and plate. It was, the Padre thought, a breathtakingly beautiful sight.

For a brief moment he was mesmerized by it. It seemed so incongruous with the act he was about to perform. Finally, reality intruded, coming in the form of a question posed to himself. How was it possible that such festivity could be going on in the face of his own sadness? In an odd way, he felt foolish, out of step. Nevertheless, his instinct was confirmed. Nobody really cared. If tragedy did not strike you or yours, it simply did not exist.

Carlotti stood in the center of the circle of waiters, like a director of a great opera performance. Each was dressed in a black uniform, a short vest with piping, wing collar, and black tie. He barked last-minute instructions, went over details that must have seemed elementary to the professionals among them. Before he had finished, a tall lady in a black evening dress and a pinched, severe expression intruded. Carlotti's fawning attested to her rank and he introduced her to the group, giving her title a resounding fullness.

"This is Miss Hartford, social secretary to the wife of the President of the United States."

With a look of disdain, her eyes roamed the faces of the waiters, alighting with obvious distaste on the thick features of the Canary. Try as he might, he would never look the part.

"It is a privilege to work in this historic house, home of Presidents," Miss Hartford intoned. "You must remember this privilege when you do your job. Each must pull his own weight. We ask for the best that is in you. Impeccable service. We are expecting that your work will help make this one of the most memorable evenings ever in the history of our republic."

She nodded, acknowledged the sporadic applause, and swept out of the room again.

The Padre had listened to the lady with half an ear. Now to business, he told himself, as he surveyed the room. He saw the method of exiting—through the pantry, up the stairs to the living quarters. He and his men were already inside. Timing would be a matter of accessibility.

"Now," someone said, handing him a silver tray of hors

d'oeuvres. He took the tray and followed another waiter into the main hall. Looking behind him, he could see the Canary carrying another tray loaded with drinks. The waiters ahead of them stayed well beyond the presidential receiving line.

Women in gowns and men in black tie snaked in a slow-moving line extending from the staircase to the right of the main entrance. Each was introduced to the King and Queen and the President and the First Lady. Pleasantries were exchanged. The President laughed. The First Lady smiled. The King bowed and the Queen offered a shy grin.

As the people came off the receiving line, waiters stepped forward offering drinks and hors d'oeuvres. The guests took them, sipped and ate, and roamed through the hallway. Some stepped into the Green Room and looked around.

The Padre thrust his tray in front of one man who studied him briefly with some curiosity. He turned his face away as quickly as was appropriate. For a moment he felt the man's eyes following him. Then, miraculously, the man seemed to give it up, turning to engage in conversation with one of the other guests. The Padre quickly moved to another part of the crowd.

Carmine moved among the guests dispensing drinks, an odd grin on his face. He saw Vinnie carrying a tray of hors d'oeuvres, looking very much the professional. Occasionally Carlotti's face would peer from the entrance of the State Dining Room as he watched the proceedings. When their eyes met, Carlotti turned away. He noted, too, that there was a circular pattern to the way in which the Secret Service men watched the President and observed the guests.

When the last guest had cleared the receiving line, the President led the Queen through the group to the dining room. The King followed, the First Lady on his arm. It was all very formal, ritualized. The waiters brought half-filled trays back to the pantry. Carlotti stood in the doorway of the pantry watching while each waiter picked up a bottle of uncorked white wine. The appetizer had already been placed before each guest.

"When?" Benjy asked. He was at the pantry bar placing an array of bottles for after-dinner drinks on a silver tray. Carlotti suddenly raised his hand, a signal for the waiters to march into the dining room to begin pouring the white wine.

As the Padre passed him, he could see the repressed panic in Carlotti's eyes. The Padre shrugged and offered a half-smile of reassurance. It did not appear to give the man any comfort.

In the dining room, the Padre surveyed the scene. The Secret Service men maintained their circular vigil. They were adept at fading into the woodwork. The President and the First Lady chatted with their dinner partners. The hum of voices rose and fell in rhythmic patterns. In his mind, the Padre worked out the final method of exit. He would proceed along the mantel wall to the swinging door of the pantry. The First Lady would have to be led forward from her seat, following in the President's wake.

Inside the entrance to the pantry, they would lock arms with the President and the First Lady and proceed up the stairs to the living quarters. Of course the Secret Service men could not be expected to sit idly by. They would be figuring out countermeasures, talking to each other on their little microphones. Maybe they had a secret plan for coping with this eventuality.

The Padre moved to the dining room with the others and poured the wine, proud of his steady hand. He went around the table to which he was assigned, knowing he was under the watchful gaze of at least one Secret Service agent, the man to the right of the mantel, who stood, hawk-eyed and alert, hands folded behind him. Peripherally, he saw the President. He was smiling and telling what seemed like a funny story to the Queen. He heard the Queen's appreciative giggle. Vinnie was serving another table at the north side of the room. The Padre could not see Carmine, who was working in the Red Room.

He finished pouring the wine and started back toward the pantry. At that moment the Padre heard a crash. Not loud, but uncommon enough to attract attention. There was a moment of silence. He could feel the sudden tension in the room. The Secret Service men standing at either end of the mantel took a few steps forward, closing ranks behind the President. After a second or two, the hum of voices began again.

Back in the pantry, the Padre saw Carmine enter. He looked crestfallen as he carried the remains of broken glasses on a tray. Behind him, he caught a glimpse of Miss Hartford, her face grim. She strode toward Carlotti, who was supervising the final details of the entrée, making sure the food was arranged perfectly on each plate. Although she did not speak loudly, her voice carried to where the Padre stood.

"Get that clod out of here," she said. The Padre turned. His eyes met Carlotti's. He moved his head, just enough for Carlotti to note his negative reaction. The color drained from Carlotti's face.

"He's a good man," Carlotti protested in a whisper.

"I will not leave here until that man is removed from this place," Miss Hartford said.

"I swear—" Carlotti said.

"Now."

She was livid with anger. Carmine seemed helpless. His knowledge of women was as inadequate as his knowledge of serving. His hands hung at his sides; his large head hung down over his shoulders. His hangdog eyes sought out those of the Padre. Easy, Carmine, the Padre's gaze told him. Without the Padre to hold him back, he could be capable of a sudden violent eruption. At that moment a Secret Service man came into the pantry.

"Who is this clown?" he asked Carlotti.

"One of my waiters," Carlotti responded weakly. His skin was the color of alabaster. The man looked at the Canary.

"You'd think it was his first job." He turned toward Carlotti. "Is this man experienced?"

Carlotti was sweating, his complexion yellowing.

"He has home problems. His wife. Very very sick. His mind is not on this job." He turned to Miss Hartford. "I'm sorry."

"I want this man out of here immediately," Miss Hartford said, showing all her meanness.

"What's your name?" the Secret Service man asked. The Padre wondered whether he would remember the fictitious name on his ID. Circumstances dictated. The time was now. He moved his head toward Vinnie and Benjy. The three of them grabbed bottles of the red wine. He waited until Vinnie and Benjy had come within striking distance of the President and his wife. Then he moved.

As he passed the Secret Service man, the Padre put his hand in his pocket, pulled out the little note, and tapped the man on the arm.

"You dropped this," he said as he passed. The Secret Service man took the paper. It was a reflex action. Before he moved back into the State Dining Room, he paused a moment to be certain that the man had begun to read. The Padre knew the words by heart.

To the Honorable Secret Service. Please read every word. We are carrying liquid explosives on our person. They can be detonated on impact. There are four of us. If you interfere with our plans in any way, we will detonate the explosives. This will surely kill the President and the First Lady. It will also kill us. We are not afraid to die.
WE ARE HOLDING THE PRESIDENT HOSTAGE.

In the dining room, the buzz of conversation had settled into normalcy. People were eating and drinking.

The Padre moved toward the President's table. Benjy was already there. Vinnie stood behind the First Lady. The two Secret Service men behind the President moved forward, then stopped suddenly. They were listening intently through their earpieces, watching the three men. Each, as if on signal, began to pour the wine, moving, but maintaining the required lethal proximity to the President and the First Lady.

As he poured, the Padre looked up. He stared at one of the Secret Service agents posted in front of the mantel and motioned with his bottle toward the President. The man hesitated, listened, spoke into his microphone, then whispered something into the President's ear. Bewildered, the President, fork in midair, looked up, meeting the Padre's gaze. The Padre nodded, then looked toward Vinnie, who stood near another Secret Service man, who now leaned over the First Lady.

"Will you excuse me," the Padre heard her say, moving toward the President as he rose from the table. Benjy, too, came forward. The First Lady walked past the President's table to the wall with the mantel, with Vinnie close behind her. Carmine, too, now materialized. They moved in a tight knot toward the pantry. The dining guests continued their conversational din, although it seemed to subside as the party moved the short distance to the north end of the room.

As they reached the pantry door, Benjy moved quickly, the Padre behind him, locking arms with the President. The maneuver was replicated with the First Lady by Vinnie and Carmine, who had somehow escaped further notice. But as the pantry door swung back, they quickly changed position, arms entwined, forming a tight circle, with their backs to the President and his wife, who were trapped in the center. The Padre led the pack as a kind of point man, with Carmine and Vinnie facing the rear, moving backward.

Around this moving circle the Secret Service men formed another circle, Uzis drawn, muzzles pointed directly at the foreheads of the four men. Additional men stood beyond the circle, all with weapons drawn. In seconds they had completely cleared the pantry of the serving personnel.

They seemed to be in a soundless vacuum. The Padre had visualized this moment, but the silence was much more than he had expected. Even the din in the other room had fully subsided.

"There is no place to go," a man's voice said. He was standing unarmed, just outside the rim of the circle made by the Secret Service men. He was tall and authoritative and did not wear a tuxedo. The man in charge, the Padre thought. Along the length of the rear of his body he felt the bodies of the President and his wife. They felt like a clot of flesh, nailed together. The Padre sucked in his breath, eyes narrowing as he studied the faces around him. He felt the cold steel of the Uzi's muzzle against his forehead.

He would wait, he decided. Perfect timing was required. The hot flame of passion must dissipate.

"Now if you would just slowly release your arms and walk forward, no one will get hurt," the man said. Obviously he was carefully trained for such an event, his voice steady, almost friendly.

"What we will do now," the Padre said, ignoring the man's instruction, "is to walk forward as a group. You must please keep your distance. Our wish, too, is that no one gets hurt."

The Padre heard his own voice. It was cool and steady, exactly the right tone. He was concerned that a tremor might indicate that he was, in some way, concerned for his own life. At all costs, they must believe that he did not fear death.

"But we can't let you do that, you see," the man said with deliberate politeness.

"I am very sorry but you have no choice in this matter," the Padre said with equal politeness. "I thought the note explained about the liquid explosives. They will go off at the slightest impact." He looked around him. "The explosives will blow up this entire room and everyone in it."

"That fellow, the big one," the man in charge said. "We know he's not carrying explosives."

"Mr. President," the Padre said.

He felt a slight movement and heard a muffled voice behind him.

"Yes."

"With respect, Mr. President. Please feel along my chest and down my sides. But very gently. This material is not as stable as I would wish."

He felt the President moving his hands along his chest and down his sides, probing.

"I take your word for it," the President said. The Padre felt his breath whiz past his left ear.

"We don't doubt you, Mr. . . . ." the man in charge said. "What did you say your name was?"

"I think we are wasting time here," the Padre said gently. "We do not wish to tire the First Lady."

"Don't worry about me," the First Lady snapped behind him. A fighter, the Padre thought, surprised that his lips could curl in a tight smile at this moment.

"What do you want?" the man in charge asked. His tactic, the Padre knew, was to stretch out the dialogue as long as possible.

"What we want," the Padre said, "is to move quietly to the President's quarters on the second floor. It will be much more comfortable for the President and the First Lady there."

"We can't let you do that," the man in charge said. The Padre noted, for the first time, a tiny tremor of anxiety in his voice.

"Well then," the Padre said, "we could stay here until we can no longer stand. If we falter or in some way move too hastily, this area of the White House will require a great deal of costly repairs. Not to mention the tremendous expense of a great number of funerals."

He looked directly into the eyes of the man in charge. Instinctively, he knew which of them would blink first, but the man held his stare for a longer time than expected. Finally, the man turned his eyes away.

"What is it you want?" he asked tersely, the pose of politeness quickly dissipating.

"A very simple request. We wish to move forward, through that door." He pointed with his head. "Up the stairs behind it."

"I mean, why have you done this?"

". . . and then we wish to be left alone for a while."

"For how long?"

"That depends."

"On what?"

"I'm sorry for the discomfort, Mr. President. But this man is very stubborn," the Padre said.

The man in charge seemed rattled. His options, it was obvious, were few.

"You'll kill yourself too," the man in charge said. "You want to die?"

"Do you?" the Padre asked.

The man in charge shrugged. He was wearing a microphone and earpiece. The Padre noted peripherally that the outside lawn was bathed in strong lights. He heard movement in the dining room, chairs being pushed back, the sound of moving feet, hushed voices.

"What is your cause? Is it publicity?"

"For crying out loud, Ike," the President snapped at the man in charge. "We're not getting anywhere. Let's move it upstairs."

"Very sensible," the Padre said.

"They obviously want something. We'll get up there, we'll talk about it," the President said. No panic in his voice, the Padre noted. The President was a man who had come a long way on a very rough course. He had learned to control himself. A good sign.

"I can't let this happen," Ike Fellows said.

"Yes, you can," the President said. "I order you to do it."

"We're Secret Service, Mr. President. Your safety is our mission. We have a right to supersede your orders."

"Are we going to stand here and have a procedural argument?

They don't want to take us out of here. Only upstairs. Hell, you've got them surrounded."

"I don't think—" Fellows began.

"For chrissakes, man, if he wanted to kill us, he would have done so already."

"Absolutely correct, Mr. President," the Padre said.

"We'll talk," the President said. "We'll work it out."

Fellows' body seemed to collapse from the inside. He shook his head, all his bravado gone.

"Step away," he said to the men who surrounded them. They moved a few feet beyond the tight little circle and the Padre started forward, feeling the pull of the others as they followed. It was an awkward, clumsy way of walking.

With each step, the circle of Secret Service men followed, although they had to make room for the Padre's circle to pass through the wide doorway. They reformed again in the corridor and moved slowly in tandem with the Padre's circle.

The staircase seemed narrower than expected. A number of Secret Service agents moved ahead of them, backward, the muzzles of their Uzis continuing to point directly at the foreheads of the Padre and his men.

The Padre led the way upward. It was difficult for those behind him to follow. And dangerous. As they moved, Carmine momentarily lost his balance and slipped backward. But he could not unlock his arms and the clot of bodies listed as they resisted his fall. The Padre pushed forward, straining like a horse in a harness. They were halfway up the stairs. A tumble would be deadly.

The Padre felt the enormous strain on his shoulders and heard the heavy breathing and grunting behind him. For a moment he felt his strength ebb. He could not hold back the enormous weight being helped by the force of gravity, carrying him downward. Husbanding his energy, he shifted his effort so that the full weight of the circle might move sideways toward the banister.

Behind him, he heard panicked voices and the clatter of shoes. He paid little attention. The circle listed further sideways. Then, suddenly, the Padre felt resistance. They had been inhibited from falling by the banister. They rested now. He could feel and hear them taking deep breaths.

"Now forward," the Padre said. His voice had weakened. But the Secret Service men who had preceded them had melted away, as well as the others who followed. They moved upward haltingly, step by step, finding a foothold, then rising in unison until they reached the upper landing.

They were in the long central hall. Quickly he took in the

brightly lit crystal chandeliers, the polished double partners' desk, the beautiful picture of the lady and her two children on the far wall, the plants and figures of animals on shelves, the gold carpet.

Secret Service agents were posted everywhere, Uzis at the ready. A line of men were stretched across the corridor, beginning at a point where a door opened to what the Padre knew was the yellow Oval Room.

Although the men were in different positions, no longer in a tight circle around them, the basic situation had not changed. It was still a stalemate. The Padre's circle had stopped moving just beyond the partners' desk at the entrance to what the Padre realized was the west sitting room.

"Now what?" Fellows asked.

"You will please order your men from the west side of the house," the Padre said.

He had studied the plans for hours, picking the best possible place for them to be with the President and First Lady. He had chosen the west quarter of the house for a variety of reasons. The plans showed that by closing off the sliding doors that separated the west sitting hall from the central hall and the corridor that connected the President's study with the master bedroom, they could effectively seal off this section from the rest of the house. Also, in that area was a small kitchen and service pantry, the family dining room, the First Lady's dressing room, and a bathroom. After all, they had to eat, had to perform ablutions, had to sleep.

"Won't we need guns?" Benjy asked the Padre, loud enough to be heard across the hall.

"No guns," Fellows said.

"We have no need for them," the Padre said.

He looked at Fellows, now nervous and pasty-faced. The Padre was certain that the exact circumstances of his actions had never been seriously considered by the Secret Service as feasible. "Now please remove your men to the east side of the central hall."

He was being deliberately specific, illustrating his expertise and sense of authority. That, too, was important. They must believe in his authority.

"Let the boundary between us be the partners' desk."

Fellows hesitated. This was his turf. He seemed humiliated by the request.

"For chrissakes, follow his instructions, Ike," the President said.

"We're setting up a command post out here," Fellows said. He was tentative and hesitant.

"I have no objection," the Padre said. "But I strongly advise that you do not pass the present line. In the interests of our mutual safety and the safety of your men."

"Thank you." Fellows sneered.

"Now there are certain ground rules that must be established," the Padre said.

"Jesus," Fellows hissed.

"Under no circumstances must you interfere with us. No sneak attacks. No heroics. We will, from time to time, give you instructions. For example, we will need meals, perhaps other necessities." He was deliberately vague. "You must follow these instructions to the letter."

"And if, for some reason, the instructions are not followed?" Fellows asked.

"That would be a mistake," the Padre said. "You must understand. We do not intend to kill the President. Or ourselves. Don't make us do it. Let us proceed under that idea."

"What is it you want?" Fellows asked.

"I will explain everything. I promise you."

"May I ask who you are?" Fellows asked.

"All in due time," the Padre said.

"All right then. How about a name? Surely we're entitled to a name."

"You know the best way we can establish a relationship?" the Padre asked. Fellows seemed momentarily at a loss for words.

"By not asking any questions," the Padre said.

It was, the Padre knew, rubbing their noses in it. The great Secret Service had been circumvented on their own turf. It was an organizational humiliation. He hoped it would not prod them to take chances. By now they would be taking all available countermeasures, bringing all their technological expertise to bear. He was very sure they would be scouring the East Room and the pantry for prints.

The Padre and his men had worn white gloves. But the Padre knew that, sooner or later, their identity would be discovered. Better later than sooner. There had been no need to worry about a credibility problem. Their choice of weapon had been more than adequate. But Fellows was still not conforming, still hesitating on the order to withdraw his men.

"Mr. Fellows," the Padre said in an effort to cement a reasonable working relationship. "All your questions will be answered. I promise you."

The Padre counted twenty men, all with Uzis drawn. They took positions behind what had become the imaginary line, and the

Padre started to move the circle backward. They reached the west sitting room. At the doorway, the Padre paused and moved the group first to one side, then to the other. They maneuvered the group inside the west sitting room and closed the sliding wooden doors. Still, he would not let them unlock their arms.

"One more simple job," the Padre said, moving the group to the presidential bedroom. He paused for a moment, surveying the connecting corridor between the bedroom and the President's study. He heard movement in the closet, behind the President's clothes.

"Mr. Fellows is not a man of his word," the Padre said. "You people there in the closet, I would suggest you tell him that."

Clothes rustled and three men hopped out from behind the clothes and dashed out toward the President's study. He closed the door. With a sigh of relief, the Padre began the process of unlocking all their arms. They were stiff, and each of them flayed the air to get the circulation going.

The Padre pointed to two chairs and signaled the President and the First Lady to be seated. Benjy, as he had been instructed, closed the draperies and tore out the pulley ropes. He threw one to Vinnie, who let out a ten-foot lead and tied one end around his waist and the other around the President's. It was a tight, complicated knot, one that could not be undone without effort. Benjy repeated the process with himself and the First Lady.

The Padre instructed Carmine to clear away the objects from the desk and place it against the door to the corridor. That task completed, the group again moved into the west sitting room. Creating a room out of this end of the large upper hall, with its huge rosette window, seemed like an afterthought. A brilliant floodlight provided a striking backlight to the window's latticework, making it look like a giant spiderweb. Such a pretty window, the Padre thought as he pulled the heavy gold draperies, shutting out the glare. Then he instructed Carmine to move the couches and place them side by side in front of the sliding doors.

"Good you came, Carmine," he said, patting the Canary's back. The big man turned and showed him a broad, partially toothless smile. A compliment from the boss was all he ever needed.

The Padre stepped into the dining room, inspected it, then moved to the upstairs pantry beside it. Although it had facilities for cooking, the pantry was sparsely equipped and looked as if the main meals were prepared in the kitchen two floors below. Then he inspected the entire suite as the others followed him with their eyes. He kneeled on the floor and looked under the furniture, then upended all the chairs.

"Maybe the chandeliers," the President said.

"Are you sure?"

"I've always suspected them."

He instructed Carmine to stand on tables and check the chandeliers for any signs of listening bugs. They waited until he went through all the rooms. Carmine returned from the dining room, his last stop, shaking his head.

"Good to know," the President said.

"Why not check behind the pictures," the First Lady said. "Saw it in a movie once."

The Padre nodded, and Carmine proceeded to look behind the pictures. He found one bug behind a painting of a beach scene hung on the south wall of the west hall, holding it up for all to see.

"Speak of the obvious," the President said. "But then they didn't have much time."

"Unless they were there all along," the Padre said.

"Nothing would surprise me," the President said, casting a quick glance at the First Lady.

Carmine found five more bugs, all wireless and remote and magnetized to metal picture hangers. They had covered each room. The Padre found an antique nutcracker on one of the tables and handed it to Carmine, who crushed each microphone one at a time.

"Do you play bridge?" the First Lady asked, looking at Benjy, to whom she was attached.

Benjy chuckled.

"A real joker," he said.

The Padre turned toward the Canary.

"Carmine, I want you to stay right there." He pointed to the entrance to the presidential bedroom, which opened off the west hall. "There are only two places where they could rush us. So watch and listen."

The Padre moved into the dining room and signaled the others to follow. He placed them around the polished rectangular table, and pulled another chair to join them.

"You could have at least let me finish my main course," the President said.

"Wasn't bad at all," the First Lady said. She sighed. "All that planning for nothing." She looked at the Padre. "You sure loused up the evening."

"Okay," the President said. "Now that we have our appointment, what are you selling?"

All this small talk and wisecracks, the Padre thought, was a defense mechanism.

"I am the father of Maria and the grandfather of Joseph Michaels," the Padre said.

"Who?"

The President turned to the First Lady, whose expression registered no recognition of the names.

"The woman and child who were taken hostage," the Padre prodded.

"Oh my God," the President said. "How stupid of me."

"Not stupid. It is simply not in the forefront of your mind."

"True. But it obviously is in yours." The President seemed to stop in mid-thought. "I understand. I want you to know that."

"We have two children—" the First Lady began.

"I am not here for understanding," the Padre said.

In the long silence that followed, the President and the First Lady exchanged glances. For the first time since they were seized, the Padre detected in their expressions a sense of tangible fear.

"I am as helpless as you are," the President said, his throat scratchy. He coughed into his fist, clearing it. "I've tried everything."

"Not quite everything," the Padre interjected.

# ✷ 16 ✷

IF YOU SHOW THEM FEAR, THE PRESIDENT THOUGHT, THEY WILL capitalize on it. Fortunately, he had been too stunned to react normally. He was sure it was the same for Amy. Not one of the scenarios ever posed by the Secret Service had mentioned this possibility. He always figured some little piece of the puzzle had been kept from him, as if he could not be trusted. That was the most difficult part of being President, coping with gaps in the flow of information. Too many middlemen deciding what he should be allowed to know. Now he was damned angry. But he kept that fury hidden as well. If he ever got out of this madness, heads would roll.

He had expected that his captors would make a play to leave the White House. It surprised him that they hadn't. Here in the living quarters, surrounded by armed agents, what did these men expect to accomplish? Sooner or later they would have to surrender. Or die. They had left themselves no middle ground.

Was the same true for him and Amy? Hell, he shrugged, summoning what he suspected was more bravado than courage, he had had a good run. If he had to choose a place to die, this one was as good as any. In fact, the best.

Thankfully, the Secret Service had not forced the issue. Biding one's time was always the best choice. If only he could resist showing his fear, hold it from their view, keep his mind clear, alert for opportunities.

He had no doubt that the men were carrying liquid explosives. Indeed, he had felt the sacks in which it was contained beneath the leader's clothing. Soft. Pliable. A kind of waterproof plastic container somehow fastened to their bodies. Able to explode on impact. He believed that implicitly as his mind searched for some countermeasure. Perhaps the slash of a razor blade, clean cut through clothes and plastic, might safely disarm them. He would think about that. Think hard.

Contemplating the havoc that these men had wrought was daunting. The very idea of the presidency was about to undergo a metamorphosis. Who the hell was in charge at this moment? He had sent the Vice President on one of those endless combination funeral and goodwill tours. The idea was to keep him out of the country, out of the political mainstream. A string of world leaders had died in recent weeks and Martin Chalmers was fast becoming the perfect mourner. He wondered how long it would take him to get home. Twenty hours. Poetic justice.

He had used Marty, used his regional clout and antecedents to get elected, but he never brought him into the fold. Now all the people on his own team, the people whose careers, ambitions, jobs, and futures depended on him, were in deep trouble. And if Marty's plane blew up or he stepped on a rusty nail, who then? The Speaker of the House. That turkey. Leadership in depth, he thought. Sarcasm aside, these men who had taken him hostage weren't as clever as they appeared. Didn't they know about the damned Twenty-fifth Amendment for chrissakes?

They were all seated around the dining-room table now. The heavy blue draperies had been drawn, a remarkably perfect fit. Not a rim of light from the powerful floodlights seeped out from where the edges joined. The crystal chandelier above them was lit. The table, an ironic counterpoint to this incongruous situation, was, as always, permanently set for four, with the usual centerpiece of fresh flowers, plates, crystal glasses, and silverware.

"I want my daughter and my grandson. I want them freed. I want them home," the man said. He spoke quickly, his tone commanding, yet surprisingly gentle.

"You know," the President said. "I really feel for you. But we have a problem. I represent two hundred and thirty-odd million souls. Any crackpot demands something, he takes an American. You tell me what I'm supposed to do."

"That, Mr. President, is why I am here," the man answered calmly.

"He's done everything humanly possible," Amy interjected. "You really are off the wall on this."

"Amy, please," the President said.

"It's an exercise in futility and he should know it," Amy persisted, directing her attention to the President. "It's wrong. What they're doing is just as inhuman as what is happening to his daughter and grandson."

She turned to the leader. "You're not really going to blow yourselves up. This whole thing is silly. . . ." Her voice trailed off. The men watched her impassively. She waited, then shook her head and said, "Just a stupid woman, right?"

They were tolerating her, waiting. In the distance, he heard the telephone's ring. It seemed so inconsistently normal under the circumstances. The men exchanged glances.

"It doesn't ring in here. Only lights up," the President said, pointing to a console device with a speaker-phone attachment on one corner of the buffet with a number of buttons, one of them flashing. "It can reach to the dining table. I'm supposed to be always in touch."

"Of course," the leader said.

The telephone continued to ring in the distance.

"Let it," the leader said.

"Can you imagine what's going on out there?" the President asked.

He could barely imagine it himself. To contemplate the ramifications staggered him. The country was a rudderless juggernaut. He wondered whether provisions had ever been made for this eventuality.

"Now, Mr. President," the leader said calmly, "all I ask is for your cooperation. I know that this is very difficult for you."

"How kind of you to understand," Amy snapped.

"And for Mrs. President," the leader continued without missing a beat, "we must try to ignore the circumstances and work together."

"May I ask you a question?" The President was genuinely confused by the man's tone.

The man contemplated the question for a moment, then nodded.

"My wife and I are here under the most terrible conditions of duress. You claim to be wearing an explosive device that could blow us all to hell. You have the entire world holding its breath. We're here, for chrissakes, in the goddamned White House, and you have the gall to ask my cooperation. Would you please tell me what the devil is going on here?"

"I have only one thought in mind," the man replied. "To get my daughter and grandson home safely. I am willing to die for that mission. I'm sorry that it has come to this. We have, it seems, a simple disagreement in method."

"He's crazy," the President said, turning to his wife, then exploring the faces of the other men seated around the table. But when his gaze lighted on the face of the man to whom he was attached by the cord, he shook his head. The man's expression had become a mass of dark wrinkles.

"Who are you?" the President asked, turning to the leader.

"My name is Padronelli," the man said.

"Who?"

"The Padre," the younger man said.

The President was genuinely confused.

"You never heard of the Padre?"

"You mean Padre, like in father?"

The President looked at his wife. Her face reflected his own puzzlement. Crackpots, he thought.

"Not important," the man called the Padre said.

"Mafiosa. Cosa Nostra. The black hand." The younger man lifted his own hand, made a fist, and punched it into the air like a hammer. "The Padre family. Little Italy. Manhattan. You never heard of us? The President. . . ."

The man called the Padre shot the younger man a withering look.

"Jesus Christ," the President said. "He's a Mafia boss."

Amy began to laugh. It started as a giggle and gained momentum, becoming throaty, then uncontrollable as it rattled through the room. Tears began to roll down her cheeks.

"I'll be damned," the President said. "They've picked up the daughter and grandson of a Mafiosa boss." He looked at the Padre and saluted. "Shades of Richard Nixon." The Padre looked at him with a blank expression. "The Watergate tapes. Remember the tapes. And Kennedy." He shook his head. "No, you wouldn't remember."

The President could not recall exact quotes, only what had lingered in his mind. Dean, the President's assistant, had suggested that what they were doing was the sort of thing the Mafia could do better and Nixon agreed. And Kennedy had suggested some shadowy arrangement with a Mafiosa to knock off Fidel Castro. Often, he had thought of such a solution himself. An organization able to bend the rules, subject to no higher authority than their leader.

"I understand, Mr. President," the Padre said. "Please. It is an exaggeration." Again, he looked at the younger man and shook his head.

"Is it?" The President glanced at his wife, who had taken a napkin from the setting and was wiping her eyes. "He's in control of the goddamned President of the United States and he says it's an exaggeration."

Then he turned back to confront the Padre. The Padre! A fantasy gone amuck. Forgive me, he wanted to say. But how can I take this seriously? He did not say it. Instead, he asked, "So what can you do that I can't?"

"As I said, all I am asking for is your cooperation."

It was too ludicrous a request to consider. He wondered if it was time to reveal the provisions of the Twenty-fifth Amendment, to lay the facts on the line for this deluded man. All right, the President told himself, he is crazed with grief and anxiety, and, despite his apparent calm, he has perpetrated an act that, if he ever gets out of this alive, will assure him a lifetime's stay in a mental hospital or a prison. Or worse.

He looked at Amy. Only Amy provided the real evidence of their danger. As President, he was the necessary ingredient for this delusion. But Amy was the hostage, the final persuader. Humor dissipated in his mind. No, it was not funny, not at all.

"You have resources," the Padre said, his voice barely above a whisper, as if he distrusted the earlier sweep of the listening bugs. "You have your intelligence services, your armies, your communications connections, your undercover teams, your . . ." The Padre paused. His tongue flicked over his lips, an odd gesture. "Your authority."

"My authority?" He considered it through a long pause, noting, too, the Padre's laundry list of presidential resources. He lifted his eyes and locked his gaze on the Padre, who returned it. "Your action has effectively destroyed my authority," the President finally said.

"We shall see," the Padre replied.

The President went over it in his mind. The Twenty-fifth Amendment. The mechanics of succession. He hadn't really thought about it much. There had not been a recent occasion for it to be considered.

When Reagan was shot, he remembered, there had been some confusion about it. But when he had undergone surgery for cancer he had written a letter handing over the power of the presidency temporarily to the Vice President. It had been in writing. Yes, it specifically said "in writing." In the event of death there were clear-cut legalities. But in the event of capture . . . Hell, it had not happened in the history of the republic. He dug deeper into his recollection of the amendment.

Barring a written acknowledgment that he was not capable of serving, the full Cabinet had to meet along with the Vice President and choose a temporary successor within, he believed, forty-eight hours. If they could not agree, Congress had to form a parallel body to choose a new President. He seemed to recall twenty-one days. For crying out loud, it was July. They were all on junkets somewhere. Maybe this fellow wasn't all that dumb.

"So what would you have me do?" the President asked.

"First we must know the circumstances."

"What circumstances?"

"Who has taken my daughter and grandson? Where are they held? What is being asked for their freedom?"

"Do you seriously believe that I keep all this information in my head?"

Must he explain the dynamics of presidential leadership? Essentially, he dealt with priorities and options. His staff presented him with information, suggested courses of action and consequences. He made decisions based on weighing the ideal and applying whatever weapons of political persuasion he could muster to achieve an effect that was as close to the ideal as possible. Much of the time, he dealt in compromises, accommodation. Sometimes abject surrender. How could he explain to this man the difference between democracy and dictatorship?

"You have people, resources," the Padre said.

"The President has people," the President corrected. "Under these circumstances, I doubt that I'm still the President." He looked toward Amy, who seemed confused.

"Well then, Mr. President," the Padre said patiently. His pose of respect was getting under the President's skin, another emotional irritant. "Who would be the person most likely to know all the circumstances that affect my daughter and grandson?"

The President turned the question over in his mind. Jack Harkins, of course. He took an odd pleasure in contemplating the prospect of Harkins' involvement. At last, the bastard would have someone who talks his language.

"Probably the CIA," he said with a touch of malevolence. "The head of the CIA would have access." The President looked toward Amy, repressing a desire to wink. "But you still have to deal with the matter of authority, specifically mine. I have, at the moment, a severe credibility problem."

The Padre nodded. Then he got up from the table and walked to the buffet, bringing the telephone console to the table and placing it in front of the President. He stretched out the wire to the speaker-phone and put it in the center of the table.

"I think any request would be useless," the President said. They were, he was certain, waiting for the kidnappers to make the first move. Undoubtedly, by now, the most authoritative crisis-management team had been mobilized. The man in charge, he knew, heaven protect us all, was the Vice President, who was surely speeding home from Asia.

"Mr. President," the Padre said. "This is a simple request."

"And if I refuse?"

"You cannot. Not under the circumstances," the Padre said calmly.

"I'm telling you, I don't have the authority. You don't understand—"

"Mr. President . . ." The Padre shook his head. Then he nodded to Benjy who was attached to Amy.

"This is not a personal thing, believe me, Mr. President."

The President looked at Amy, who had gotten the message.

"I'm not afraid of them," she said. "Let's call their bluff." She stood up abruptly. The cord that attached her to the young man tightened and he stood up in tandem. For a moment she faced them, fearless and defiant. She started to take a step backward. Benjy closed the distance between them and held her in a viselike grip. She struggled briefly.

"Amy," the President shouted. "For crying out loud."

The younger man held her, then deftly twisted one arm behind her. She grimaced in pain but did not cry out.

"This is not necessary," the Padre said quietly, his features showing no emotion or concern.

"Tell him to get his hands off of her," the President commanded.

He watched as Amy tried desperately to repress any expression of pain.

"Please," the President said. Benjy loosened his grip.

"Bastards," Amy hissed.

"Please, Amy." She looked at the President for a moment. Then she shook her head in disgust. Tears welled in her eyes. But the man did not release her. He guided her back to her chair and he stood behind her, his forearm locked around her neck.

"Leave her alone," the President commanded.

She could not speak. But she shook her head in defiance.

"After the call, Mr. President."

Reluctantly, the President reached for the phone.

"What could be more simple? We are inviting him here for a talk."

"They will not grant it. I promise you. . . ."

He glanced at the clock on the buffet.

"You tell him we will expect him in a half hour, precisely. Eleven-thirty." The President punched in a button.

"Yes, Mr. President." It was an operator's voice, hollowed and amplified by the speaker-phone. The Padre rose and stood beside the President.

He felt a warm hand on his own. The touch of the man's flesh was surprisingly warm. He had expected it to be cold and clammy. "Only the request. Nothing more," he whispered.

"It won't do any good." The President shrugged. The Padre offered no comment and lifted his hand from the President's.

"Jack Harkins, please." He heard his voice. It did not sound like his own. Then there were other sounds.

"This is Vic Proctor, Mr. President."

The President looked toward the Padre. So they were routing all calls to the crisis-management team.

"The Secretary of State," the President said. The Padre nodded and motioned with his hand, a signal to continue.

"I would like you to have Jack Harkins here in precisely one half hour."

"Yes, Mr. President." There was a brief pause. Then a whooshing sound. He knew that they had patched in another line.

Damn them, the President thought. Why must they still call him Mr. President? Why hadn't they figured out a way to fire him?

Suddenly the Padre touched the connecting button. The line went dead. At the same time, he noted that the younger man released his grip on Amy and returned to his seat.

"He won't come," the President said. "You just don't understand how these things work."

"We shall see," the Padre said.

# ⋆ 17 ⋆

MARTIN CHALMERS, VICE PRESIDENT OF THE UNITED STATES, SAT IN
the front cabin of Air Force Two. He wore a light headset and
microphone attached to an open line that led to a conference room
in the Executive Office Building, a gingerbread building next door
to the White House.

He was alone in the front cabin by choice. He did not completely
trust his traveling staff. Some were a conduit to the President's
men. Unfortunately, this knowledge induced a paranoia that was
counterproductive. He needed a clear head, an alertness to subtlety and nuance.

The stakes, he assured himself, were larger than mere personal
ambition. Yet the dilemma was unavoidable. He was, indeed, next
in line. The President was a hostage and he, the Vice President,
had been, to the President's men, an outsider. Now they would
consider him a usurper. The thought made him exceedingly uncomfortable.

No Vice President in history had ever been caught in such a
situation. Others, he knew, would characterize it as a catastrophe.
Surely, in national terms, it was a crisis of the first magnitude. As
soon as he arrived in Washington he would take charge—fully,
completely, speedily. They would have to accept him now. Indeed,
it was their patriotic duty.

Earlier they had patched him in to the conference room devoted
to the crisis management of this situation. He was waiting for Vic
Proctor, the Secretary of State, to report to him on the results of
any conversation with the President.

Despite his paranoia, despite his suspicions and uncertainties,
Martin Chalmers, in fact, had never felt more whole, more alive,
less frightened. He savored the thrill that trickled up and down his
spine. His main worry, of course, was his own worthiness. Would
he have the resources, the talent to be, well, presidential? Such a
condition was wholly apart from performing as Vice President,
which was essentially a waiting game.

He also worried that he would be equal to maintaining the image
and tone of a man meeting his destiny. Think of Lyndon Johnson,
he urged himself, remembering those days nearly thirty years ago
when the whole world became a camera eye focusing on the Kennedy assassination. Old Lyndon had pulled it off with dignity.

Martin Chalmers searched his heart for the levers of magna-
nimity, even forgiveness. The President's men had put him down,

ignored him, insulted him with their indifference and silence. Above all else, he hated being patronized. Nor did he have any illusions. Attitudes like that filtered down from the top. Suddenly he heard a momentary burst of crackling static, then a whooshing sound.

"Martin." It was Vic Proctor's voice coming through again. Chalmers had put the Secretary of State in charge until he got home. Whatever his faults, Vic had probity. Never mind that he would be one of the first to go in a Chalmers administration. Most of them would in any event. No vindictiveness there, he assured himself. A leader needs people around him with whom he could be comfortable.

"Yes, Vic."

He wanted his voice to sound purposeful, commanding. He had ordered that the conversations between him and the crisis team be recorded. The world must have evidence of his leadership.

Paul had picked him as his running mate for his region, the Southwest sun belt, his antecedents—his father had been the beloved senator from Texas, Tad Chalmers—and his innocuousness. All his life he had been a figurehead, a one-term governor of Texas, the chairman of the board of Chalmers Industries, a professional board member of a dozen corporations. When you need a good rubber stamp, get old Marty. He was, above all, a professional ingratiator. It was a role he despised. Coming up at last was the moment he had waited for all his life.

"The President has asked to see Jack Harkins. No reason given."

"You spoke directly to him?"

"Directly. No other conversation."

"Did you mention the . . ."

"The procedure?" Proctor asked. They had chosen the word for the euphemism.

"Yes."

He would have to be cautious. Procedure meant the legalities of the Twenty-fifth Amendment, specifically the necessity for the President to put in writing his admission that he was unable to govern. It was explicit in the amendment. Section three. For the Vice President the Twenty-fifth Amendment was holy writ. The words were engraved in his mind. The amendment read:

"Whenever the President transmits to the President pro tempore of the Senate and the Speaker of the House of Representatives his written declaration that he is unable to discharge the powers and duties of his office, and until he transmits to them a written declaration to the contrary, such powers and duties shall be discharged by the Vice President as Acting President."

"He said nothing about that," Proctor said. "But then he has a gun to his head." Proctor paused. "A figure of speech. But it means the same thing."

"Perhaps we had better put the procedure for Section Four on standby," the Vice President said calmly. He felt the pounding of his accelerating heartbeat. It was, after all, explicit: *in writing*. He supposed the President could scribble the words on a piece of toilet paper and get it out through Harkins. It was possible to do it if he was clever, and it would save them all the back-biting and trouble. Section Four could be a real problem. The Cabinet would have to decide. He had that down too.

"Whenever the Vice President and a majority of either the principal officers of the executive departments, or of such other body as Congress may by law provide, transmit to the President pro tempore of the Senate and the Speaker of the House of Representatives their written declaration that the President is unable to discharge the powers and duties of his office, the Vice President shall immediately assume the powers and duties of the office as Acting President."

It got more complicated after that. One step at a time, he told himself, although a black thought lapped at the edges of his mind, despite his conscious refusal to acknowledge it. Blow him up. Jesus, Marty, he told himself, you bloodthirsty bastard.

"Shall we give them Harkins?" Chalmers asked.

Proctor hesitated at his end of the line. For a moment the Vice President confronted the statical void.

"I . . . I didn't think we had a choice," Proctor said. "It was a request from the President."

"The man's a hostage, Vic." It took a great effort of will to keep his voice down.

"But he's still the President."

His paranoia flared.

"What about Harkins' life?" Chalmers asked. Of all the President's gang, he detested Harkins the most.

"We gave him the option of not going," Proctor said.

"Since when is that bastard calling the shots," Chalmers blurted, immediately regretting the outburst. Proctor's hesitation was diplomatic. Both knew that the heart of the problem was the recognition of the President's authority. Proctor, of all people, would stick to the most orthodox legalities.

"I must say, he has got a lot of courage stepping into the eye of the storm," Proctor said with the barest hint of deflection.

"I think it's very stupid," Chalmers muttered. He hoped the man would get his ass blown up.

"Maybe"—Chalmers paused to calm himself—"we should have that Cabinet meeting. Explore Section Four just in case."

"I'll get them together."

"And I'd like to be kept informed."

"Of course," Proctor snapped. Chalmers heard the man suck in his breath. "TOA still the same?"

"About seven hours to go," Chalmers said, looking at his watch.

"They'll be here waiting," Proctor said.

Chalmers thought he had detected a slight note of deference.

# ★ 18 ★

NED FOREMAN SAT AT THE CONFERENCE TABLE AND BLEW HIS NOSE into a Kleenex. A cold in July, he thought with disgust. In fact, everything that was happening was ludicrous. Foreman, the national Security Advisor, had spent the last couple of hours on a mission of reassurance. He had called the foreign ministers of all the NATO allies, of France, of Japan, of India, and, of course, of the Soviet Union.

To all the message was the same. The machinery of government would operate smoothly in this crisis, as it had in previous circumstances. Not to worry. Some crazies have got the President holed up, but we'll figure out a way to get the situation resolved.

"What are their demands?" Dimitri Karkov, the Soviet Foreign Minister, had asked in his remarkably unaccented English. He had seemed genuinely shocked, expressing deep concern. He and the General Secretary liked the President. Endangering the American President was not in their interests.

"We are not yet certain."

"That is very bad," the Russian said.

Foreman, although unseen, nodded in agreement. He was tempted to ask what he knew had been asked many times before when American hostages had been taken. Is this a KGB-inspired operation? If not, what is your influence? Do you control these people through surrogates? Surely, if you tried, you could get them out. Always the answer had been the same. *Nyet.*

"They are in no way connected to us," Karkov assured him.

"We studied that possibility. It was quickly rejected, Minister."

It had been a carefully measured response. He wanted the Russian to be certain that the matter had been under deep consideration. Nor had it been rejected out of hand.

"Of course you realize that we may have to put the armed forces on worldwide alert," the Foreign Minister said. "But, I assure you, it will be routine."

"It could be viewed as a provocation," Foreman said cautiously.

"We have studied that possibility."

It occurred to Foreman that they were talking in the same language but at cross-purposes. He remembered a line from a movie: "What we have here is a failure of communication."

"You think this hostage incident was arranged by our side to provoke yours?"

"A thought," the minister responded, "but quickly rejected."

Foreman doubted that he spoke the truth. The Soviets were always testing America's motives. Devious bastards. He would have to arrange another clandestine meeting with Peter Vashevsky to confirm the Russian's real intentions. Peter Vashevsky was the top KGB operative in the United States, with a direct pipeline to the General Secretary. He and Vashevsky had no communication problem. The Soviets were only comfortable operating on two tracks. One public. One private.

"I hope your alert doesn't get our people nervous," Foreman said.

"You must assure them. But certain things are necessary."

"I understand, Minister."

"So who is running your country?" the Russian asked. In his voice Foreman detected an unmistakable note of contempt.

"At the moment"—Foreman hesitated—"the Secretary of State is nominally in charge."

"Nominally?"

"Actually, he is reporting to the Vice President, who is on his way home from the Far East."

Always futile, he thought, to define the intricacies of the democratic process to the Soviets. To begin to define the Twenty-fifth Amendment to him would be unthinkable. Besides, no one was quite certain how it applied in this case. He could sense the wheels going around in the Russian's mind.

"Everything is under complete control here," Foreman added, but thought to himself, bullshit.

"Do you know anything about these people who have the President?" the Russian said, his voice demanding.

"We'll have something soon."

"They have a great prize. They could demand the impossible."

"We will keep you informed, Minister."

His conversation with the Russian reinforced his sense that something was nagging at Karkov, something he could not distinguish through the murk of these swift-moving events.

The White House staff had set up a crisis center in a conference room on the basement level of the Executive Office Building. The Vice President was theoretically in charge. However, he was so far outside the circle of power that, as the saying goes, he did not even have the keys to the men's room.

Until this incident he had been barely tolerated, and the prevailing opinion was that God did not give him his fair share of gray matter. At least he had the good grace to be separated by distance. Once he arrived on the scene, the situation could only go downhill. At the moment any shred of hope was invested in the director of the CIA, Jack Harkins, a smart son of a bitch.

Foreman studied the faces of the men around the table. At the head of it sat Vic Proctor, the Secretary of State, an old nemesis of the Vice President but too much of a pro to refuse the call to close ranks. Already, in his mind, the conference room had become the bunker.

Others around the table were Steve Potter, the President's press secretary, Lou Shore, counsel to the President, and Bob Nickels, the Chief of Staff, the old-boy team, the death-till-us-part triplets he called them, but never to their faces. Also present, the chairman of the Joint Chiefs of Staff, Admiral Bill Kendall, who sat quietly in a chair at a far end of the table directing the so-called siege, which was not a siege at all, in fact, was no more than a small cordon of men who had no practical function except to show the world that, somehow, America was still in charge of itself.

The Secretary of Defense, Harley Fox, was also present, as usual, scaring them to death about the Soviets taking advantage. He had orchestrated a presentation by some general who was sure that his elite military SWAT team could do the job with a fifty-fifty chance of getting the President out unharmed. Good odds, considering, the Secretary of Defense had offered.

"Considering what?" someone had asked.

Fox grunted. He hated to have his military options put down. Then someone said, "Suppose it was you, Harley?"

He seemed to be considering a comeback until someone said, "Anyone can walk through the detectors in the Pentagon carrying the same material."

"Then we'll authorize a body frisk for everyone," Fox snapped.

"Body frisk thirty thousand people a day?" Vic Proctor asked.

By then everyone in the room realized the futility of the discussion and Steve Potter put it in perspective. "Fact is," the President's Press Secretary said, "none of us are really safe. There are holes in the system. That's a given. Besides, the body frisk is just not American." Invoking what was or was not American had a soothing effect on the tense gathering.

A bank of telephones had been swiftly installed. When they spoke on the phones their voices were low, controlled. These were men who under most circumstances knew the value of tone. Outwardly, they were cool, although, Foreman knew, most were genuinely frightened. If the President were blown up, the ball game was over for them as far as government was concerned. Chalmers would bring in his own team.

A telephone button flashed suddenly. The men looked up from their various conversations. Vic Proctor picked up the instrument.

"Good. Right now."

He nodded and tapped lightly on the table with his free hand. Then he replaced the receiver and looked up.

"Halloran," he said. Halloran was the head of the FBI.

The interrogation of the caterer was taking place a few doors down from the conference room, a makeshift filing office pressed into service for its proximity and lack of windows.

They did not have to wait long. Halloran arrived. He and his wife had been guests at the state dinner. He was still wearing his tuxedo. The ready-made black tie hung awry on one collar point. Halloran appeared as a big, bluff, red-faced man whose face was the map of the Emerald Isle and whose speech contained the sounds of Bean Town. He had given the FBI back the glamour that had seeped out of the organization over the last decade. Once a big-city cop, he developed into a hands-on manager who, like Hoover, often led the posse and conducted the big investigations himself. He had done so in this case.

"I got good news and bad news," he began. His eyes surveyed the faces around the table. He did not sit down, knowing that he was about to impart something momentous. He waited to create the perfect sense of drama.

"Mafiosa," he said, pausing for a long moment. "The man who has the President is Salvatore Padronelli, better known as the Padre, probably the most important don in this country. Second generation. A racket network of powerful proportions. The other three are his top capos, loyal to the death. One of them, the Canary, is a known murderer and hit man. The other, the Prune, has a rap sheet as long as your arm. The young one is Benjy Mustoni, known as the Kid, an ambitious enforcer. This caterer, poor bastard, was, as they say, given a deal he couldn't refuse."

"What the hell do they want?"

"They want Maria and Joseph Michaels, the Padre's only daughter and grandson."

"Who?" the Secretary of State asked.

"The woman and kid, the hostages who were picked up in Egypt."

"You're joking," Steve Potter said.

"Notice my laughter," the FBI chief said. "Joke's on me, too. He served me a drink. The Padre himself. I knew he looked familiar, but I couldn't place him. Dammit. Not in that atmosphere. He's slippery and efficient as hell, a master motivator. But stand in his way . . ."

Halloran remained silent for a moment, then continued. "In his group of people, they worship him. It is no accident that he is called the Padre."

Halloran shook his head. "He's sixty-nine years old. I'm sending his file over. Makes good reading. He's seen it all. Not a scratch on him. Knows his business. Worse, he subscribes to a mythology that makes him truly believe he is a man of honor. Gives him total justification for any act of thievery or brutality. Yet, he's supposed to live modestly, although he's richer than Croesus."

He looked at Potter. "Now you got something to feed the animals."

"Depends on how stupid you want us to look," the press secretary said gloomily. "Those Arabs who got her and the kid will be laughing for a millennium. The fucking Mafia. Who would believe it?"

"At least we know they're not fanatics," Bob Nickels, the Chief of Staff, said.

Inexplicably, Foreman noted, the tension seemed to ease. Even in himself. Perhaps it was because the Mafia was perceived to be, under all the hoopla, business people. Lou Shore, presidential counsel, seemed to put it in perspective for all of them.

"They know the value of a deal," Shore said. "Also, I doubt if they're suicidal. That's the key. We might just have to wait them out."

"You been dealing with them, Lou?" Halloran asked with unmistakable sarcasm. He did not wait for an answer. "The world's best police brains have been trying to break them for years. No way. They know what they want and that old bastard up there will die trying. If necessary, he will blow himself to kingdom come. I shit you not."

"That doesn't mean he would stand in the way of negotiations," Vic Proctor said.

"You can call it that if you want to," Halloran said, meeting Proctor's gaze. "Just ask the caterer."

"Are you saying he won't negotiate?" Shore asked.

"All day long. But he won't settle for anything less than the delivery of his daughter and grandson harm-free."

"But we've done everything we can," Foreman interjected. "Jack Harkins will explain that to him."

"The Padre doesn't think so," Halloran said stubbornly. "That's the whole point of this exercise."

"Got to get him out of the line of fire," Proctor said wearily.

The National Security Advisor sensed his meaning. Force the President out of office. Leave the Padre no one to negotiate with. Halloran appeared uncertain as to how to bow out. He seemed disappointed that his advice was not being solicited. But the Secretary of State was lost in his own thoughts.

"Shall I go out and toss the fish to the seals?" Potter asked.

The question brought Proctor back to alertness.

"We've got to ask Chalmers," he said with obvious distaste.

"In that case . . ." Whatever came next was swallowed, unheard.

"No way out on that," Proctor said, looking toward Potter with obvious sympathy.

"Too juicy an opportunity for him to miss," Potter sighed.

"You might want to knock out a statement," Proctor said.

"For him?"

"He's the man." Proctor looked about him, searching the faces. "Unless someone's got a better idea."

"We've got nearly seven hours before the Vice President touches down. You'd think all you superbrains would find an answer," Lou Shore interjected, his expression growing more harried by the minute.

He had less to lose than the others, Foreman thought. The President's childhood friend, he would be perceived by Chalmers as a fanatic loyalist and marked as one of the first to go.

"All right," Proctor said, glaring at Shore. "What's your pleasure?"

Shore lowered his eyes and cracked his knuckles. "Try gas or something. Hell, that's what some of you get paid for."

"Whistling Dixie," Halloran said.

"You're the head of the fucking FBI," Shore said, raising his voice. "What the hell have you got to offer?"

Illogic was taking hold now. Shore, striking out blindly, had begun to reflect everyone's frustration. And panic. Halloran flushed red. He shifted his weight from foot to foot.

"You people haven't been listening," he muttered. All eyes in the room had once again turned to him. "There are no alternatives," he said, lowering his voice. "Bottom line. Get the woman and the boy out. End of story."

The room filled with silence.

"Problem is . . ." Foreman said. The elusive notion hiding in his mind suddenly burst into his consciousness along with the words of the Russian: They have a great prize. They could demand the impossible. "They will up the ante," Foreman finished.

"In the end, we'll have to meet whatever they ask," Halloran said.

"And if not?" Foreman asked. Awful scenarios were dancing in his head. One in particular. It was definitely the wrong time to put it into words.

"Then you've got, among others, one very dead president up there," Halloran said solemnly.

## ✻ 19 ✻

EVERY MAN WAS GIVEN A MOMENT, JACK HARKINS BELIEVED. IT could only be defined as a lightning bolt. If the tip of the bolt reached out and touched you, then you were obliged to slip through the seam of the flash into the void of destiny. Jack Harkins was certain that such a moment had arrived.

As he walked up the winding stairway of the White House to the central hall, he felt the adrenaline of anticipation. All the vectors of his life were converging, the Phi Beta Kappa key, the four athletic letters, the six-year doctorate in political science, his slog through the maze of government service. If this new phase was life-threatening, so be it. It added all the more excitement to the joy and pleasure of it.

Harkins walked through a gauntlet of armed men. Another line ranged itself across the upstairs width of the central hall. The men wore helmets and battle gear, an incongruous form of dress in the elegant hallway. Between this line and the closed door of the west sitting hall was a kind of no-man's-land.

Moments before, the CIA Director had been in the basement command post at the Executive Office Building, where the Secretary of State had briefed him on the situation. The man had been apologetic, weary, but not vague by choice. It was, Harkins thought, an astonishing can of worms.

"You realize the risk you are taking," the Secretary of State said gloomily.

"I think you might be exaggerating. They need contact with the outside. That's essential to them."

Without hesitating, Harkins walked through the line of men, across the no-man's land to the closed west-sitting-room entrance. He looked back at the faces of the tense men across the hall, smiled, then rapped on the door. He waited, rapped again.

He heard movement within. The door slid open slowly. Just a sliver at first. He saw an eye staring at him. The door opened farther. He sensed the tension rise behind him, imagined movement, the leveling of guns. The door opened farther. Hands came out and scooped him in. He felt himself embraced by the arms of a big man. Another moved furniture into place behind the closed door.

Locked in position, he waited until the job was completed. Then the man who had moved the furniture, an older man, turned directly toward him. A calm face, he thought, stubbled, with alert eyes, which studied him. He knew at once it was the Padre referred to in his briefing.

"If you'll follow me, Mr. Harkins," the man said. He waited while the bigger man, behind him, frisked him thoroughly.

"Don't be silly," he said.

There was no response. He followed the older man into the dining room. The setting was serene, peculiar. The President sat at one end of the table, Mrs. Bernard at the other. They looked at him with expressions that might have been characterized as wry amusement.

Two men sat at either side of the table. It took him a few seconds more to see the attachments of cord. Beyond that, there was little sign of disarray. What was most bizarre were the waiters' uniforms the men wore. They somehow clashed with the stark seriousness of the situation.

The man he had followed went toward the wall with the sideboard, pulled another chair forward, and waved for him to sit down. He did so. The chandelier above them glistened, its reflection scattered into thousands of sparkles on the crystal, plates, and silver. The situation did not even strike him as threatening to the President.

"Sorry about this, Jack. It's definitely not my idea," the President said.

"Nor mine," the First Lady said.

Harkins shrugged.

"Caused a bit of a stir out there . . ." the President said, also looking toward the Padre, who remained silent, listening to the exchange.

"A bit," Harkins said.

"They know what we have here . . ." the President said.

"Apparently," Harkins said.

"Crazy, right?"

"Different," Harkins said.

"You'll find this fellow very polite."

"There's little enough of that," Harkins responded, looking at the Padre, whose face was impassive.

"You know why we've been taken?" the President asked.

"Yes. I've been informed."

The Padre rubbed his chin, his eyes vague, as they looked downward at the table. Then suddenly he lifted his head, fully alert.

"Do you know where my daughter and my grandson are being kept?"

Harkins looked at the President. There were numerous questions still to be considered. How forthright must he be? How accurate? When should evasions begin? Yes, he knew approximately where the woman and child were being held. Indeed, he knew a lot more than he had ever told the President.

"Information is very vague," Harkins said, stalling for time to assemble a strategy.

"But you have some information?"

Harkins nodded.

"He has assets," the President said. The Padre seemed confused by the word.

"People on the inside," the President explained. "It's in the computer." Harkins did not like the President's mocking tone. He wished he would hold his tongue.

"We can hook into this computer here?" the Padre asked.

"Yes." No point in evading that answer, Harkins thought. The man might be a rough diamond on the outside, but he was no fool. He must be prepared to accept that fact as an axiom.

Harkins' attention became acute, his mind's antenna tuned to its most sensitive frequency. As always, he had trained himself to confront every man without preconditions. His mind would eventually categorize him, but at the beginning he started with a clean slate. Although this man called Padre came packaged in a carton of media clichés, the wrapping seemed inappropriate. Perhaps his strategy was to present himself as scrupulously unimpressive, badly groomed, world-weary.

Yet this man could not be evaluated in a vacuum. He was, after all, holding hostage the President of the United States in the White House. The method of entry was not simply a lucky guess. Beating the security machine was the stock-in-trade of men who earned their living going into places where they did not belong. Everything and everyone was vulnerable. Rule one of the spook game. But the actual hostage-taking required both inspired loyalty and, in the case of the caterer, pinpointed intimidation. For that kind of intimidation, history was important and had to be respected.

"Who are the people who have taken them?" the Padre asked.

"A radical Arab group," he answered. There were so many he had eschewed committing them to memory.

"Is there someone in charge of this group?"

Harkins saw a crossroad ahead. He took the one that would make it simple, cut and dried.

"Yes."

"And you know who he is?"

"Yes."

The Padre prodded, paused, then began again.

"Where does the money come from?"

Harkins hadn't expected that question. It threw him off for a moment. He hesitated, something he had not intended to do.

"The money," the Padre prodded.

Harkins backtracked to the crossroad. The explanation defied simplicity.

"We are dealing here with the byzantine ways of Middle East politics. I guess you could begin at the beginning. There is a kind of blackmail in this. The conservative states—"

"Please," the Padre said. "I have no interest in the history of these things."

Harkins felt at a disadvantage. He was annoyed with himself. He looked helplessly at the President, who wore a thin sardonic smile, as if he were enjoying the proceedings.

"Well, for one, the Saudis. They pay a kind of ransom to these people. The Iranians. The Libyans. Those are the principal bankers." Harkins paused long enough to see if he had the Padre's attention, confirmed it, then slogged on.

"But even that does not explain everything. These people have emissaries who meet with each other. They plot and plan. And they are united, allegedly, in one public idea. Their hatred of Israel. But to many of them, the existence of Israel is merely the fuel that drives the engine. Each has diverse goals. And there are others who try to get into the fray for their own ends. The Druse, the Shiites, the Sunnis, the Maronite Christians, their splinter groups, and the splinter groups of the splinter groups. And the Western powers and the Soviets and profiteers. It is a smorgasbord of competing interests. Then there are the Syrians who hide behind their own sinister facade of respectability. I'm sorry. I'm compressing it as best I can."

"So you think, those countries you mentioned, they are the money people?"

"Yes." Futile to go beyond that explanation, Harkins thought. The man went right for the jugular. His logic was beginning to emerge.

"These people on the inside," the Padre said. "You can reach them?"

He looked at the President. The smile had disappeared. The man was cutting very close to the famous bone of contention. Harkins felt his adrenaline surge.

"We have a highly efficient covert action organization. What you call people on the inside."

"They can get things done?"

"Absolutely." He looked at the President. "Once set in motion."

"Anywhere in the world?"

"Most places where it counts. Like the Middle East," Harkins said cautiously. He was sure now he was catching the man's drift, locking into his mind set.

"You give them orders, they obey?" the Padre asked.

"That's the general idea," Harkins responded, pausing. Again he looked at the President, who evaded his eyes. "But in specific terms you can't set any action in motion without an order to pursue a covert operation coming directly from the President of the United States."

"I wouldn't get any ideas in that direction," the President interjected. "Besides, my presidency is a moot point.

"You ordered them to get you this man," the Padre said calmly. "They did."

"Tell him about the Twenty-fifth Amendment," the President said, thrusting a thumb in Harkins' direction.

"What is that?" the Padre asked.

"It spells out a method of succession," Harkins began.

"You should have read it before you began this . . . this absurdity," the President interrupted. "You'd know that there are provisions for a situation in which I cannot perform my official duties or functions. Which means I will be replaced, at least temporarily. You may hold me hostage, of course. Which puts this situation in another category."

It was, Harkins saw, an obvious setback for the Padre. It could not be glossed over or hidden. He got up from the table and walked around it, rubbing his chin.

The President turned to Harkins, who addressed the Padre. "Soon the cabinet will be meeting. Perhaps to pick another man under Section Four of the Twenty-fifth Amendment. The Vice President is constitutionally next in line for the presidency. He is also in charge of the committee assessing this problem. At this moment he is on his way back from the Far East. When he lands the Cabinet will hold its meeting."

Harkins turned to face the President. Play this ploy gingerly, he cautioned himself. "Could be that in a few hours Chalmers will be the President of the United States."

"Chalmers. Pity us all," the President muttered.

"A temporary measure, Mr. President," Harkins said. He looked at the Padre. "Until this matter is resolved."

"So what you have in your power is a potential has-been, Mr. Padre," the President said. His tone struck Harkins as a blend of sarcasm and regret.

The Padre had remained silent for a long time. His thoughts and desires were, of course, setting the pace. No action could be performed without his consent. Harkins turned this over in his mind and waited. Was it possible to break the lock this man had over them? He looked so benign. The others were thugs, human weapons of the Padre's will.

"What does this mean, official duties?" the Padre asked, directing his question to the President.

Once again he had come to the heart of the matter. Now Harkins locked himself into the Padre's wavelength. The President answered it too eagerly, heading blindly into the trap the Padre had set. Instantly, Harkins knew the role he had been assigned.

"Be available to function. The Executive department is a vast bureaucracy. There are decisions to be made," the President said. "How can I be expected to operate tied to these, this human bomb. You'll have to admit, it does hamper the decision-making process."

Harkins noted that the President was growing bolder. "The fact is, you're finished. There's nothing I can do for you. Oh, you might hold out to trade me for your daughter and grandson. But don't bank on them playing your game. Our enemies love this situation. They love seeing the President of the United States in this position."

The President smiled. He enjoyed telescoping the sardonic message he was about to launch. "If I were you, considering the realities, I would be better off bargaining for a presidential pardon."

The Padre listened patiently. "You have your mind, your brains," the Padre said. "You can speak."

The President seemed confused. He turned to Harkins. "What the hell is he getting at?"

Harkins was having no trouble understanding where the Padre was going. But he chose to remain silent, let his ideas sink in.

"I have no intention of preventing you from doing your official duties," the Padre said.

"You're releasing me then?" the President asked.

The Padre ignored the question.

"We have telephones here. People can come." He pointed to Harkins. "Here is your CIA chief. Anyone you need, we get."

"One of your fans," Amy said. "He wants you to stay in office. Better than having Chalmers." She giggled compulsively, as if confused by her own remark.

"So where am I wrong?" the Padre asked.

The President looked at him for a moment, then smiled. "How am I supposed to conduct Cabinet meetings?"

"On the telephone."

"And you expect me to conduct foreign policy tied to this man?" He looked at Vinnie with disdain.

"What would you do if you had a cold, Mr. President? Perhaps a little fever. The doctor would ask that you stay in bed. Nothing more. No Twenty-fifth Amendment."

"I don't understand any of this," the President said, shaking his head. "Is this in the context of a suggestion?"

"I am simply asking if you think it is possible," the Padre said.

One-track mind, Harkins thought. He simply edits out what is not relevant.

"I wouldn't consent to it in any event," the President said.

The Padre nodded to Benjy, who rose suddenly. The First Lady, feeling the tug around her waist, rose in tandem. She turned pale.

"Where are you going?" the President asked.

The younger man started to move toward the entrance of the dining room. The First Lady looked toward her husband.

"I'm not afraid," she said, her voice tremulous under the pose of defiance.

"I demand . . ." the President began, standing up suddenly. His attached companion did the same. The cord stretched. Aware of the pressure, the President buckled slightly, his fingers held stiffly against the table, his back slightly arched. He was not a foolish man, but he was having a difficult time dealing with his frustration.

Finally, after a long moment, he sat down. A politician, Harkins knew, was, above all, a practitioner of the possible. There was no point in calling the Padre's bluff.

"Just leave her alone," the President said.

Again, the Padre nodded and the younger man led the First Lady back to the dining-room table.

"Cold-blooded bastards," Amy said. The color had come back to her cheeks. Nevertheless, Harkins saw, the gesture had made its point.

"May I repeat the question?" the Padre asked when they had settled down. His voice was steady, calm.

The President sucked in a deep breath. It was now obvious that few choices were open to him. Bravado was futile. Courage was merely a word.

"I doubt it," the President said. "It's never been tried. A President operating under these conditions. Push comes to shove, they'd throw it into Congress."

"And in the meantime you would be able to act?" the Padre asked. "All you have to do is to tell them that you are capable of carrying out your duties?"

"Telling isn't doing," the President muttered, looking at Harkins with eyes hard as agates.

By then Harkins had had time to consider possibilities. Like himself, the Padre was a man of plans. This one had taken a detour, but the premise still existed, and it was the premise that the Padre was fighting for. Harkins, too, fully understood that premise. Wild, yes. But there was a bizarre logic to it. More important, it heralded the arrival of Harkins' long-sought moment. Again, he cautioned himself.

"He wants you to remain in office," Harkins said into the silence that followed. He hoped he had mustered the appropriate skepticism. Harkins paused. He looked at the Padre. Their eyes locked for a moment, acknowledging an alliance.

Harkins' mind raced as he compressed reflection. The idea was the concoction of a totally amoral man. Harkins could empathize with that. He must be careful, he warned himself, to maintain his neutrality. At some point there would be an accounting. Above all, he must come out of this situation unscathed, celebrated.

"What he's doing is giving us an opportunity."

"What opportunity?" the President asked.

"To act in the only way possible," Harkins said.

"Your way."

"The only way."

"Which I certainly won't agree with," the President said.

"Maybe."

"Maybe? What the hell does that mean?"

"Taking you hostage waives the rules. You now have permission to proceed without restraints." He hoped he was getting the idea across. He shot a glance at the Padre's eyes. He could detect approval there.

"Permission?"

"In a manner of speaking," Harkins said.

"How would it guarantee the safe return of his daughter and grandson?" the President asked. From protest to debate, Harkins thought with some satisfaction.

"I understand the mentality of these people," the Padre said. It was his way of signaling agreement with Harkins' analysis.

"I was doing my damndest to get them back. All of them." The President glared at the Padre. "Apparently you had no faith in the way I've been going about this?"

The President looked at Amy. Her nostrils quivered with anger.

"I have considerable experience in these matters," the Padre continued.

"I'll bet you do."

"I am not offering you any choices, Mr. President," the Padre said calmly.

"All you want me to do is put the madmen in charge of the madhouse."

"In a way, Mr. President, the insane are already in charge," Harkins said. He wondered if the right moment had arrived for him to commit himself.

"What the hell is going on here?" the President asked. His face flushed as he fought to keep himself under control. "Are you in on this, Jack? Is this one of your spook tricks?"

"Ashamed to say, I don't think I would have the imagination, Mr. President," Harkins said, knowing he was treading on dangerous ground.

Again Harkins and the Padre exchanged glances. The Padre nodded.

"The CIA meets the Mafia. Perfect marriage," the President snickered.

"An odd couple, I'll admit," Harkins said. "But look at the opportunity." Harkins paused. Why didn't the President grasp the logic of it? "The fact is that we are in a bind over the hostages. Nothing has worked. We're caught between a rock and a hard place. He may not realize it, but he's giving us an out. Now we can throw inhibitions to the winds. I'm not sure he has the answers. But I am sure of one thing. For whatever reasons, we don't."

"Blame it all on him," the President said. "The devil made me do it." He turned toward the Padre. "Offense intended."

The Padre showed no reaction. He didn't have to. Harkins knew he had permission to carry the ball. He pressed forward.

"He's taken this risk because he believes he has the answers. All right. What's to lose if we try it his way?" He raised his palms. "I'm not saying I know what he's up to. It's obvious he wants to use our covert operation. It's all set up, ready to go. I'm only saying that you can do things because he's got you under the gun that you might not be doing if he wasn't here. You don't have to worry about our so-called allies second-guessing you. As long as you retain your authority, you can use your power."

The President crossed his arms over his chest. Protection or defiance, Harkins wondered. He wasn't sure which.

"Suppose it doesn't work, even if I follow your instructions and it doesn't get your daughter and grandson back safely. We're dealing with ruthless bastards. They could kill them without batting an eye. Then what?"

"That is thinking too far ahead," the Padre said.

"And if I don't go along in the first place?"

"I told you, Mr. President. I did not offer you a choice."

"You'd actually blow us up?" the President asked, looking at his wife, who had gone pale again. "Yourself as well."

"I am a man of my word," the Padre whispered.

The President looked at his fingers, obviously contemplating his options.

"Even if I resign?"

"I have tried to be reasonable," the Padre said.

"But they will act. My situation is obvious."

"Then they should realize this."

The fact was, Harkins saw, there were no options. Compromise was not in the man's vocabulary.

"Without veto power on your suggestions, how can I be a President?" the President asked.

"I am a man who always welcomes suggestions," the Padre said.

"Can't ask for anything more than that," Amy said sarcastically. They paid no attention to her outburst. "Macho men," she said with contempt.

Harkins' mind was already heading in other directions. He was excited. He knew he was absolutely central to any idea the Padre might have. Finally, he would be able to fully utilize the full power of the CIA machinery.

The President bit his lip and tapped his fingers on the table.

"Suppose they don't let me continue in office?" he asked.

"You must convince them."

"A man goes to these lengths . . ." Harkins began.

"No need to explain, Mr. Interlocutor," the President said to Harkins.

After a long pause, he turned to the Padre. "Can you put the plug in this way or do I have to bend over?"

# ✷ 20 ✷

ROBERT MICHAELS SAT IN THE MISTY PUNGENCY OF MRS. SANtorelli's kitchen watching the portly woman stir pasta sauce with a wooden spoon. She shuffled around in worn slippers, offering benign smiles when she looked at him, winking at him as she tasted the sauce from her wooden spoon.

Because of the heat, he had stripped down to his T-shirt. Yet he had chosen to sit in the kitchen rather than the cooler living room because he did not want to be alone. Not that he and Mrs. Santorelli had much to say to each other. Her frame of reference was only that of her dead husband, the sainted Giovanni, and almost no sentence escaped her mouth without a reference to what her Giovanni used to say.

When he was not watching Mrs. Santorelli's movements in front of her old-fashioned gas range, his eyes drifted to the black and white television set on her Formica kitchen table. From where he sat, he could also see Angelo, the Pencil, sitting at the dining-room table speaking softly into the black telephone. The heat did not faze him. In fact, little fazed him. He seemed to be a man wearing blinders, his eyes wandering only as far as his little notes, which he consulted periodically, after which he dialed a number and whispered into the phone.

Agitation and frustration had given way to helplessness. He felt childlike, half-made, ravaged by the triple demons of guilt, uncertainty, and depression.

"Not to worry," Angelo had assured him.

It was only when he heard the first announcement on television that the enormity of the act blasted into his consciousness. To hear it in this manner, stark and blatant, shattered his hopes.

"Madness," he said aloud. Angelo had looked at him and frowned. It was a conclusion he had not allowed himself to make during the planning stages. Salvatore had made it seem so simple, so logical. We will take the President hostage and not give him up until Maria and Joey are released. An eye for an eye.

Now he blamed himself for encouraging it to happen. Not that he could have stopped the vaunted Padre from doing anything.

"They will surely kill them now," he sighed. By then, Angelo merely ignored him. Robert knew why. There was no role for a Cassandra in the organization. Not now or ever. They were simply geared to believe that they could perform the impossible.

Mrs. Santorelli began to slap meat into meatballs, clapping her hands around the little globs of beef as if she were cheering the tenor in some Verdi opera. It was such an incongruous sight, he could not, despite his gloom, keep himself from smiling.

At that moment Rocco burst in the door. He was out of breath, sweating from walking two flights. He grunted in Robert's direction, passing him to where Angelo was sitting in the dining room. Robert listened as the men spoke in low tones.

"The Pole," Rocco, the Talker, said.

"Again," Angelo said. "We trashed his trucks."

"He still makes trouble."

"It was not enough of a message," the Pencil said.

"No."

"Not a warning this time," the Pencil said. "He has made his bed."

The Talker nodded. The Pencil made a note.

"Something to do with Salvatore?" Robert asked. He knew better, but needed to ask the question.

"Just business," the Pencil said. The Talker grunted.

"You're going to have a man killed, aren't you?"

They both looked at him, ignoring his question.

"Considering what we're involved with now"—Robert pointed to the television set—"how can you, it boggles the mind."

"It is business, Robert," Rocco said in a gravelly voice.

"It is the Padre's orders," the Pencil said, "to conduct business."

Robert did not expect an answer. He felt imprisoned in a value system that he could never really understand.

Rocco moved into the kitchen. Mrs. Santorelli looked up and nodded a greeting.

"You want some, Rocco?" she asked.

"Later," he said. His expression was dark and gloomy. For a moment he looked at the television set.

"It was a stupid idea," Robert said testily.

Rocco glowered at the television, then left.

Luigi came into the apartment without knocking. He looked agitated. His face was red and he, too, was sweating.

"They know. The FBI is everywhere, even in the restaurant."

"Did you think it would be a secret?" Robert said sarcastically.

"But the Padre is inside the White House," Luigi said, after he had cooled down. "Right in the bonanz. You'll see, they will succeed." He looked at Robert, then bent over and patted his hand. "Your Maria and Joey will be coming home soon."

"Blind faith," Robert said. Inside himself, he was churning. Did he feel pride in his father-in-law's incredible achievement? It was awesome, beyond madness.

Mrs. Santorelli slid the meatballs from a wooden board into a pot of boiling water. Something in the act panicked him, as if she were throwing bits of Maria and Joey into the pot. He imagined their pain and felt it himself.

"Those people are animals," Luigi said, watching the television screen. They saw images of the dead after a recent airport terrorist attack.

Mrs. Santorelli muttered something in Italian.

"What did she say?" Robert asked Luigi.

" 'Without a heart, they will lose every time.' An old Italian saying."

Considering what he had heard earlier, he did not savor the irony.

"We are all flesh and blood," he whispered. It was then that the idea occurred to him. With the all-seeing media eye focused on the issue of hostage-taking, perhaps the time had come for another bold step. He would get on television. Surely he would be a commodity of news value, the son-in-law of the man who held the President hostage. He would make an appeal, let the world see a husband and father's anguish. Appeal to the hostage-takers, to his father-in-law, to the world. He would certainly have their attention.

Suddenly his interest was drawn back to the television set. The commentator was making an announcement: "Another American hostage has been murdered."

"Oh my God," Robert shouted.

"We have been provided with these tapes, distributed by the group calling itself the Islamic Jihad," the commentator continued. "They are not for the squeamish."

Mrs. Santorelli turned from her pots. The Pencil came in from the living room to watch the television set.

On the screen was a man sitting on a chair in a barren room, his face bearded, his eyes glazed and fearful. Beside him were two smiling young men waving weapons. Suddenly they leveled their guns and took aim at the man's body. There was a burst of silent gunfire. The man's body bounced in a macabre St. Vitus dance. Then, bloody and riddled with bullets, the body slumped to the floor in a gruesome closeup.

Robert ran to the bathroom, knelt beside the toilet, and vomited.

# ✯ 21 ✯

"AN ELABORATE TRICK," THE YOUNG MAN SAID, HIS FACE PINK WITH little puddles of natural red flush on either cheek. Ahmed watched him with pleasure, thinking how well he had absorbed the lesson. Trust few people. Trust only actions. Never words. He patted the boy's blond hair, the texture soft and fluffy to his touch. An aberration in the genetic pool, a blond Arab, product of some horny Crusader who had poked his way eastward in the name of Christ, spoils, and pleasure.

"You think so?" Ahmed said, pouring another spill of scotch into the tumbler and lifting it to the light of the single naked bulb. Then he tipped the tumbler in the direction of the boy, who stood posing against the wall in his tailored camouflage greens, a delicate hand poised on a polished leather holster. My toy soldier, Ahmed thought, upending the drink as he watched the flickering image on the television screen.

"They want us to think that," the boy said, encouraged by Ahmed's air of approval. Ahmed smiled and poured again. He knew that the news was true. By way of celebration, he told himself. At first the news had stunned him. Then it had recalled to him an emotion he had not observed in himself for years. Fear. Not a simple fear of death, but of immensity.

Less than a half hour had passed since the news had flashed over Beirut radio. It played constantly, plugging him into the outside world. Prior to this new announcement, the killing of an American hostage had been the only news of importance. Everything else had been repetitive. The killing had annoyed him. It had removed him momentarily from center stage.

He had been listening with half an ear, his mind concentrating on the process of inveiglement. He had planned to seduce the boy as a diversion, had set him up for this moment, had plotted, as always when an innocent was about to be initiated. Then this new

· 112 ·

announcement had exploded into his consciousness, emptying him of desire.

Three quick shots of scotch steadied him. Yet he did not wish the boy to see his uncertainty. Worse, he suddenly did not trust the boy or any of the others whom he had spotted about the building. The legitimate dwellers had long since fled.

The woman and her son had been placed in an apartment on the third floor of a building in West Beirut. Men from his group lived above and below the apartment. Others inhabited adjacent apartments, one of which he used for himself.

He had organized everything in shifts, food preparation, guard duty, time off. He had also devised a pattern to the captivity. Every few days they would move to another building. Sometimes it would be for only a few hours. The object was to keep moving in a pattern much like a child's drawing in which lines were drawn in numbered sequence.

Most of the gunmen he chose from among the militias were very young. Some, like the boy who stood before him, were barely sixteen. Through the clever use of myth, ritual, and mystery, he had found that the youngest were the easiest to manipulate. Thus, he could easily take full advantage of the fanatacism that had been built into these boys from earliest memory. Boys of this age had no concept of death and dying. They yearned for martyrdom, assured by some crazy mullahs that death was merely an unpleasant interlude between pain and paradise.

He had, of course, been ridiculed for his bungling of this last caper. A woman and a child. Of no value. They wanted this Assistant Secretary of State from America and would pay for none other. Even the Arab press had demeaned him. But when they had discovered the real value of this currency, he would be catapulted to fame.

The value of the woman and the child had increased a millionfold. He had in his possession one of the great political prizes of all time. A mere exchange of prisoners was hardly fitting for such a prize.

"We must leave in a few hours," he told the boy.

"Because of that?" The boy moved his head in the direction of the television. A short time ago, Ahmed might have permitted the intimacy of truth.

"No," he lied.

"It is a trick. I'm sure of it," the boy said.

Ahmed smiled and patted the boy's head. He wrote down the address of the apartment building he had chosen, a damaged structure a mile away.

"You will reconnoiter and set up a new place."

"Yes, Ahmed."

Ahmed embraced him and kissed him on both cheeks, his usual gesture of soldierly camaraderie, a subtle step removed from a more intimate embrace.

When he had gone, Ahmed stepped into the corridor, where one of his men snapped his AK47 into firing position, then slowly shifted the muzzle. It had been his own instructions. Trust no one. The axiom of his trade.

He carried the portable television set with him to the apartment where he kept the woman and the boy. He stepped inside and relocked it from the inside, a precautionary step he might not have taken previously. His weight made the barren wooden floor creak as he moved farther inside, listening for the telltale signs of the chain links.

The apartment consisted of two rooms as well as a tiny kitchen and a bathroom. The windows had been tightly boarded from both the exterior and interior wall, with tiny holes for ventilation. The woman and the boy were chained by the ankle to a pipe, with the links long enough to permit them to reach their sleeping bags.

Compared to how it had been in Egypt, it was a comparatively benign imprisonment. He had made sure the food was nourishing, and access to the bathroom was allowed for a minimum of personal hygiene. The rooms were barren. He did not trust beds or furniture. Pieces could be pulled apart and used as weapons. He put the television set on the floor.

"Who is it?"

The woman's panicked voice came from the corner where the sleeping bags had been placed.

"Mommy?"

"Only an old friend," Ahmed said.

His English had come from two years of high school and American television programs. He had established, he believed, a workable system of communication with the woman. Like all women, she was irascible and sarcastic, and, of course, her disposition was not improved by her situation. The child he had bribed with candies and comic books.

There was no point in holding back the news. In fact, he was anxious to impart it. They were now colleagues of a sort, certainly co-conspirators. He chuckled at the thought. American Mafiosa. The idea of it had the ring of comedy.

He flicked the light switch. A bare bulb of weak wattage lit the room. The woman stirred in the sleeping bag and sat up rubbing her eyes. The boy opened his eyes and looked fearfully at Ahmed.

"It's all right, sweets," the woman said soothingly. "Go back to sleep."

The boy looked at her tentatively, then, reassured, closed his eyes again.

Ahmed squatted down and settled himself cross-legged beside the woman, an uncommon gesture for him. The woman looked at him curiously.

"I have news," he murmured, smiling.

"You're letting us go?" the woman asked expectantly.

"Depends," Ahmed replied, "on how your father handles the situation."

"My father!" She unzipped the sleeping bag and sprung upward like a missile released. She was sleeping in a man's shirt, which served as a kind of nightgown.

"You've been a naughty girl," Ahmed said, waving a finger at her. "Not telling me whose daughter you were."

"It was none of your business."

"I could have saved the lives of my men, plucked you right off the parking lot of the Egyptian Museum. You, my dear, are the real prize."

"All right, so you know," she said. She moved around the room on her bare feet, as far as the chain would take her. Then she turned suddenly. "Most men in your position would be paralyzed with fright. My father is not a forgiving man when it comes to his family."

"So the world has discovered," he said with a wry chuckle.

Her face expressed puzzlement. He debated keeping her in suspense, then decided to plunge forward.

"He has taken the President of the United States hostage."

"My father?"

"The Padre himself."

She shook her head in disbelief. A hysterical giggling sound bubbled up from her chest.

"Oh Jesus," she cried.

"He has him in the White House. Along with the President's wife."

"I can't believe it."

"You are welcome to see for yourself." He stood up and plugged in the television set. It warmed slowly, then burst into light. He waited while she absorbed the confirmation. It was clear in any language. The hostage-taking of the President was the dominant theme of all the channels he flipped through.

She paced the room as far as the chain allowed, then moved back to where he was squatting, towering over him. His eyes met hers.

"You want to hear something funny? I kept saying to myself, he finds out, there'll be hell to pay. Now I'll tell you something funnier. I don't think I'm as surprised as I should be."

Ahmed laughed, a belly laugh, which grew in great waves until his eyes began to glisten. The boy sat up and rubbed his eyes.

"It's all right, sweets," the woman said, bending over him and kissing him on the forehead. He slipped lower down in the sleeping bag and she kissed him again on both cheeks.

"He must love you very much," Ahmed said, wiping his eyes on his sleeve.

"Not half as much as he must hate you," the woman snapped.

"Does he seriously believe that you and the child are worth the price of the President himself?"

"You don't know my father."

"Perhaps I will meet him someday."

"Oh, you'll meet him. One way or another. If I were you, I wouldn't be making any long-term plans."

Despite himself, Ahmed felt a brief tremor of fear, which rattled him for a moment and left him suddenly angry. It passed quickly. What he must do is consider all aspects of the situation, especially the political realities within the Arab world. As always, they would fight among themselves. Some would see it in its true light, as a major victory, rejoicing, urging more blood, hoping that the President would be blown away. Some would see it as a standard to be matched, perhaps upstaged.

No, he decided, this was the summit of such action. However they pushed the tide of terror further and further into the dark oceans of intimidation and blood, few, perhaps none, would be able to match the reaction he had achieved. He savored the sense of it, the exhilaration of owning power, of manipulating events on the vast world stage. One could not characterize these events as mere fantasy. He was not a puppet on a string any longer, to be jerked and pulled to fit the design of others. He was the fingers now, manipulated by his own brain.

"So what do you think you are worth?" Ahmed asked. "To get you back. What should we ask for?" Yes, he thought, enjoying the special irony of the collective pronoun.

"You will soon get something you didn't ask for."

He ignored her belligerence. "No. I am serious. You know the man. Think what lengths he has gone to. It is beyond conception. The boldness. The daring. What is in his mind?"

"That should be easy for a man like you to figure out."

"A man like me?"

"A man totally devoid of moral scruples," the woman said, her voice tinged with regret.

So her father's act had puffed up her courage, engaged her hope. He smiled.

"If I were you," the woman said, "I would just get us out of here and send us on our way."

"Good idea. Get dressed."

The woman looked at him warily, studying his expression. Ahmed watched her run the gamut of uncertainty, warmed by her confusion.

"Now?" she asked, looking toward the boy.

"Now."

"We're going home?"

"That would be strictly up to your father. He will decide."

I will decide, he silently corrected himself.

He did not move, but continued to stare silently at her as her confusion increased. Finally she turned away, moved toward her son, bent down, and shook him gently. Again he opened up cranky eyes and she managed to get him out of the sleeping bag.

Ahmed watched her dress the child with a mother's care. Briefly he thought of his own mother, her gentle touch, the soft cool lips on his forehead. For a moment his thoughts drifted to another time, his childhood, the billowing safety found between his mother's breasts. Often he had found comfort there.

His gaze turned inward, explored another landscape, a place where he had been before, narrow streets of pounded dirt, the smell of cooking oil and sweat, raindrops on the roof of corrugated steel, the feel of the cold metal of his first rifle. Where does the road to hate lead? Hate Israel. Hate America. Allah had decreed his destiny. The door to paradise led through a curtain of blood.

He had pushed such speculations far out of his mind. Until now. They were wrong. All of them. Paradise was power. Of course. Allah was merely the idea. He looked upward at the naked bulb and nodded.

Suddenly the woman's actions intruded. She had unbuttoned the shirt. Now she removed it. She was totally naked, but she paid no attention to him, as if he were some inanimate object. Her figure was full, high large breasts, small waist, a thick bush of pubic hair.

Again she was flaunting herself, showing her contempt. Arrogant bitch, he thought. Anger welled up inside him. Was this the prize? He tried in his mind to calculate the worth of this woman, daughter of the Mafiosa Padre. Hardly something so paltry as a king's ransom. She seemed to be deliberately stalling, holding back, determined to show him her body, mocking him. You fucking fag. Had he heard those words?

Then it came to him, what he should ask in trade for this bitch and her boy. Black void for black void. All that must be done would be to light the fuse. Perhaps he was not technically correct, but the image would suffice. He chuckled. A very fair trade indeed.

# ⋆ 22 ⋆

AIR FORCE TWO TAXIED TO A STOP IN A REMOTE CORNER OF ANDREWS Air Force Base. Armed men packed into a tight circle surrounded the plane. A man dressed in one of Chalmers' suits stepped out of the opened cabin door, saluted, and rushed down the stairs. The tight circle opened briefly, the man stepped into a waiting limousine, and a convoy of armed vehicles took its place in a phalanx that quickly moved down the tarmac. Others began to file down the stairs.

A man in battle dress burst into his cabin. He had been instructed to stay inside, alone. The man saluted and Chalmers returned the salute.

"Put this on, sir," the man said crisply. He obeyed without protest, sliding into the bulletproof vest, then putting his hands through the sleeves of an oversized camouflage jacket.

"The height of fashion," Chalmers said. He felt testy, annoyed. The words echoed and reechoed in his mind. Proctor's voice had been hoarse with strain. "We have a problem," he had said over the line. "No kidding," Chalmers had responded, but then had come that long pause.

"No kidding," Proctor had repeated, like a blow struck at his solar plexus. Then the Secretary of State had said, "I wouldn't use this line to tell you what's going on. Just in case. We've got to keep it out of the press. I'm sorry. Wait until you get here."

He followed the man down the center aisle, moving quickly toward the rear of the cabin. Other men, who had been posted along the cabin windows, followed behind him, automatic weapons drawn. Perhaps, he thought, the President is dead.

It was a thought to be chased away, not to be dwelled upon in its raw unconfirmed state. Unthinkable, he told himself, not wishing to experiment with his own sense of guilt and inadequacy. He was not quite ready to handle the situation. Not with Proctor's ominous words ringing in his ears.

At the rear cabin door the man who led him stopped, using his arm as a turnstile. Chalmers waited, sucking in deep breaths. It was all so mysterious, like a child's game.

"Now," the man said.

He followed him quickly down the stairs to a waiting car. In the distance he heard a chopper's staccato chomp. The car, he noted, was brownish, nondescript. There were no flags on the fenders. As soon as he got into the back seat, the car began to move.

"Welcome home," Vic Proctor said. Chalmers turned to find a pale, tired face offering a grim smile. At that moment the driver, too, turned to show his profile. Ned Foreman, the President's National Security Advisor. He waved two fingers in acknowledgment.

"We bring you greetings from the snakepit."

"What the hell is going on?" Chalmers demanded.

The car had gone barely a few feet when it moved upward suddenly into a dark space. Foreman cut the motor.

"It's the latest form of transportation," Proctor said. "Silly. But, the Secret Service says, very effective. At least in theory."

He felt movement below him, but it wasn't the car. They were obviously in some kind of moving van.

"The meeting is still set?" Chalmers asked.

"It may be academic," Proctor sighed. "He says he can govern."

"He must be out of his mind." The comment had seeped out too quickly for Chalmers to stop it.

"Maybe." Foreman shrugged.

Suddenly Chalmers was seized by a sense of unfairness. He wanted to protest. They were paying it out like a fishing line, torturing him deliberately. He wanted to strike out at them.

"It's a dilemma," Proctor was saying. Chalmers wondered if he had already missed the explanation. "We have it in writing, too. His own hand." The Secretary of State reached into his inside pocket and pulled out a letter on presidential stationery written in a firm, unmistakable hand. Chalmers read it, then reread it while the words swam randomly in his head.

"Despite my present circumstances, I am physically and mentally able to carry out the duties of my presidency." It was signed Paul Bernard, President of the United States.

"It's one bitch of a catastrophe," Proctor said. "There's only the three of us who have the word."

"So far."

Chalmers licked his lips, which had suddenly dried. "Seems pretty clear to me. We ignore it."

"The Twenty-fifth Amendment?"

"Fuck the Twenty-fifth Amendment," Chalmers snapped. "The man can't operate. He can't move freely. It's a matter of national security."

"But there is no precedent," Proctor said.

"Precedent, hell. We can vote him out."

"Not so easy according to the Twenty-fifth," the Secretary of State cautioned. "If he says he can govern, we have to throw it over to Congress. They can impeach him."

"This is crap, Victor, and you know it. We just go ahead, have our little meeting, and appoint me Acting President. The man obviously cannot function. You know it. I know it. Every goddamned person in this country knows it. He's out. That's final. So let's get on with it."

It felt good, but just for the moment. They were moving, but no one in the car had any control over their movement. Foreman looked at him archly.

"Comes down to, are we a country of men or laws?" the National Security Advisor said.

"Jesus, Ned," Chalmers responded.

He was furious. But it was the kind of fury without an outlet. He felt it sticking in his throat.

"Then we call their bluff," Chalmers said.

"Who gives that order?" Proctor sighed.

"I do," Chalmers said.

"Under what authority?" Foreman asked, but gently.

"We're . . ." Chalmers faltered. "We're responsible men. Millions of people throughout the world depend on us. There are predators out there. People who would take advantage. The Soviets . . ."

"Let the string run out," Proctor said.

"What the hell does that mean?" Chalmers asked.

"He says he can govern," Foreman answered. "Let him govern. Meanwhile we throw it to Congress. Impeachment may be the only solution. Should take a few days to bring them home. The thing might resolve itself in a day or two. Surely the country can get through forty-eight hours without a President. Meanwhile we do our job. He thinks he can do his job. Remains to be seen."

"And this Mafia man, this Padre, what happens to him?" Chalmers asked.

Foreman shrugged.

"He's got his own ax to grind. Maybe he'll frighten them into giving up his daughter and grandson."

"Sounds like you're grasping at straws," Chalmers said.

"I suppose we are," Proctor mused. "The trick is not to panic. If we panic, the country will panic. Indeed, the world will panic."

"I think it's dangerous as hell," Chalmers said.

"Any way you look at it, it's a tough call," Foreman said.

They exchanged glances. Suddenly the movement stopped. They heard the van door squeak open. Light flooded into the space.

So they will try to put it off as long as possible, Chalmers thought, wondering if the idea was prompted by paranoia, ambition, or an inordinate respect for the law.

"There's only one issue here," Chalmers said. Above all, he would keep his dignity.

"What is that?" Proctor asked.

"What's best for America."

Chalmers wondered if he sounded sufficiently presidential.


# ✯ 23 ✯


THE PADRE WATCHED HARKINS' FINGERS GLIDE LIGHTLY OVER THE keyboard of the monitor. The President had ordered it to be brought in. A man had placed the console in front of the entrance to the west sitting room and the Canary had scooped it up. It had a built-in modem and Harkins had connected it to telephone lines.

At times Harkins' stubby fingers would stop their keyboard dance and the man would contemplate the monitor screen.

The Padre had sat stiffly watching Harkins' performance. Perhaps he had dozed. He wasn't certain. At intervals the computer beeped or buzzed. But it was only the absence of sound that jogged the Padre to alertness. On the buffet they had placed a television set, moving aside the expensive candelabra. They had shut off the sound, although the images continued to flicker throughout the night.

Most of the network stations were on twenty-four-hour alert, as they were during the Kennedy assassination. Since the gruesome killing of the hostage, there was little to report, except speculation.

It did not surprise him that they had not yet reported the President's announcement about his insistence that he was willing and able to govern the country. But Harkins had expressed his suspicion that they would not put out that information until the Vice President had met with the Cabinet.

Earlier, the coverage had become dizzying. The Padre had listened with half an ear. He saw his own face on the screen and a long segment on his organization. He did not like to see his face on TV, but he was mildly amused by what was said about him by commentators.

They called him ruthless and cold-blooded, a man who controlled a network of rackets, hijacking, prostitution, protection, and a myriad of legitimate businesses, a man who bought and sold politicians and judges, a man who had ordered hundreds to their deaths.

As always, it was an exaggeration, mostly pandering lies. They had deliberately excised from this so-called biography the concept of honor and family, which was fundamental to his character. As for the reason for the organization, there was no way they could understand the necessity of rebellion against authority, its lies and hypocrisies.

They had also shown Maria in her high school graduation picture with a cap and gown. At that point he changed the channel. There was, incredibly, a game show on one of the independent stations. People were jumping wildly up and down, celebrating their winnings.

Finally he had switched back to one of the networks. This one showed pictures of the outside of the White House ringed with troops in full battle gear, guns at the ready. There was also old footage of the President's living quarters, then a live shot of the windows outside.

After a while the coverage became boring and repetitious. World leaders had been interviewed ad nauseam. There were even interviews with official and unofficial Middle Eastern leaders in Beirut, Libya, Syria, Egypt, and Israel. Yassir Arafat also got in his two cents' worth. Everybody had differing points of view, speculations, analysis.

Terrorism and hostage-taking, some agreed, had gone too far. Others believed that terrorism, hostage-taking, and other forms of intimidation were the ways to get the message across. The world was drowning in bullshit, the Padre thought. What has all this got to do with my daughter and grandson? What did they know about a father's pain?

Occasionally the Canary would poke his big face into the room, survey the situation, and leave. He had been given the role of inspector. His job was to patrol the premises, keep a watchful eye. Like the Padre, he did not need sleep.

They had organized the routine with an eye both to security and comfort. This was, after all, the White House, and a certain modicum of dignity was required. Food had come up from the downstairs kitchen by dumbwaiter, trays of excellent fare prepared by the chef. It showed a very sensible acceptance of reality. They had apparently yielded to the idea that it was better to cooperate than risk the President's life, which meant that the Padre and his men had won the battle for credibility.

As a gesture of good faith for the President's cooperation, the First Lady was released from her cord attachment to Benjy, who, nevertheless, stuck close to her despite her protestations. The Padre trusted his instincts about the President, who was essentially an honorable man. Unfortunately, he was also a political animal. All of his reactions seemed to be considered in the context of politics. It was a good thing, because it was the hook that Harkins had used to persuade him. Now he understood why the President had so much difficulty taking the necessary action to free the hostages. A pity the government could not be run like his organization.

Of course he did not fully trust the President. Nor did he order Vinnie to untie the cord that attached him to the man. That proximity was his most effective weapon.

The two of them, Carmine had reported, were now dozing peacefully together in the master bedroom. The First Lady was sleeping in her dressing room. She had been allowed a bath and to perform her usual female ablutions. Considering the situation, he decided, his adventure into hostage-taking was extraordinarily civilized and humanitarian. He wished the same treatment for his daughter and grandson, although he doubted it.

The Padre had, of course, expected difficulties. In the end, he knew he would get the President's cooperation. No one ever wanted to give up power.

"You see, Mr. President," the Padre had told him after they had brought in the monitor. "They obey your orders as before."

The President had looked at him and shaken his head.

"They won't buy it for long," he had said.

"Perhaps it won't be for long," the Padre had suggested.

With the exception of the threatening gesture against the First Lady, it had all been remarkably nonviolent. The Padre liked that. Nevertheless, he knew he must be wary of Harkins. Harkins was clever, but as crafty and venomous as a snake.

Earlier, Harkins had revealed what the Padre had merely suspected. That the CIA did indeed have people stashed all over the world, that they had the ability to act in the shadows, behind the scenes of authority and legitimacy. Harkins had characterized them as agents, but it sounded to the Padre as though they were organized tightly in a hierarchy of information gatherers, transmitters, and doers.

The doers, translated into the Padre's terms, were more like button men hired out for whatever jobs that came along. Harkins called them "coverts," a nice clean way to portray them. "They are trained to play dirty," Harkins had explained. The Padre was amused by the characterization. Dirty was a matter of perception.

Harkins also had his "pencil," a computer network with secret access codes that kept track of missions. It also gave orders and transmitted information. It was airtight, Harkins had assured him. No hacker, amateur or pro, had ever been known to access it. He wondered if such machines would improve the operations of his own organization. He doubted it. A machine could be loyal only to itself.

"You would be surprised at our reach," Harkins had explained as he pounded the keyboard. Sitting in front of the monitor, he seemed very much at home.

"Reach?"

"We can place our people anywhere. There are no boundaries. We have the necessary assets and the ability to use them. As a matter of fact," Harkins added proudly, "we are not as inefficient as we are portrayed in the media. The truth is, we court the image. Gives us more leverage in the short strokes."

"Good." The Padre nodded, not completely understanding the language, but thoroughly understanding the implications.

For most of the early morning, banging on his keyboard, consulting his monitor, Harkins was able to provide the Padre with the information to concoct any scenario that might have occurred to him. The Padre absorbed this information, sifted and refined it in his mind. It became a cram course on terrorism and the groups that perpetrated these acts.

The names of these groups formed what appeared to be an endless parade on the monitor. They were not confined to the Middle East. There were the Irish, the Basques, the Sikhs, the Croats, and on and on, espousing causes that sometimes were centuries old. Impossible causes, pursued by people with obsessive fantasies and implausible dreams.

Harkins relished his presentation. Although the Padre was interested primarily only in what affected his daughter and grandson, he watched and listened with respect. It was, he agreed, a remarkable system. More important, it held the key to releasing Maria and Joey.

"The man who leads the group that holds your daughter is Ahmed Safari, thirty-seven, a hard case, a homosexual, a wife and sick teenage son in Jordan. Born in a Lebanese refugee camp." The intelligence became microscopic, tracing every aspect of the man's life and his present circumstances.

The Padre nodded at intervals, continuing to absorb the information, keeping what was essential, rejecting what was not useful, translating it into organizational terms he could understand, searching for vulnerabilities that would strike fear.

"And you know where she is being kept?" the Padre asked.

"She and the boy are being moved around and held in various safe places in the Muslim section of Beirut. We have an asset in the group. But the man is clever. He rotates his people. Mostly young boys."

"And you have your own groups that could go in, button men?"

"Yes, we do."

"They will obey?"

"If we pay them enough. In our business, people are mercenaries."

"Of course," the Padre said.

"And how fast can you transmit orders?"

"Remarkably so."

"And weapons?"

"We have access to those as well." Harkins smiled and coughed into his fist. His face darkened. "Problem is . . ."

"Yes."

"We have to cover our tracks. Legitimize our actions, clean it up for public consumption. The fact is, you can't run a covert action program with those Congressional oversight idiots having to know every move beforehand. It's ridiculous. But they do hold the purse strings. In the end, though, the authority for all our actions still flows from the President."

The Padre was getting the message. Harkins was asserting his own power in this situation. He would act, of course, but only on orders from the President, tendered after manipulative and vague briefings. So, the Padre thought, he needed presidential authority to cover his ass. Yet he was also telling the Padre that this computer was his weapon and he was the only one present who could fire it.

The Padre stood up and paced the dining room. Then he

stopped at the buffet and poured a glass of water from a crystal decanter. The ice had melted. It was warm, but he drank it anyway. He was conscious of Harkins studying him, waiting.

"The leaders of these countries who finance them . . ." The Padre paused. His thoughts were coming together now. "They have families, of course."

"Of course."

"Are they heavily protected?"

"Some," Harkins replied. "Many have children or grandchildren in school in this country."

The Padre smiled. Harkins remained poker-faced, but the Padre knew now where they were both headed.

"You know where?"

"Yes." Now Harkins smiled too. "But we have no mandate to operate within our borders."

"We would, of course, respect each other's territory," the Padre said.

"Of course."

"And this fellow who holds my daughter?"

"In Jordan he has a son he adores," Harkins answered eagerly.

The Padre remained silent. He had learned that certain characteristics were common to all men. Some feared death. Some feared dishonor. Some feared losing loved ones, especially children, who represented a sense of continuity, of immortality. Some feared a loss of power, cojones sliced off, a worse fate than death to a man who knew its full meaning. There were others, of course. Every man had his fears.

"Tell me, Mr. Harkins," the Padre asked. It was a question that was nagging at him, although he had not been fully conscious of it. "What plans did you people consider?"

Harkins wet his lips.

"It was only gamesmanship," he said, his Adam's apple bobbing nervously. "You know, making up scenarios, concocting different situations, most of which are politically impossible to carry out."

"Like what?"

"A kind of tit for tat. Do unto them what they did unto us. They hijack planes. We hijack planes. They shoot up airports. We shoot up airports. They plant bombs. We plant bombs. They take people . . . You get my drift. Problem is, wherever you put these ideas forward in a kind of committee, they get sidetracked. Too inflammatory. Too immoral. The beast in us gets like the beast in them. You know the arguments."

Harkins hesitated suddenly. Despite his earlier eagerness, he seemed to pull back. He had drawn his line.

"I just give options and take orders," Harkins said.

The Padre nodded.

"All right then, Mr. Harkins. I think it is time we woke the President."

# ✮ 24 ✮

FROM THE MOMENT THEY HAD BEEN BROUGHT TO THE LIVING QUAR-ters, Amy Bernard had been thinking about the little silver-plated .22-caliber pistol that lay in the rear of the drawer of the table next to her side of their king-size bed. Without her husband's knowledge, she had put it into an empty metal pastille box and had brought it with her from their home in the Kalorama section of Washington where they had lived when Paul was a senator.

Was it fear or simply whim that made her take it with her? Certainly she had been frightened at the prospect of living in the goldfish bowl of the presidency. It was not comforting to remember what had happened to Jack Kennedy and Ronald Reagan. Sometimes the knowledge of its presence passed vaguely across her mind. No one had ever asked her about the pastille box. Indeed, she frequently opened the drawer where she kept a set of reading glasses, a roll of Tums, and a box of tissues.

She knew it was loaded, six rounds. And accurate only at close range.

She had taken a bath, amused by the incongruity of soaking in the warm comfortable steamy water while strangers kept her imprisoned in her own home. She had taken off her evening gown and dressed in comfortable slacks and a blouse, ideal captive wear.

Then, instead of her bedroom, which was reserved for Paul and his constant companion, they had allowed her to use the bed in her dressing room. An interesting cell, all orange, with its white leaf prints and the dressing table deliberately put in front of the window for better light. Useless now. They had drawn the blinds of both windows.

Her "keeper" had carefully sat down on the upholstered straight chair and put his feet on the round antique table, a travesty that she ignored. No point in raising issues that had nothing to do with her objective, which was to get her hands on that pistol.

"May I read?" she asked pleasantly.

The young man shrugged an indifferent consent.

She looked about the room. On a little table she found a book in an antique binding. She had never opened it. She had been sitting on the edge of the couch where she had often taken catnaps. Cautiously, she got up, walked to the table, opened the book. To her surprise it was printed in French.

"My glasses," she said coyly.

"Where are they?"

She paused. All make-believe, she decided, like when she was in a school play. Pause briefly, flutter eyelids, smile thinly, show uncertainty.

"In the drawer in the master bedroom, the table next to my bed. May I get them?"

Her mind had devised a half-formed plan. She would open the drawer, remove her glasses, and the pastille box. He would be watching her.

"The President is sleeping there," the young man said. "I wouldn't wake him. He'll need his rest."

"How thoughtful," she said, angered by her own sarcasm. She wasn't following the stage directions.

"You should be getting rest yourself. Keep you in a better mental state."

For what, she wondered.

"I won't wake him," she said, ignoring what she decided was a preposterous remark. Why would he care?

He thought for a moment, then nodded his okay and stood up.

They moved through the doorway into the darkened bedroom. She could see her husband's form on the bed. He was under the covers on his side of the bed. On top of the covers, fully dressed, occupying her side of the bed, attached by the ubiquitous umbilical cord, was the ugly man, Vinnie. He was instantly alert. The other man, Carmine, sat near the desk, his chair slanted against the wall, his feet flung out in front of him.

"She wants her glasses," the young man said.

She walked toward the bed, opened the drawer, felt around for her glasses, then quickly moved her hand to grasp the pastille box. Even in the half-light he was alert to her movements, watching her hand. She drew out her glasses and held the pastille box in the other.

"What's that?" he asked.

"Candy," she replied, ignoring the pounding of her heart.

She walked calmly through the door to her dressing room and arranged herself lengthwise on the couch, book in hand. Please let him move to the other side of the room. He followed her, stood over her for a moment, studying her. Then he bent over. Her insides clenched and a sudden chill made her body tremble. He was looking at the candy label, squinting.

"Pastilles," she said. "French." She showed him the open pages of the book she was reading. "Like the book I'm reading. *Parlez vous français?*"

He watched her for a moment more, then moved back to the chair, again putting his feet on the antique table. After a while she flicked the switch of the lamp that provided light for the couch, moved the pastille box under one of the pillows, and closed her eyes. Yes, she decided, she would need her rest. Her alertness was essential.

# ✱ 25 ✱

"YOU'RE NOT SERIOUS?" THE PRESIDENT ASKED. HAD HE ACTUALLY asked the question or was it some repetitive tape gone awry, zipping away in his mind? He sat in the dining room, beside him the ever-present Vinnie, whose sour odor seemed to have become a staple of the air they shared. He had slept beside the man in the same bed. There was something obscene in the memory.

Strangely, he had actually slumbered. His mind had clamped shut, as if he had slipped into a deep black pit of emptiness, rising without an iota of residual dream memory.

His first thought had been of Amy, whose missing presence set off the alarms of thirty years' awakenings. He couldn't bound out of bed, of course. Vinnie was attached, and they had taken the precaution, sometime after he had dozed off, of taping his ankles to a leg of the bed.

"My wife?" the President had asked.

"The other room."

"I must see her."

The man shrugged and followed him into the dressing room. She was still sleeping. He had leaned close to her cheek, moved a wisp of errant hair, and kissed her on the forehead. The young man, who had risen from a chair when they came into the room, looked haggard from his night of surveillance.

"She's sleeping like a baby," he said with a cocky smile.

The President did not answer. He returned to the bedroom and started to undress.

"I'm not going to stink all day, pal," he said. "Bad enough I've got to carry you along."

His captors' communication system revolved around the big man with the heavy face, who seemed always lurking behind them. They had these mysterious little eye and body signals between them. The big man disappeared and came back with consent, and the two men stayed by him as he was untied. They also followed him into the bathroom.

"I'm going to try and ignore you guys," he said. He began to shave. The blade glided over his face. Then he remembered what he had thought earlier about the plastic sacks holding the liquid explosive. A razor's slash, quick, sharp, direct. Would it empty the liquid, seep away the danger? He tried to dismiss the thought, couldn't, then he replaced the blade and palmed the one he had just used.

To deflect their attention, he held up the razor. "Old faithful. Real gold." As they looked he put the palmed blade in the pocket of his robe. Never know, he told himself. Then he patted his face with after-shave and pinched his cheeks. Old habits never die, he thought. "I know it looks kind of silly."

Neither man responded while the President kept up his bouncy monologue. "Sorry, fellas," he said sitting on the toilet. "You remind me of my mama standing over me a hundred years ago, urging me on to duty. Making birdies, she called it. Funny, haven't thought about this since the kids were being housebroken. Might have been how old—two, three?"

He looked at the men. "You have mamas, guys?" He shook his head. "Doubt it. God, you both are ugly. No self-respecting woman would have spawned either of you."

He put up his palms. "Sorry. I don't mean to be so outspoken, but hell, it throws you off your feed to have to take a crap with two guys observing the process." He stood up. "Want to inspect the results?"

They were impassive. He flushed the toilet and jumped into the shower, sticking his head out as he regulated the taps.

"Come on in and play. Wouldn't drop the soap in front of you guys." He felt giddy as he moved into the stream, turning the knobs to make the water as hot as he could stand it, then reversing the process. Must clear out the cobwebs, he thought, raise the adrenaline.

He came out of the shower and toweled himself off. The two men leaned against the wall and watched him. They followed him back into the bedroom, where he dressed. With more sleight of hand, he transferred the blade from his robe to a pocket of his slacks. Then he put on a sport shirt and a cardigan with a Camp David logo stitched over the breast.

"I'm at home, after all. Why not be casual?" he said, really to himself.

Aside from the observing men, the situation struck him as routine. After he had dressed, they reattached him to the cord. Even that act felt expected. He tried to find some reference to a similar situation, one that might act as an anchor of logic. It came to him suddenly. He was Alice and he had walked through the looking glass.

"So let's get on to the tea party," he said, striding across the bedroom threshold, traversing the west sitting room with its doorway piled high with couches, like some decorator's nightmare. "And there's the mad hatter," he muttered. "And the March hare." A strange sight.

They were sitting calmly across the table from each other, the Padre, still in his waiter's uniform, his bow tie removed, and Harkins, who looked up from his keyboard and offered a thin, hesitant smile. The President was instantly on his guard.

Despite the obvious fact that both men seemed to have been up all night, they looked strangely alert. On the table stood a pot of coffee and rolls and butter.

The Padre, as if he were the host, pointed to the President's accustomed chair. The President smirked, sat down, putting a strain on the cord that attached him to Vinnie, who quickly sat down beside him. He poured himself some coffee, but had no appetite for anything more.

"The wonders of the computer age," the President said.

"Greatest invention since the wheel," Harkins said.

"Or curse," the President mumbled. They were bantering with clichés. He watched as Harkins turned toward the Padre, signaling. So he had picked up the eye and body signals.

"There is a certain logic to what he has in mind," Harkins began. The President clasped his arms across his chest. It was, he knew, an uncharacteristic gesture on his part, a kind of protective act. Here it comes, he thought, wondering just how much caution and subtlety Harkins would be able to muster.

"He insists he understands these people, the hostage-takers," Harkins continued, nodding his head toward the Padre, who blinked his eyes in mysterious acknowledgment. "Kind of a new way of looking at the eye-for-an-eye concept. Like two eyes for one."

"I like the way you put things, Jack," the President said, sipping his coffee.

"It's important to place all this in the proper context," Harkins said.

"Of course," the President replied, looking toward the Padre, who returned his gaze impassively.

"It boils down to the following," Harkins said cautiously, again looking toward the Padre. His delivery had the appearance of a well-rehearsed script. Harkins pointed to the monitor.

"In our data banks we have the names of most of the big players in the Middle East terrorist game and some of the little ones. The financiers, the bosses and underbosses, some legal heads of state, the rest hustlers, renegades, opportunists, many hiding under arguably legitimate causes."

Again he looked toward the Padre. "Like what you call consigliatoros and capos and button men." He was being transparently patronizing. The Padre showed no reaction.

"So chicanery is universal. How profound," the President said, noting that his mocking tone was ignored. He had the impression that Harkins was making this presentation merely as a courtesy.

The President looked at the Padre and addressed him. "Okay, you've got his motor running. You want your daughter and your grandson. Just lay it out. Tell me how you think you can do it. I said I'd go along if I thought it would work. I don't want a catalog of the bad guys. I've been through it all before ad nauseam." He felt his anger rise. The Padre listened, unruffled and thoughtful.

"You have the means," the Padre said, darting a glance at Harkins.

"What he wants to do . . ." Harkins said.

"Let him speak for himself," the President said testily.

The Padre put up one hand like a traffic cop, playing the role of peacemaker. Unreality, the President assured himself, seeing the image of the tea party unreel again in his mind.

"He is a good talker, this fellow," the Padre said pleasantly. "We have discussed the situation and made suggestions."

"Options," Harkins corrected.

"A rose by any other name . . ." the President said, his words drifting off. Probably sold the man a bill of goods that he knows how to handle me, the President thought.

"I'm an interpreter," Harkins said, summoning up whatever humility he could muster. Again the President saw the signals pass between them. They are brothers, he decided. This man Harkins was like a pig in dung.

"May I continue?" the CIA Director asked. There was something touchingly childish in his request. The President looked toward the Padre and turned away quickly, suddenly fearful that he was contracting this strange virus of obedience. Okay, the President told himself. It's only an option.

"Ahmed Safari," Harkins said. "The man who holds his daughter. Although he is a known homosexual, he has a wife and son in Amman. He cares nothing for the wife. An arranged marriage, typical in the Arab world. But he does adore his son. The boy is seventeen and sickly. Rheumatic heart."

"I can't be a party to that," the President snapped.

"We have the assets in Jordan. We can have him in custody in hours."

The President shook his head. Harkins again looked toward the Padre.

"Mr. President. It is a viable option," Harkins said.

"Not for me."

"But it would be deniable," Harkins pressed.

"And obvious." He felt his gut pinch and harden. "Also, this Ahmed will know that we could not harm the boy. You know we can't be a party to that. It would be too transparent." He turned toward the Padre. "What is his motive for releasing your daughter and grandson if he knows that his boy will be safe?"

"It's only a part of the plan," Harkins muttered. "We will have to illustrate to him that we mean business."

"And how do we do that?" the President asked. He had relaxed, curious to hook in to their logic.

"You are absolutely right, Mr. President. This is the heart of the matter," the Padre said.

"We must establish our credentials," Harkins said.

"For what?" the President asked. A moot question. He knew the answer.

"I told him how the Soviets had handled a similar episode," Harkins said. When the President did not interrupt, he continued. "A group had picked up four Soviet diplomats in their embassy in Lebanon. They killed one. Then the Soviets retaliated by kidnapping one of leaders of the group that had perpetrated the kidnapping. No fanfare. Quite simple. They cut his balls off, stuffed them in his mouth, and dispatched him back to his cohorts. The three Soviet hostages were released in the flash of an eyelash."

"And you want me to be a party to that kind of tactic?" the President asked.

"To the concept," Harkins said.

"You liked that?" the President asked.

"It is a question of credibility," Harkins said, again looking at the Padre.

"I'm sorry," the President said. "We've spent nearly two and a half centuries establishing other credentials. We don't castrate, gouge eyes, or crack kneecaps." He looked pointedly at the Padre.

"But we haven't dealt with this kind of warfare before. It's a new phenomena requiring a novel way to deal with it. Aside from the moral judgments," Harkins said, "a threat requires believability. Our antagonists are very good on that score."

"On average," the President muttered. Despite himself, he felt engaged, dangled on the hook of Harkins' presentation.

"It is their most effective weapon," Harkins said.

The Padre nodded. The President grew thoughtful. He knew that they were waiting for his next question. But he delayed asking it. They were right, of course. America was afflicted with ethical inhibitions, and such moral strictures created by the Ten Commandments and various rules flowing from them. Not that he was a purist, but there were tolerable limits to any violations. Their suggestions were not within such limits.

"So what are you suggesting?" the President asked. "Cut off the kid's ear and send it as proof of our resolve?"

"You might also get an ear in the mail," Harkins replied.

"I don't like that talk," the Padre said darkly.

"We need something bigger than that, less likely to stimulate such a reprisal. We need something to make our threat credible. Most of all, we need chips to play with.

"What we must do," Harkins said. He looked toward the Padre. "It is the Padre's suggestion. But the concept is quite logical. We take Safari's boy. That's a given. But we also take some blood kin among the other top players. We've searched the data banks. We have names, places, possibilities." Harkins paused. "Even in the States. You would be surprised who is attending our schools. They would be an easy job."

"You're not serious?" the President repeated. He wondered just how credible his own protestations were becoming.

Harkins was working up a good head of steam, throwing an occasional glance toward the Padre, as if he were performing just for him. In a night of mad planning, the two had devised a wicked brew that flew in the face of every philosophical tenet of the Judeo-Christian ethic.

"Of course we're considering only the most impressive options," Harkins continued. "The computer has spit out its choices. In fact, most of the actual missions have already been worked out in theoretical scenarios."

"I never knew," the President said. Self-righteousness was turning to self-delusion. Of course he knew they played these games.

"Verisimilitude," Harkins said, pressing on. Nothing was going to stop him now. "How many times have you said in your public statements that we would go after these bastards if you could make a clean surgical strike against those responsible? Problem—it's never clean. Remember Libya. In an odd way we lost more than we gave. With due respect, Mr. President, we rattle our swords and do little that is truly effective. They bash our people and we tweak their noses. They just don't believe we will act with the same degree of ruthlessness. Well, here is the perfect ploy. Do unto them as they do unto us. Only more so."

"I wish you could give me guarantees that it could work," the President said.

"I'm sorry, Mr. President, I can't."

"He is a good talker," the President said, looking at the Padre, who nodded.

"It is the only way to get Ahmed to release the woman and the boy," Harkins said. "He will be pressed to do so by those who support groups like his, people whose children we will have as hostage. We need just enough to make the point. A favorite Saudi prince at Berkeley. The daughter of the President of Syria attending school in New England. The grandson of Khomeini, who teaches in Teheran. The teenage son of Colonel Qaddafi himself, who can be snatched in Tripoli by our people. We have watched him for months. A mere five."

"You really think you can pull this off?" the President asked.

Harkins nodded. "Except in the States. The CIA has no mandate for that."

"You're joking. I must have missed something in this scenario. Why suddenly the attention to the legal scruples?"

"There is no need for us to violate domestic American laws."

"How decent of you," the President said. Harkins' use of the collective pronoun "us" struck him as ironic.

"The Padre's organization will do the work in the States," Harkins said.

The President felt himself holding down an inner panic. "Are you serious?" he asked.

"We can't be responsible for what the Mafia does, Mr. President." Harkins shot the Padre a quick glance.

"Got all the answers," the President said.

"Some," Harkins said. He smiled.

The President tried to summon up an attitude of great indignation. It was difficult and it frightened him.

"Are you asking me to condone the use of kidnapping as a national policy? In effect to practically sanction the perpetration of a capital crime by the number one outlaw group in this country? The idea of hostage-taking is repugnant in itself. It is bad enough to be victimized by it. But to authorize it." He shook his head. "Dammit. It's a heinous crime."

"Yes it is, Mr. President," Harkins said, perhaps too swiftly, as if he had been waiting in ambush for the idea to reappear. "It is on a par with murder." He coughed into his hand. "We all know that war is state-authorized murder. In effect, what is happening out there can be characterized a a brutal no-holds-barred war. In that case kidnapping is a legitimate weapon."

"These are innocent people," the President protested.

"Yes they are," Harkins retorted.

The President twisted in his chair. It went against all moral justification. He looked at the Padre. The man stood up suddenly and came closer. An arm's length away, the President thought as his hand reached casually into his pocket. He fingered the blade that lay there. One slash. He wondered what the others would do once the Padre was "disarmed."

Yet he resisted taking any action. He slipped his hand out of his pocket. He fleetingly wondered whether such inaction constituted approval of Harkins' plan. It was a question he did not choose to answer.

Looking up, he saw the Padre's calm, serene face. There was not the slightest hint of hesitation. They simply occupied different moral space. And yet he allowed his mind to drift along an untrod path. Each step forward was painful. Ahead was blackness, deeper than mere darkness. And yet he could not deny, independent of his predicament, that the idea had some force to it. Vengeance, after all, had a compelling magnetism of its own.

"And if I don't agree?" the President asked.

"It is do-able, Mr. President," Harkins said. "I'm not saying that it will be perfectly executed. These things never are. But it will send the message once and for all."

Harkins had, of course, evaded the President's question. Had it already been answered by the Padre? Did he really have a choice? Absolutely not, he assured himself. To live or to die. Those were apparently his only alternatives.

But wouldn't his consent legitimize the idea? And yet did he dare admit to himself that such a tactic had a grotesque attraction?

Of course it was possible they just might achieve their goal without bloodshed. Presidents have taken chances in the past, lost lives, blundered. The world would know he was making such decisions under duress. And if it achieved its purpose? He counted his political capital. To collect, he'd have to be alive. That, of course, was the most seductive persuader of all.

"And after these people are collected. What then?"

"Someone will have to respond at their end," Harkins said.

"But how will they know we really mean business?" the President asked. "There is no way that I would order the killing of innocent people in cold blood."

There, he thought, he had found a moral imperative, a bit of indignant flotsam to hold on to against the rushing river of action.

"But there could be bloodshed, Mr. President," Harkins said coolly. "You can't have any illusions about that."

He had gone under for a moment, then surfaced.

"I said I can't justify killing in cold blood."

"Of course not," Harkins said, shooting a disturbing glance at the Padre, who shook his head in affirmation.

The President tapped the table. "I don't like it," he said. Like Harkins' pose of reluctance to act without orders, it was a voice for posterity's evidence. On balance, in theory, even transcending the magnetic seductiveness of it, he did like the idea intellectually. It had verisimilitude.

"It is necessary," the Padre said, as if reading his mind. "Power is nothing without respect."

The Padre watched him rubbing his chin. The President felt the chill of his own nakedness. He both feared and loved the use of power to subvert the conventional means and plunge directly into the enemy's heartland. The old bastard was right, and Harkins was right about the old bastard.

His presence was an excuse for the unconventional treatment of this international illness. Let's go get the sons of bitches. As for consequences, hell, he could always go back to the old hypocrisies. Politics was his business, for crying out loud.

"All right," the President said, his voice low. He was determined not to show them his exhilaration.

"Now, Mr. President?" Harkins asked, his fingers on the computer keyboard.

"Do it then," the President said, his voice affirming his authority.

He was, of course, covering only his end. What the Padre and his cohorts did was none of his business. Render unto Caesar what is Caesar's and to God—he looked at the Padre—what was God's.

They watched as Harkins' fingers darted over the keyboard. His eyes became mesmerized by the screen. After a few minutes Harkins' fingers rested. He looked at the screen again. Hit the keyboard keys, then paused.

"Failsafe confirmations," he whispered. "Trick is to avoid using the phone. This scrambles and only comes out whole through unscrambling." Harkins paused again. Then he tapped out another message. "Turkey in the oven," he said, looking up, offering them all a broad smile.

"What hath God wrought," the President said. Well hidden behind his mask of concern, he smiled. He looked toward the Padre. The Padre's face was grim.

## ✱ 26 ✱

THIS SUMMIT WAS BEING HELD IN AN UNDERGROUND BUNKER. AHMED enjoyed the irony. He also took pleasure in sitting at a round table as an equal. In this game personal symbols were important. Dress, facial hair, hat, sidearms, and, above all, the illusion of noncontrivance. Arafat was a master at it. His barber must be a genius to keep that seven-day growth immaculately authentic.

He had dressed for the occasion. Tailored khakis, a powder-blue beret and matching silk cravat, a pair of wrap-around sun goggles, a Smith & Wesson 9-mm automatic pistol tucked into a spring shoulder holster, and a waist belt with pockets for four eight-shot magazines. He had trimmed his bushy mustache and cut off its side droops.

There were eight of them around the table. Number twos mostly. It would be unseemly for the number ones to appear, responding to this summons by an upstart. At one time or another he had worked for all of them.

His contacts were with those on the third and fourth levels, buying his expertise in managing these enterprises. Most of them, over the years, had become nameless, then faceless, finally merely ciphers. Also, he claimed ideological neutrality, a strong asset, considering the competing religious and national animosities. He was a professional among fanatics.

"I am a gun," he would tell them. "A gun has no ideology, only accuracy."

Iranians, Syrians, Libyans, Palestinians of three factions, and Shiites were represented, whoever had organizational strength, finances, the big boys in this business. Remarkably, it had taken less than twelve hours to get them all together.

Of course they were uneasy, not knowing what to expect. Only yesterday he had been characterized as a blunderer, a misguided missile, although his boldness had given him a kind of cachet. Boldness was currency in this business.

He had taken the woman and her child as an afterthought, a booby prize. As it turned out it was the hottest ticket in the hostage game. His once-faltering status had skyrocketed overnight.

There had been the usual preliminaries and rituals of Arab politeness, an exchange of pleasantries that transcended the fierce and often bloody competition. But the rule, as he well knew, was to bring the rhetoric but leave the weapons at the door.

It took some time for the politeness to run its course. The fundamental question before the group was how best to use this sudden windfall of power. For Ahmed the question was how to use his prizes for his own purposes.

Ahmed's objective was to get them to coalesce behind him, to follow his lead. Quite simply, and they all knew it, he had the President of the United States by the balls.

"What are you suggesting then?" the Libyan asked. It seemed to Ahmed a consensus-type question.

"We've got to demand more than we have been asking," Ahmed said.

"But they haven't caved in to our original demand to release our brothers," the Libyan said. He was a middle-aged man with a head of tight gray curls, thick moist lips, and hooded brown eyes. In this group he had spread Qaddafi's money around in great buttery gobs, which, he felt, gave him the right to wear the mantle of spokesman.

"That's the point. We have to make the kind of demand that will force them all to take notice."

"So then," the Libyan said. He did not look at the others for approval. "I agree that we might ask for something larger. But the ultimate humiliation for the U.S. would be to get them to negotiate with us. That would be a victory in itself."

"A victory, yes. But not a route."

"I don't understand."

Ahmed had their attention. He must be cautious, he told himself.

"Up to now we have been delivering gnat bites to the rump of the horse. Annoying, yes. But nothing has occurred to bring our cause one step closer to fruition." He was deliberately vague here, since they all harbored variations of the cause.

"What we need to do now is to deliver a hammer blow, to get the horse to go berserk, to scare the shit out of the whole world. Only then will they realize that we mean business." He felt a sudden surge of the old fanaticism.

"So what sort of a brew do you propose for our great Satan to drink?" the Iranian said, a thin handsome man with a mustache. Although he was dressed neatly in Western-style clothes, Ahmed suspected him of being a mullah.

Ahmed deliberately took his time before continuing, studying each man's face, bracing for their reaction. He felt tingles in his crotch and a radiant warmth crawl up his spine.

"I throw this gathering open for your suggestions," he said. He needed to draw them in.

"We ask for the release of every Palestinian from every jail in the world," one of the Palestinians said, a fierce man with eyes that glowed like burning charcoal.

"Not all," the Syrian said.

"That is very shortsighted," another of the Palestinians said. "We are all brothers."

"Some are only half brothers," the Syrian shot back.

"But our general goals are the same," the third Palestinian said.

"Not completely," the Iranian said, obviously injecting a religious note. The meeting seemed to be heading for contention.

"My friends. Please. The suggestion of our esteemed brother, while heartfelt, is still far from the mark. Considering what we have, it is still not enough," Ahmed said.

"Not enough?" the Palestinian shouted, his voice high-pitched, strident.

"I have a better idea," the Libyan said, slapping the table. "A delicious idea." He looked around the table before speaking again. Then his tongue licked his heavy lower lip, wetting it until it glistened. "We ask for an atomic bomb."

"Thank you," the Syrian said, chuckling derisively. "Why not ask them to give up Texas?"

"Maybe not the latest version," the Libyan continued, surprised at the derision. "But one with just enough power to effectively render harmless a small country of three million people."

He heard a loud chuckle come from one of the Palestinians, then silence.

"But you know that will never happen," the Syrian said.

"But think of the fear we will sow by the demand alone. Our point has always been the same. We have a respectable bargaining chip now. Why settle for bodies? This is the ultimate fear of our enemies."

"It will goad them to some massive retaliation," the Iranian said. "We can't discount their armaments."

"And the Israelis?" the Syrian asked.

"We will freeze their bowels with fear," the Libyan said. "But we will give them no real justification for retaliation." He smiled. "It is a splendid opportunity. After all, we have the President of the United States."

"We don't have the President," the Syrian corrected. "We have a surrogate. There is also another problem."

"And what is that?" Ahmed asked.

The Syrian had a pleasant face and smiled easily, which, to Ahmed, meant he was very dangerous. "Whatever is negotiated is best done through us. Only we maintain relations with the United States."

Their narrow view amazed Ahmed. They were doomed to petty fighting, constant jabbering among themselves. They lacked vision, imagination.

"And what will you negotiate?" Ahmed asked.

The Syrian waved his arm in a sweeping gesture.

"Whatever we decide. Aren't we, after all, the Islamic Jihad?"

It was so pleasantly put that it disarmed them all. Except for Ahmed. Vipers, he told himself. They would come out of this affair as the great white knights. Whatever private concessions they would get from the Americans would be valueless to Ahmed. He didn't want settlements. His business was chaos. His objective was the sweet heady joy of power and celebrity. Did they think they would manipulate him? Lily-livered swine.

"There is only one resolution," Ahmed said. It was, of course, the heart stopper, and he listened with pleasure to the silence. "The Mafia has given us a great prize. They boast of their honor. Well, we should allow them the opportunity to show it. After all, gentlemen, I have lit the fuse."

"You mean force them to blow up the American President," the Syrian said, unable to contain himself. He suddenly looked upset. "Madness."

"No," Ahmed responded. "It is a logical step, the ultimate act of terrorism. We have acquired the means to assassinate the President of the United States. We will never have this opportunity again."

"And what will it achieve for our cause?" the Syrian asked.

"Once and for all, it will validate that we are people to be reckoned with, a force that cannot be ignored," Ahmed continued. "We will slay the beast in his own den."

The Palestinians had been remarkably silent. Although the three groups and their adherents hated each other, the commonality of interest, their mutual hate for the enemy, held them together.

"It would be wise to keep us anonymous in this affair," one of them said. He was the representative of the PLO, a shadowy figure whose name, Ahmed was certain, was a pseudonym. "Although we will cooperate fully behind the scenes." He cleared his throat. "As always."

"So you intend the Libyans and the Shiites to take the brunt, as usual," the Libyan declared.

"Are you frightened?" Ahmed asked. It was always the ultimate question to these macho-oriented types, sure to get them riled.

"None of us at this table have to present our credentials of courage."

Suddenly the discipline within the group broke down. They all began to talk at once.

"Friends. My brothers," Ahmed cried, slamming his fist down on the table. "I am not here to divide us. I am here to unite us. Believe me, I am happy to take all the credit myself. Let it be my contribution to the cause. Think of what it will do. It will make the world sit up and take notice. It is a boldness beyond anything that we have ever concocted. I ask only for your trust and support. No need for anyone to reveal themselves. I can handle this myself."

His words drifted away. He had called this meeting to test the water, confirm his power.

"You realize that we will have to publicly disassociate ourselves from you," the Syrian said.

"Of course."

The Libyan nodded concurrence.

"I am aware of that," Ahmed said.

Ahmed looked at the men around the table. Without a word being exchanged, he knew that consensus had passed between them.

"Then tell us, Ahmed, what can we do to help?" the Syrian asked.

# ★ 27 ★

TO THE PADRE THERE WAS NO NOVELTY IN DEFYING GOVERNMENTAL authority. It was a solemn duty. His values demanded it. The government represented repression, rigid conduct, straitjacketed ideas. Governments were created to force order, to demand adherence to a system of law that inhibited man's natural state of freedom. Its so-called much-vaunted ethical system favored the few who manipulated the many. If the system failed the needs of the leadership, then the leadership had to change the system to meet its needs.

This, to the Padre, was the heart of the government's corruption. Until now he had never realized how truly corrupt it was. His lifelong antagonist, the government, had stolen some of the methods of his organization to further its own corruption.

An entire operation was devoted to this pursuit. They actually had set up and financed an entity that could deal in murder, intimidation, theft, and kidnapping. This entity acted under orders from the President.

Talk about injustice, the Padre thought. Might just as well have licensed his organization or others like it to do the same job. Wouldn't have to waste energy fighting the system. He would be able to operate inside it.

He had thought it would be difficult to coerce the authorities into following his advice. It turned out to be easier than he had believed. They were ready. It was like lighting a match to dry tinder.

Harkins sat at one end of the table tapping out instructions on his keyboard, receiving reports on his monitor. The President sat at the other end of the table near the telephone console. Occasionally their eyes would drift toward the images on the television set, which kept them remarkably informed about events happening outside the White House.

Apparently those officials charged by law to take action in the event the President was unfit to perform his official duties had accepted his assertion that he was, in fact, willing and able to govern. They had tested this assertion all day and he had patiently responded with ideas, orders, and approvals. The presidency, the Padre had discovered, was a job similar to his own. Put out fires, settle or compromise disputes, perform rituals, make decisions, exercise leadership.

He felt remarkably compatible with the President. The man,

after a little tap dance of opposition and disapproval, had an affinity for his ideas. Despite his protestations, he knew the hidden meaning of power and manipulation.

But the woman was a problem. He had taken her to apply more pressure on the President. Now he wasn't so sure it was a good idea. Yet he would be a fool to release her now.

Women baffled him. He often wondered whether he had ever truly known his beloved Rosa. Rosa, too, had been reluctant to give his business her blanket blessing, but she had never resisted him, had understood her role.

This Harkins was a superb organizer. He had even devised a way to get confidential information to the Pencil. By hand-delivered message, no less. He punched out info, then one of their covert operatives passed the word directly.

All the Pencil needed was names and places. The Saudi's favorite son was a student at Berkeley, the daughter of the Syrian President a student at Amherst. The Pencil would know what to do with that kind of information. Those operations under his control did not worry the Padre. It was the government that worried him. Above all, they had better not fail in Jordan. This Safari boy must be taken. He was the key to the operation.

The Padre's eyes drifted toward the television set. He had lowered the sound. Besides, the images themselves had become too tiresome and repetitive.

"Our Iranian operation is completed," Harkins said, looking at the monitor.

"The Libyan?"

"In progress."

"And Jordan?" the Padre asked.

"No word yet."

The President looked up. He had been talking on the telephone and making notes on a pad. He looked toward the television set, then returned to his conversation. The Padre had listened to the conversation with half an ear. The President was talking import quotas with someone. He had heard the beginning of the conversation. The President had said:

"Pretend all things are normal. Let's just stick to the issues."

Remarkable, the Padre thought. The man had the kind of discipline required for the job. The government was functioning. The idea had begun to take hold. It was all grist for the television mill.

Nevertheless, a task force continued to operate from its headquarters in the basement of the Executive Office Building. Vice President Chalmers, as the heir apparent to the presidency, was the man in charge. Congress had been summoned to return and would soon meet to debate the question of accession.

The miracles of satellite communication allowed everyone to have their say. Television had reported the views of the Soviets, the Syrians, the Israelis, the Libyans, the Egyptians, and on and on.

The foreigners were confused as to why the President had not been superseded by the Vice President. This situation had been explained from every conceivable vantage point. The President himself had been pressed to appear on television, but the Padre had vetoed that idea. He did not yet wish to relinquish any control he might have over him. He knew that the President's phone conversations were being recorded, but they were not being publicly aired.

Harkins' fingers bounced endlessly on the keyboard. He had assured the Padre that the computer was foolproof. It could not be tapped by anyone who was not authorized. The CIA had commissioned computer experts to attempt to infiltrate the covert data base, and these included teenage hackers. Some had actually broken in, but the method was swiftly analyzed and the system debugged to prevent it.

Suddenly something flashed across the computer screen that startled Harkins.

"What?" he cried.

The Padre felt a cold, pinching sensation in his guts. The President, once again, turned from his conversation and looked at both men.

"What is it?" the President asked.

Harkins looked up at the television screen.

"We always get it first," he said. The pride did not erase the sense of dread. The Jordan operation, the Padre thought. If that failed . . .

At that moment the First Lady, followed by Benjy, came into the dining room from the pantry.

"A call to a Beirut newspaper. Soon it will be released to every corner of the world. A demand from our friend Ahmed on behalf of the Islamic Jihad."

"What is it they want?" the President asked.

"You won't believe this," Harkins said.

"Try me."

"An atomic bomb," Harkins said. He looked toward the Padre. "In return for the delivery of your daughter and grandson."

"Quite an idea," the President said.

Of course they would raise the ante. A perfectly logical expecta-

· 145 ·

tion, the Padre thought. In an odd way, he was relieved. Although he had not admitted it to himself, the absence of any reaction from the kidnappers was cause for worry. Now he could assume that Maria and Joey were still alive.

"Why not?" Harkins said rhetorically.

"It's impossible," the President said.

"They know that, Mr. President," Harkins said.

"Then why demand it?"

"To tell us how much leverage they have." He turned toward the Padre. "They must have something else up their sleeves."

The President's wife, who had been uncharacteristically silent, suddenly spoke:

"He's unleashed the beast, that's what," she said with disdain. The woman had not been taken into their confidence. If she knew what was happening, the Padre thought, she would be even more excited.

The Padre signaled with his eyes, and Benjy turned up the sound on the television set.

"There," Harkins said, looking up at the television screen. "It's moving now." He looked at his watch. "Beat the bastards by five," he said. He got up from the chair and turned up the sound. A correspondent in Beirut was providing the information that Harkins had just imparted along with various speculations and a picture of Ahmed Safari.

"Next thing we can expect is an interview with your daughter and grandson," Amy said. "And now, direct from the cell of Maria and Joey Michaels—"

"Amy, for crying out loud," the President said.

"They know it's impossible to grant," Harkins said.

"But it serves their purposes to frighten the hell out of all of us," the President roared. "And remind us of the ultimate nightmare, the big bomb in the hands of some crazy." He paused to concentrate on what the commentator was saying.

"Even the size of the bomb was specified. Something to knock out a nation of three million people." The commentator's face had turned ashen.

"What of the Jordan operation?" the Padre asked calmly.

"It has gone forward," Harkins said. "We would not get word until the boy is safely in our hands."

"What boy?" the President's wife asked. She looked at her husband. The President turned to the Padre, who shrugged. Her reaction is immaterial, he thought. No harm in telling her.

"This man, Ahmed Safari. We are referring to his own son," the Padre said.

She did not need any further explanation. Her lips trembled, her nostrils flared. She turned to the President.

"So you've sold out to them," she said.

"Not quite," the President said.

Before she could reply, the commentator was offering another bulletin. A Saudi prince, grandson of the King, had disappeared from Berkeley.

"My God," the First Lady exclaimed.

"No one has been harmed," the President began.

"You've authorized kidnapping," she said.

The Padre signaled to Benjy, who grabbed the woman from behind, lifted her out of the chair, and moved her, kicking and screaming, out of the room. The President paled and stood up. The tautness of the connecting cord brought back the reality of his situation.

"If you hurt her . . ."

"Of course we won't, but we can't deal with a hysterical woman. Benjy will be careful, I assure you," the Padre said.

The voice of the commentator compelled them to silence again. He explained that there were no clues to the disappearance of the Saudi prince. Someone in the apartment complex in which he lived saw three men, but he wasn't sure.

"We are handling our end. What about yours?" the Padre pressed.

Harkins tapped away on the keyboard.

"No word yet."

"Perhaps the CIA should take a lesson from the Mafia," the President said. The color had come back into his face. The Canary, who had been in the other room, poked his head into the dining room.

"She is in the bedroom," he said. "She is all right."

"She had better be," the President said, but he seemed relieved.

The President's telephone lights began to blink. He picked up the instrument. The Vice President spoke:

"You've got to give it up, Mr. President," he said. "We've got a worldwide panic on our hands."

"Don't exaggerate, Martin."

"All you have to do is say the word."

"I am governing," the President said. "Stop letting a bunch of tinhorn terrorists make you crazy."

"Make me crazy? You're the hostage. You realize that this is a totally irresponsible act on your part."

"Do you think for one moment that I would entertain such a request?"

"No, I guess not," the Vice President said, retreating from his earlier belligerence. "But this bomb business is unsettling."

"It's an absurd demand."

"But if you stepped down, Mr. President. Got out of the line of fire."

"Then what, Martin?" the President asked pointedly, letting the question hang ominously in the air.

"This is irrational, there is the country to think about, the people."

"Stop it, Martin. Nobility does not become you."

There was a long pause.

"And in the meantime, Mr. President, what are we supposed to do?"

"Hang in there."

"I might if I knew what the hell was going on."

The President hung up.

Harkins continued to tap away at his keyboard, watching the monitor.

"The boy?" the Padre asked.

"No. But here's something. The Libyan. Right in their own backyard. In Tripoli. Now you've got to admit, Teheran, then Tripoli, that's something. That's one helluva coup. Damn, we're good."

He tapped the monitor. Then he looked at the President. "It's what I kept telling you, Mr. President. We've got the means. We've got the reach. And we can move these people out of the country."

"Like where?" the President asked.

Harkins smiled.

"The Libyan will be in Morocco in a few hours. The Iranian in Oman. All set up."

"And they will not be hurt?"

"Those kids will never have it so good. They'll come out loving the United States."

"And when they get out will they know who did this to them?"

"Mr. President," Harkins said. "This is a covert operation. And that's the way it will remain. I've been telling you this for months. We've got the greatest underused weapon in the world."

A braggart, the Padre thought. Yet there was something miraculous in the operation. A man directing a vast operation from a computer.

"Louder," the President said, pointing to the television screen. "What is that man saying?" Benjy turned up the sound.

"Sonya Rashid, the daughter of the Syrian President, has disappeared." The commentator's voice was high-pitched with excitement. His forehead glistened with sweat.

"We have an open line to our Boston correspondent," the commentator said. "Tell me, Bob, when was Miss Rashid last seen?"

"Last night," the correspondent said. "She said she was going out to a movie. She loves the movies. She never came back to the dorm."

"Was she alone?"

"She left alone."

"Is there any evidence of foul play?"

"None whatsoever. The police are combing the area. For Miss Rashid not to return to her dorm for curfew is very uncharacteristic conduct. The police have concluded, at least unofficially, that she is a missing person."

"Is it fair to speculate that she is another casualty of what is presently occurring, in other words, connected in some way to the hostage-taking of the President and the disappearance of the Saudi prince?" the correspondent asked.

"I would not want to speculate."

Then came the usual round of comments as the busy satellite bounced signals around the world. Most agreed that the disappearance of the Saudi prince and the daughter of the President of Syria was, indeed, connected to the current situation. The interviews became repetitive. Voices droned on. The Padre got up and lowered the sound.

"Can't understand it," Harkins said. "We should have had it first."

"Nobody's perfect," the President said, obviously enjoying the spectacle of Harkins' tiny defeat. Then he turned to the Padre. "I don't want those people hurt. Under any circumstances."

"Mr. President. This is not a government operation," Harkins said, glancing toward the Padre. "Not in our purview."

The Padre stiffened. All were accounted for now, except the boy in Jordan.

"Only a fool will believe that these actions are not connected to us," the President said.

"That's the point, Mr. President. They will, however, have to draw their own conclusions," Harkins said.

The Padre felt no remorse or pity for the hostages they had taken. As always, the Pencil had gotten the job done.

"The FBI is deeply involved," Harkins said, watching the monitor. "They've dispatched investigative teams to Berkeley and Amherst."

"You think I should talk to Joe Halloran, the head of our FBI?" the President asked tentatively.

"Why?" the Padre asked.

"I would advise that you keep your distance, Mr. President," Harkins said.

"But they'll think . . ."

"We want them to think that, Mr. President. It is the heart of the strategy."

"And say nothing," the Padre added.

"Then how will they know that these people are hostages?"

The Padre nodded to the television set.

"That will do our work for us."

"But they will blame us," the President said with mounting frustration. "Maybe . . ." He paused and bit his lip, as if trying to stop the words from coming. "Maybe we should put out a statement."

"If asked, we deny. Only deny," Harkins said.

"But suppose the FBI finds these people, the perpetrators as well? And they trace them back to here." He shook his head.

"You are looking at the dark side, Mr. President," the Padre said gently. What else is a politician if not an intriguer, the Padre thought. Of course he knew the consequences. For whose benefit was he making this speech? Perhaps his own.

"I hadn't bargained for all this," the President said.

"Yes you did, Mr. President," the Padre said curtly.

# ✯ 28 ✯

DESPITE THE FAMILIAR DOMESTICITY OF MRS. SANTORELLI'S APARTment, Robert's anxiety was corroding his ability to defend himself from within. The separation from Maria and Joey, who represented the very core of his life, had left him dangling and inert. Helplessness and frustration had wreaked havoc on his nervous system.

Only a few weeks ago he had been content in his superiority. After all, wasn't he privy to the most intimate secrets of an entire civilization, one that had defied the understanding of those who lived through it? The ancient Egyptians had believed that paying obeisance to a sacred animal or sending their dead into tombs with all their possessions would assure them immortality in paradise. If his academic discipline would have allowed him to be judgmental by today's values, he would have called them naive fools.

Lying awake in one of Mrs. Santorelli's spare bedrooms, tossing and sweating on tumbled sheets, he tried to lift himself out of the contemporary world, push his sense of time forward a few thousand years, then look back with all the investigatory instincts of an archaeologist.

Civilization around the year 2000, he concluded, was technologically superior but morally bankrupt. People killed, maimed, and tortured each other indiscriminately. They worshiped the mechanics of destruction. They threw bombs in airports and bus stations. They took people hostage for obscure reasons. Murder was an honorable tactic in the service of political aspiration. Creatures of that era even showed pictures of murder and suffering as entertainment. If one were to be judgmental, one would conclude that they would have been better off worshiping dogs.

A light knock at the front door alerted him. He might have been dozing. He was never sure. Lifting himself off the damp sheets, he put on his pants and walked barefoot to the doorway, peering along the corridor. All night long he had heard whispered voices. Did these people ever sleep? Even Mrs. Santorelli's flapping slippers seemed to echo perpetually through the apartment, a sound as ubiquitous as the garlicky smells of her cooking.

He had seen on television pictures of Maria in the cap and gown of her graduation. It was too painful to watch, too heartrending. It merely triggered his imagination, taking his thoughts down dark alleys of speculation. My Maria. My Joey. When he thought of them his body went numb with fright.

It was the Pencil who opened the door. A man entered. He was youngish, grim-faced. He carried a briefcase. Robert knew instantly that he was a stranger. The man followed the Pencil to the dining room. Robert moved cautiously along the corridor. He was sure the stranger's presence had something to do with Maria and Joey, with the President. Perhaps it was part of the negotiation.

When he reached the edge of the dining room he flattened himself against the wall and listened. He heard the tearing of paper. Oddly, there was little conversation between them. It was possible the man was not even sitting down.

"And the Padre, he is all right?" the Pencil asked.

"I am only the courier," the man said. "But it had to be put in your hands personally."

"This place is still safe?" the Pencil asked.

"Apparently. Besides, your people seemed to have it well staked out. I was stopped three times."

"Good," the Pencil said. There was silence. They might have been shaking hands. Robert remained flattened against the wall as the man turned down the corridor and let himself out the door.

When he had gone, Robert went into the dining room. The Pencil looked up, startled, then quickly settled.

"Only a paper with names from the CIA," he said.

"So something has begun to happen," Robert said. He looked intently at the Pencil, who held the paper in his hands. "That then is my business."

"They are only names." He seemed oddly hesitant, then handed the paper to Robert. He looked at it, immediately recognizing both names and the references to Berkeley and Amherst. Robert watched as the paper trembled in his hands.

The Pencil shrugged. He would stonewall now, Robert knew. He saw his eyes dart to the telephone.

"If it gets Maria and Joey home, what difference does it make?" the Pencil said.

Incredibly, the Padre had gotten the government to act in tandem with his organization.

"Then there are things you must do," Robert said. No, he decided, he would not be judgmental. It would be futile. The Padre did, indeed, have an acute understanding of human motivation. As Robert turned to leave the room, he stopped. The Pencil had picked up the phone. He had already dialed one number.

Suddenly Robert spoke. The Pencil's dialing finger paused in midair.

"Please don't hurt them," he said.

The Pencil resumed his dialing.

# ✭ 29 ✭

"THEY'VE GONE BERSERK," CHALMERS WAS SAYING FOR THE THIRD OR fourth time in the last hour. He was giving himself the once-over with a cordless electric razor. He had also changed his shirt three times since coming into the conference room nearly twenty-four hours before.

A number of television sets had been placed strategically around the room. Each passing moment brought a new and startling revelation. To make matters even more bizarre, the networks and the local stations had begun to run commercials again. He's right, Foreman thought. They have gone berserk. Not just the little group in the White House. The whole country.

With cots brought in by the military, they had set up a kind of dormitory, utilizing various nearby rooms. Foreman had tried to get some rest. The National Security Advisor was not sure whether he had slept or merely floated in some subconscious haze on the murky edge of a nightmare. Concocting scenarios was the literal spine of his expertise. His job was to deal with present realities on the basis of an imagined future. His tools for this enterprise were logic, experience, knowledge, and intuition. Had somebody stolen his tools?

The military had also set up a mess kitchen. A duty roster had been posted outside the room. Since the crisis began, Foreman had been spending most of his time sitting around this table or talking to world leaders. Now, once again, he was reporting on his latest conversations with the Soviet Foreign Minister.

"And what does the President say?" Chalmers asked, nodding his head in the direction of the White House.

Foreman had been in touch with the President a number of times during the day. He had suggested that he speak directly with the Soviet General Secretary.

"Why?" the President had asked.

"To soothe his fears. They are getting more and more nervous, Mr. President. This nuclear thing has them up the wall."

"Good," the President had countered. "Teach them not to mess around with those terrorist crackpots."

"And our own allies. I've been in touch with all of them. They're terrified."

"Their problem. They've never gone along with any of our ideas and suggestions about terrorism. Let them stew."

"They've alerted their forces."

"Let them," the President had countered.

"You still do not want to put our forces on full alert," Foreman said.

"No," the President had said. "No more saber-rattling for us." He recalled waiting for the President to complete what seemed to be a half-articulated thought. He didn't, but, despite the denial, the message was clear. No more paralysis. Only action.

The media was adding fuel to the fire. What he reported to the group was almost simultaneous with the reportage on the tube. Information seemed to be careening forward like a brakeless truck going down a steep incline. It was almost impossible to absorb what was being said.

Khomeini, one of whose grandsons had been kidnapped, had fumed once more about the Great Satan and threatened massive retaliation. The Syrian President offered his own threats, and the

Saudis, as always, expressed extreme caution. Qaddafi was ominously silent, as were the Israelis. With the four television sets blaring out their cacophony, it was the Tower of Babel come alive in the twentieth century.

They sat around the table going over the same ground endlessly. At one point Steve Potter, the President's press secretary, burst into the room.

"Poll results are in," he said, his face flushed with excitement. "A quickie, really. But the results are phenomenal."

"Who authorized that?" Chalmers asked.

"The party people. Damned clever of them, too. The networks are also doing them. Gives us a good handle on the situation."

No one in the room had the temerity to ask the results, although Potter's face was an excellent barometer.

"Eighty-nine percent approval. Highest in history."

"Jesus." Chalmers swallowed any further comment.

"They figure the President knows what he's doing," Potter said.

"Politics as usual," Vic Proctor said.

Nervous politicians would never risk disturbing any calibration that went against an enormously popular act by the President, hostage or not. But didn't everyone know that the President was acting under duress? Nonsense, the polls indicated. It was the other way around. The President was manipulating the kidnappers. So the world was topsy-turvy, after all, Foreman decided. The country must be out for lunch.

"Might as well send everyone home," Chalmers said. "The President is in charge."

As if in response to his remarks, the other networks came on with their poll results. All were remarkably similar.

The system was eating itself from within, Foreman thought.

# ☆ 30 ☆

"SO NOW WE ARE INTERNATIONAL CELEBRITIES," AHMED SAID, UP-ending yet another shot glass of scotch and tousling the blond boy's hair. Maria, an arm thrown around Joey's shoulders as he nestled at her side, squatted, her back against the wall.

A television set stood on a chair in a corner of the room blaring out, mostly in Arabic, bits and pieces of the number one news story in the world. She watched the panorama of images. The TV screen showed the White House, stock film of the President and his family, interviews with other international figures, with a heavy emphasis on Arab leaders.

Then a still picture of Ahmed flashed on the screen along with the sound of an interview done with him over the telephone in Arabic in which he reiterated his demand for an atomic bomb in return for the daughter and grandson of the Mafiosa boss. This segment was followed once again by a picture of her in her high school yearbook. She had begun to hate the picture.

"You did not seem very happy," Ahmed said, his tongue thick with drink and laughter.

"I hated to smile then," Maria said.

"You look funny, Mommy," Joey said.

"It's the braces," Maria said, trying to maintain a facade of indifference. "I hated them."

It was ludicrous. The four of them sitting around in this barren place watching television. Yet she was determined not to show them her fear. However her father's act might be characterized by others—mad, courageous, or cowardly—for her it had a deeper connotation. Out of simple fatherly love, he had sent her a message of hope. She no longer felt completely powerless and alone.

Earlier, under cover of darkness, they had moved them to this present apartment, which, she assumed, was also in one of the teeming nondescript blocks in the heart of West Beirut. From outside she could hear the sounds of a loud and raucous street life.

As before, they chained her and the boy to a pipe. Yet it was not too uncomfortable in their sleeping bags at night, and the food, mostly vegetables, had been, if not of gourmet quality, passable. Oddly, she felt herself adapting to the circumstances. Even Joey seemed to cry less in his sleep.

Apparently the arrangement between her and her captors had reached a certain plateau of understanding. She had even sensed a certain gratitude in herself for being allowed to watch television. Incomprehensible events were unfolding. Was this really about her and Joey, about her father? About this terrible man, Ahmed Safari? Why wasn't she home with Robert? At times the events depicted seemed like some dream fantasy.

Ahmed took delight in making taunting sallies at the people pictured in the television images, providing a kind of multimedia entertainment system that both fascinated and disgusted her.

Satellites had picked up numerous remotes from all over the world in English as well as other languages, and she was able to follow the events. At first she had been frightened by her father's action. Yet it did not baffle her. Except for the enormity of the act, it seemed absolutely consistent with his way of life, his motives and methods.

Her father's love for her had always been obsessive, as it had been for her brothers and her mother. She knew what she and Joey represented to her father. The loss of her mother, hard on the heels of her brothers' treachery and death, had left a deep hollowness in him, space that only she and Joey could fill.

Ahmed's admiration for her father's action did not surprise her. The criminal mind, too, was susceptible to role models, and her father was made to order. The effect on Ahmed by his sudden ascendancy into the international limelight was dramatic. His ruthlessness had graduated to self-importance.

Somehow he had come to believe that his lucky hit was a product of his own genius. The man was now reveling in his notoriety. American television commentators, with their penchant for hyperbole, had dubbed him the most resourceful, cunning, and cruel of all the terrorists, which, as Arab commentators attested, merely boosted his stock in the Arab world.

"I am the hero of the hour," he had told her.

It was the denouement that worried her. She had tried to barter herself for Joey's freedom, but that hadn't worked. And she thought longingly about Robert. There was hardly a word about him on the television. Undoubtedly, he was frantic.

Ahmed's taunts at the television screen had accelerated with his drinking. Whenever his name was not mentioned for some period of time, he would rant and rave.

"They are ignoring me." He would toss her a look of complicity. "You, as well, my little prizes." Then he would laugh and toss off another shot of whiskey.

But beneath the mask of arrogance, she could detect a tiny sliver of uncertainty, barely a crease really, but promising.

There was no telephone in this new hideout. Alert to every nuance of her captivity, Maria noted that Ahmed had taken elaborate precautions to keep their whereabouts secret.

They had been shuttled around from one place to another. She noted, too, that the number of young men around Ahmed had decreased. She counted only five now, from what had been a high of around a dozen. There was the uncommon blond boy, Ahmed's obvious favorite, and four scrubby and dour men in their twenties, all interchangeable look-alikes, with just enough differences in their dress to tell them apart. One wore a red bandanna around his neck, another a heavy gold Muslim half-moon. One was balding, and the fourth wore a carefully trimmed goatee, the only aspect of him that was neat.

One or another of them brought in their food. At some point in the day, Ahmed had stopped one of the men, the fellow with the red bandanna. He had whispered something in his ear that she could not hear. They had looked in her direction for a moment. Ahmed had smiled and the young man had left the room.

"We will be an international sensation," Ahmed said, slapping the table. The blond boy giggled.

"You already are," Maria sneered.

"We are talking show business," Ahmed said. "The three of us." He leered. "The hostage sisters. I have sent for the equipment."

She grasped where his hints were leading. He would tape some sort of interview, sell it to the television people, greedy for information. The idea disgusted her. No. She would not allow herself to be sold for such purposes.

The boy with the red bandanna returned to the apartment carrying two large boxes. In one was a television camera, in the other a VCR. Incredible, she thought, adding a further factor to the reality of her incarceration. With impunity, they could simply go into a store and buy this equipment.

They shut off the television set to connect the VCR, then tested the equipment. With great delight, the blond young man mugged for the camera, watching gleefully as he appeared on the screen.

"Now," Ahmed said, turning to her, "you must clean yourself up. You still have some makeup?"

She nodded hesitantly, her gaze alighting on her pocketbook, which they had let her keep. "You and the boy must look healthy, smiling, a visitor enjoying our hospitality."

"You'll never get away with it," she said, unable to raise her voice above a whisper.

"A little gasoline here." He touched Joey's ear. "A dab here. Believe me, one more child's dead body would make little difference in this lovely country."

The trembling in her body increased. Her breath came in short gasps.

"You can't." Her rage finally defeated her and tears of frustration rolled down her cheeks.

He reached out and pulled her up roughly. He seemed to have sobered completely. She wanted to lash out at him, gouge out his eyes. The boy tried to move beside her. Ahmed restrained him.

"Leave the boy here," Ahmed said. The boy struggled to be released. He patted the boy's head while he held him securely in an iron grip. "Just get ready."

Her legs shook so hard, she could barely move. With his freed hand he grabbed her under the elbow and directed her toward the bathroom.

"If you hurt him . . ." she began. His response was to thrust her forward. He threw her pocketbook after her.

"A good job, Maria," he ordered, still holding the boy in his grip. The boy did not make it easy for him, squirming like an eel, until the grip tightened and he was quiet. Yet he did not cry. For that she was grateful.

In the mirror, she saw her ashen face. Her hair was unkempt. She looked awful. Nevertheless, she made an attempt to put herself in order. He was too ruthless, too unmerciful, quite capable of carrying out any threats to hurt Joey. There was nothing to do but surrender. Patience, she urged herself. Play his game. Hurry, Daddy, she cried to herself. Hurry.

She came back into the room. They had set up a kind of makeshift set, two chairs, catty-corner. Joey, frightened and sad, looking like a whipped puppy, sat on the floor.

"You must tell him to be a good little boy, to look smiling into the camera."

"Please," she whispered. "I promise you. He will be a good boy."

She bent over the boy, embraced him and kissed him. He was shivering. "It's all right, sweets. All right."

"Sure, Mommy."

"He is a very mean man," she whispered. "But we must do as he says."

"I hate him," Joey said.

"You wait. He'll be punished," she told him.

"Yeah. Grandpa will get him." She was not sure he had fully understood the events he had seen on television. His response surprised her. She smiled and hugged him.

"No question about that, sweets. No question at all."

The boy clung to her neck and she kissed his face.

"Enough," Ahmed called. "We're ready."

Like an automaton, she obeyed his instructions to the letter. She sat on the chair opposite him and composed herself. Anything, she thought. I will say anything. Joey climbed on her lap. "Smile," she whispered. The boy obediently arranged his features to resemble a smile. The room was quiet now. They had turned off the television set. The blond boy stood behind the camera.

"And after, we will go on a nice little trip."

So he was running again, she thought. What did that mean? She was still too overwrought to analyze it.

"Now, my little prizes, let us start the interview," Ahmed said, nodding toward the blond boy. She heard the low moan of the camera's mechanism as he switched it on.

"Are we treating you well, Mrs. Michaels?" Ahmed asked.

She looked at him and forced a smile. But she could not stop her lips from trembling.

"Stop," Ahmed said, gentle now, like a director imposing his charm to extract a good performance from one of his actors. "You must calm down."

"I am calm," she said.

"A broader smile, please."

"I'm doing my best."

He nodded toward the blond boy.

"Again."

The camera mechanism purred, Ahmed smiled broadly into the lens, then turned toward her.

"Are we treating you well, Mrs. Michaels?"

"Oh yes. It is wonderful—"

"Dammit," Ahmed said. "It sounds unnatural."

"Too enthusiastic?" she asked innocently. She felt her courage rising.

"You must seem natural. After all, you are making the best of a bad situation for yourself. But you understand why this is being done to you. That is the feeling we must have."

"Of course," she said.

"Now!"

Again the camera purred.

"Are we treating you well, Mrs. Michaels?"

But before she could begin, another boy, a surly type, the one with the gold half-moon around his neck, rushed into the room. His dark eyes seemed to mirror his fear. He was nervous and upset. He conversed with Ahmed in brief bursts of Arabic. Ahmed stood up, grabbed a handful of the boy's shirt, and pulled him menacingly toward him. The boy rose on his toes and pleaded. Then Ahmed let him go and paced the room. He was angry. Beads of sweat rolled down his cheeks. It was obvious to Maria that the boy had brought him news that did not please him. She held Joey closer and patted his arm.

"Everything will be fine, sweets," she whispered. "We mustn't let him frighten us." Joey's response was to press his body closer to her.

The blond boy had put down the camera and picked up his automatic weapon, pointing it menacingly at Maria and the boy. Maria forced herself not to react. They had done this to her before. A few moments more pacing and Ahmed walked toward the television and flicked the switch. He seemed to have forgotten her presence.

Again the images crowded into the room as the information-gathering juggernaut hopped around the world at a dizzying pace. There was Ahmed's picture flashed across the screen, but one look at him told her that he was not pleased. A grim commentator stood in front of a backdrop that appeared to be an Arab city street. Children peeked into the camera behind him.

"The linkage has now come full circle. The son of Ahmed Safari, the man identified as the kidnapper of Maria and Joseph Michaels, daughter and grandson of the man who holds the President of the United States hostage, has vanished from—" the man turned and pointed with his head—"this home in Amman. There are no witnesses. Speculation centers on the obvious."

Ahmed banged the top of the television set. The screen cracked and went blank. "Liars. Bastards. A sick boy." He pointed his finger at the blank screen. "You touch one hair. You will see what I can do." He was livid with rage.

"We must not be afraid," she whispered to her son. He nodded, showing that he understood.

It took some time for Ahmed to get himself under control. Finally he acknowledged her presence again.

"They touch him, you are a dead woman," he said.

"They have already touched him," Maria whispered, studying his reactions, forcing her mind to divorce itself from emotion. They had found his Achilles' heel.

"They will do nothing," he said, suddenly becoming calm. "It is just another silly ineffective CIA ploy." He continued to pace the room, speaking more to himself than to her. But he could not seem to shake himself free of his concern. "They want to play their little games, then play we shall." He looked at her and the boy. "On with the show. The more sympathetic we appear, the more the people in your country will protest."

He sat on the chair again and the blond boy put down his gun and picked up the camera. But Ahmed was a changed man, Maria noted. He seemed, despite his bravado, somehow less deadly. He waved his hand impatiently at the blond boy.

"Now," he said. The camera purred. He turned toward Maria. "And how are you being treated, Mrs. Michaels?"

She lifted her eyes, staring at him directly, lips pursed. Daddy, she thought. Her father's face materialized in her mind. Do it, she begged herself. Find the courage.

"Brutally. Without regard to human decency. These people are monsters—"

Ahmed sprang from his chair. The blond boy, out of surprise or mental paralysis, continued to record the scene. Ahmed's arm flashed and the camera fell to the floor. The blond boy lost his balance and tumbled beside it. Then Ahmed focused his attention on Maria. Something, she noted, had changed in the calibration of his arrogance. "You'll pay the price for this, you bitch."

He reached his hand out to touch the boy's head. She sprang up and, still holding the boy, moved away. He did not follow her. Instead, he waved a finger at her. "I swear to you." He was suddenly speechless, snarling impotently.

"So, Ahmed," she said, her tone measured, "there is a human side to you. Congratulations." She had found her strength. His vulnerability was quite defined now. "You had better treat your bargaining chip with some respect."

"He is a sick boy."

"I feel for him, Ahmed," she said.

Again he paced the room, then sat down on the table. He began to write on a piece of paper. She watched him. He wrote, paused, waited, grew thoughtful, wrote again. Then he waved to the blond boy and said something to him in Arabic. The boy took the paper and left the room.

"I have given them a deadline," he said, his voice gravelly.

Her heartbeat pounded in her throat. His eyes had narrowed; the whites seemed to have disappeared. They looked cruel, snake-like. His lips, too, had tightened, and when he spoke they barely moved.

"The boy will deliver the message. He will call the newspapers. Soon the world will know. A simple request, really. Your CIA will release my son by tomorrow noon our time."

"What makes you so sure?" Maria asked.

He looked toward her and pointed his chin.

"You do," Ahmed said. "And if they do not react, we will make a show of it, so they will know we mean business. I assure you, your people will get the message, especially your father."

She tightened her grip around her son. My father, she thought. Whatever happens, she thought, he will write his answer on your corpse.

OF COURSE IT WAS POSSIBLE TO IMAGINE, AMY ASSURED HERSELF. SHE was in the middle of a computerized experience, a special-effects thrill concocted for Disneyland. Action transpired according to however Jack Harkins programmed a sequence of events. The results of these sequences were then displayed on television. They were then assessed and further sequences arranged to continue to manipulate the experience. Such convictions made the reality of what she was experiencing bearable.

Once again they had let her join the "adults" in the dining room. But only after she had promised that she would behave. It was pointless to do otherwise. Her protests were totally ineffectual. They had shunted her off to the bedroom, a kind of child's Siberia. She had lain on the bed pouting and resentful, frustrated by the indignity.

Then it had occurred to her that perhaps she was wrong. Perhaps these kidnappings were merely a setup. Perhaps all that was happening, the computer-directed events, the television images, were a contrivance designed to lull the Padre into acceptance before striking back.

It was these doubts that made her delay going forward with her plan. In actuality, it was a weapon, and it rode, like a piece of ice, on the bare skin above her right hip. Its presence was a goading reminder, forcing her to think about alternatives.

"I'll be good," she had promised Benjy, her eyes imploring him to let her go back to the dining room. "I'd rather be with my husband." Her mimicking of a child's contrition seemed to impress him.

"Now you're getting smart," Benjy said, with what seemed gentler tones than before. She had little doubt about his reason for acting this way. She had assumed her rightful woman's place in their manly universe.

"Don't make waves. They know what they're doing," Benjy told her.

"So it seems," she offered fatuously. Her apparent reasonableness put in motion their odd but effective communication system. The big man, who was ubiquitous, shuttled Benjy's message to the Padre, who consented, and they had let her come back into the dining room.

Paul was on the telephone. He looked up at her and nodded. Behave yourself. That seemed to be his message as well. Beside him was his ever-present human attachment, his face rutted and wrinkled, his eyes watchful.

In the dining room, the television set was on. Harkins watched the computer and the Padre sat quietly slumped in a chair appearing to be half asleep. If she did not know better, she might have characterized him as bored. Nothing here was as it seemed.

She sat on one of the dining-room chairs and concentrated on what was transpiring. Harkins, she noted, was more agitated than he had been earlier. He was working feverishly with the computer, mumbling curses under his breath. Paul wound up his conversation on the telephone and shook his head.

"Gridlock," he said. "That was the Speaker. He's appointed a committee, but he assures me they probably won't act. The polls have taken the wind out of everybody's sails." He looked at the Padre. "In other words, the people like what we're doing."

He glanced at Amy, but turned away quickly. He seemed deeper into it than before, his face flushed, as it became when he was feverish with excitement. "This is not to say that they aren't nervous. All that military activity has them worried. Not to mention the edgy Soviets. Be good for them to fret a while."

Harkins looked up from the computer screen.

"The assessment boys still stick with their conclusion. The Saudis and the Syrians won't stir. They make a move and the Israelis will clobber them. They've called up their reserves. Nice move on their part. Scares the shit out of everybody. The Iranians haven't got the assets. Too bogged down with Iraq."

"And crazy Qaddafi?" the President asked.

"He's jumping up and down," Harkins said, sucking in a deep breath. "Not to worry. They have nowhere to go, not with the Egyptians staring down their noses. But there's always a chance he might go off the deep end, except that his council won't let him."

"No more talk of atomic bombs?" the President asked. He looked at Amy.

"None," Harkins said.

The President laughed and slapped the table.

"On the outside it might look like brinkmanship," Harkins said. "Trick is to scare enough people into putting a stop to this terrorist crap." He looked at the Padre, who ignored him.

She had heard variations of this conversation before, always one-sided reconstructions by Paul. Hearing it at first hand was more chilling than she had imagined. To avoid listening further, she looked up at the television screen. She felt like a child who had missed an important lesson and was now working hard to catch up.

The television commentator had begun to update the situation.

There were now five kidnap victims. Three overseas. Two in the States. She listened in horror. He, too, seemed overly excited by events. For him it was the story of a lifetime.

"There is still no word on the condition of any of the victims," the commentator announced in his frenetic staccato. "Nor has anyone claimed credit, although speculation all over the world insists that this is the work of our own CIA on orders from the President. The President, despite the accusations and his own tenuous position, is reported to have denied any complicity. Nor would any responsible official confirm that this was an American-sponsored enterprise. Of course the head of the CIA is with the President, but no statement has been forthcoming."

"Keeps 'em guessing," the President said. He and Harkins seemed to have been emboldened by events, as if their captivity had not occurred. A conspiracy, Amy decided. They were all in it together.

But the Padre, Amy noted, showed no such delight. He seemed deep in thought, his concentration elsewhere.

Harkins went back to working the keyboard.

"No word?" the Padre asked, suddenly reunited with events. The question perked up her own curiosity.

The Padre turned toward Harkins, who looked up from the screen.

"I'm sorry," Harkins said.

"The others?" the President asked.

"All accounted for," Harkins said. "In safe houses. Well cared for." He looked at the Padre. "What about your people?" Harkins looked first to the President, then back at the Padre. "We don't know where you've . . . where they are."

"Still nothing about the boy?" the Padre asked pointedly, ignoring Harkins' question. Beneath the mask of calm, Amy saw the cold, cruel resolve.

"Just taking them longer to respond," Harkins said. His mood had changed. He was obviously distressed.

She struggled to piece things together without calling attention to herself. The television commentator was beginning to fill in the blanks, including more details about Ahmed's son, who had been taken from his home in Jordan. These revelations had only compounded the shock. The boy was weak, sickly, a rheumatic heart. He was only seventeen. In fact, all five were under twenty. Five innocent children. Terrorism in reverse.

Still, Amy did not show them her disgust. The general assumption, as reported by the commentator and seconded by various pundits, was that negotiations were currently under way by all parties for the release of all hostages, that the Americans, although it was denied, had demonstrated their ability to reach out anywhere in the world. Their willingness to cross the moral line and kidnap other innocents for barter was the latest escalation. As always in the media, the question was debated, analyzed, dissected ad infinitum.

"We will pay the price," someone said. They had arranged a panel show to fill the time between bulletins. Above all, don't let it get boring, she thought. As usual, a confrontation had been contrived.

"We've descended to their level," the panelist declared. Despite her cynicism, her inclination was to agree. They are going mad, she thought.

"The Mafia have not only kidnapped the President. They've brainwashed him," another said. Not really, she decided. They've merely broken down the artificial barriers.

"Damned bleeding heart," the President said with contempt. It was not a term he used very often and it puzzled her.

She turned away from the set. It was too painful to watch. Both her disgust and her doubts were accelerating. She wished it would all go away. Harkins continued to beat on his keyboard. The Padre stood near him, watching.

It was obvious that all was not well. What she had determined was that they did not yet know the whereabouts of Ahmed's son. The most essential ingredient of the operation was to have the boy in their possession.

"Any definitive terms yet?" the President asked.

"Everyone is waiting for someone else to make the first move," Harkins said.

"What happens when they do?" the President asked. "How do we hide behind the denials?"

"Our people will make a deal," Harkins said, looking toward the Padre. "All hostages for all hostages. We don't have to confirm or deny our complicity. Just arrange the exchange. Isn't that the way you see it, Padre?"

The Padre nodded. "As long as my daughter and grandson are part of the package, I do not care about the others."

The Padre began to pace the floor. Amy watched him, then looked at her husband, whose elation of moments before had disappeared.

"We must know about the boy," the Padre muttered.

At this point a commentator interrupted the ongoing panel discussion on television.

"This just in," the commentator said with appropriate solemnity.

"Ahmed Safari, the man who is holding the daughter and grand-son of Salvatore Padronelli hostage, has just communicated with a Beirut radio station. He has issued the following ultimatum. If his son is not released by noon tomorrow without conditions, then Maria Michaels will be killed."

The Padre had turned ashen.

"I am sure it's only a bluff," Harkins said. "These people—"

"Where is the boy?" the Padre asked. His expression had darkened despite Harkins' assurances.

"Our people have lost contact."

"Your people are not competent . . ." the Padre began, his calm shattered. "Without the boy, we have nothing."

"He won't do it," Harkins said, but without much conviction. He turned back to the keyboard and pounded out a message. "I have ordered our asset in his group. . . . What?" He was not satisfied with his answer on the monitor. Again he typed out a message. "Gone," he said, swallowing the word. "He's changed his people."

"What does that mean?"

"He's no longer got one of his assets on the inside," the President explained.

"You mean we're out of touch?" the Padre asked.

"For the moment."

"We know of his attachment to his boy," Harkins added. Beads of sweat had sprouted on his upper lip. "He won't risk it."

"But we haven't got the boy," the President said.

"Ahmed thinks we do," Harkins said.

"He will expect us to respond," the Padre said.

"Our people can get word to him. Say we have him," Harkins said nervously. "Anyway, it's only a threat. No point in hurting your daughter. He won't. I'm sure of it."

"He is testing us," the Padre said.

"How?" the President asked.

"By our willingness to kill," the Padre said.

Amy felt an iciness crawl down her spine.

"He does not believe that we will respond in kind. If we don't, he will kill my daughter. He will then bargain for my grandson."

"Now really," the President began.

The Padre raised his hand for silence. "We must send the only message he will understand."

"I don't like the sound of that," the President said.

"We could play it in kind, give him the same deadline," Harkins said. "Contact a Beirut radio station. Get the word out to him and the others whose people we have. Tell them, release your daughter and grandson without conditions or . . ."

"Or what?" the President asked.

"Mr. President," the Padre said slowly. "The problem is that you are not taken seriously."

"Because I refuse to sanction cold-blooded killing."

"The decision is not in your hands, Mr. President," the Padre said.

"The hell it isn't," the President said, looking at Harkins, who turned his eyes away.

Amy's finger groped for the trigger of the gun.

"And yet you would stand by and let them kill my daughter. Let them kill others at will."

"But I'm not ordering that."

"Not directly," the Padre said.

"I can't."

"There is no choice for you." His meaning was unmistakable.

"Ah, but there is," the President shot back. "I can refuse to govern. I can step down."

"It is too late for that," the Padre said. "I will not permit it."

"Who the hell do you think you are?" the President shot back.

"I can decide who lives and dies in this place."

Silence seemed to crackle in the room. Although frightened, Amy discovered that her fear was not incapacitating. One thing was certain, she told herself. I will not go quietly. But she still could not find the courage to remove the gun from her waistband. The Padre had his back turned to her. How easily she could end his life. One bullet to the head.

"We shall see," the President said calmly.

His hand reached out for the phone. There was only the briefest hesitation, but Amy saw it. She was sure the Padre saw it as well. They all knew it. A feeble ploy at rebellion. The prune-faced man's arm shot forward and quickly removed the phone from the president's hand.

The President seemed to crumble. His shoulders gave way. He leaned back in his chair. She had seen him like that before, finding his second wind. Yet despite her instinct for blind loyalty, a trait she had demonstrated time and time again, she tried to distance herself from that role, to maintain some degree of objectivity.

"Perhaps we can say it and not do it," the President said quietly, indicating what she had suspected. His mind still searched for alternatives. No, she decided, he is not going to roll over easily.

"Facts not words," the Padre said. "We must show him."

"One of his," Harkins said to the President, cocking his head toward the Padre. "After all, you are under duress. The country knows this is so. I can get word to his people." He looked at the

Padre, who shrugged, an obvious sign of his willingness. The issue of who was to die as a sacrifice for credibility was immaterial to him.

Amy continued to stroke the trigger of the gun. Surely her husband was simply playing out a strategy that he had worked out in his mind.

The Padre said, "We will make sure the body is found."

"Then we deny any complicity," Harkins said, looking toward the Padre for approval. The Padre responded with a nod. "He'll get the message. He'll know we mean business and that we are capable of retaliating against his son."

"All this talk of killing," the President said, shaking his head.

"It is not talk, Mr. President," the Padre said. "We must deal with it."

"He's right, Mr. President," Harkins said.

Harkins watched him, obviously waiting for consent. Slippery bastard, Amy thought. Once again he was absolving himself of responsibility. She felt a surge of emotion. Her practiced effort at control fell apart.

"Resist them, Paul," she cried. They all turned to face her as if noticing her for the first time. "You don't have to."

"He has no choice, Mrs. Bernard," Harkins said.

Images of her own children, Tad and Barbara, burst into her mind. She felt the remembered pain of birthing, the exquisite joys of motherhood and nurturing. My children, she screamed inside herself. And theirs. Was there any crime more monstrous than to hurt innocent children?

"Weakness now is a death warrant for my daughter," the Padre said.

"Paul, I beg of you," Amy began. But she did not stand up, maintaining enough presence of mind to keep the gun in her waistband, hidden beneath the table. She reached for it again, her finger settling around the trigger. A plan had jumped into her mind. She would put a bullet in Harkins' head. Only Harkins knew the various codes to operate that vast mysterious empire of evil.

At that moment the computer came alive. It deflected their attention. Harkins watched the monitor, then began to respond on the keyboard.

"What is it?" the President asked, a man grasping for straws.

"They're reporting in," Harkins said. With a finger he flicked away the perspiration on his lower lip.

"We have him." He looked at the Padre, who nodded approval.

"A hospital in Rome," Harkins said.

Harkins turned from the monitor and looked at the Padre. Something, Amy noted, had passed between them. Then he directed his concentration back to the computer monitor. He worked the keyboard, studied the monitor again. His eyes blinked and his lips betrayed a nervous tremor. He turned away and his gaze roamed the faces in the room. Amy's fingers remained clutched around the trigger of the gun, although it was still in the waistband of her slacks.

"Intensive care," he whispered. "Critical."

# ☆ 32 ☆

NED FOREMAN, THE NATIONAL SECURITY ADVISOR, STOOD BEHIND A large oak and watched the footpath in the patch of park behind his apartment house. Vashevsky, wily as ever, rarely approached from the same direction. His journey was always the difficult one, since he had to get out of the Soviet Embassy compound unobserved by American surveillance, then find his way to the strip of parkland bounded by Massachusetts and New Mexico avenues. The senior KGB operative in the United States, he was, of course, resourceful and clever.

They had set up the rules years before, as if it were a kind of floating crap game. Meeting places were arranged by sequence. There were six preagreed sites, all outdoors, an imagined neutral turf, theoretically safe from unwanted listening devices. To police these devices, Foreman carried an electronic sensor. Its mechanism had never been triggered. Perhaps Vashevsky carried one as well. Foreman's instinct was to trust the man.

It wasn't easy for Foreman to leave what was now referred to sarcastically as the command bunker. Chalmers was frustrated. Most of those around him were exhausted. The country appeared trapped in the entrails of its own system.

He had insisted that he must go back to his own apartment. An hour, no more, he had promised. Milly had called, reporting that Vashevsky's signal had come. Two rings on his private number followed by an interval of one minute, then two rings. Repeated twice. Milly actually had no knowledge about the signal's origin. Foreman was, after all, the President's National Security Advisor. Such mysterious goings-on required no explanation.

He had expected Vashevsky to step forward in response to the crisis. Indeed, it had surprised him that he had not done so sooner.

Peter Vashevsky, a general in rank, had direct and mostly secret access to the Premier of the Soviet Union, who was also the General Secretary of the Communist Party.

A burly man with a jolly manner and a brilliant mind, Vashevsky was highly educated and, most important, well-informed, especially on matters of infighting and intrigue among the bureaucrats who ran the Soviet Union. Foreman offered similar credentials. Both men enjoyed their roles, especially the subterfuge, which seemed to satisfy some childish urge for secrecy.

Alert to the sounds around him, he heard Vashevsky's footfalls as they moved cautiously along the little-used path.

"Pete," he whispered. "Here."

Vashevsky halted behind the tree. From there they had a clear view of both ends of the path.

"Ned," Vashevsky said, offering his hand. Foreman took it and shook it warmly.

"Goes from bad to worse," Foreman said, kicking his toe into the dirt for emphasis.

"They are confused at home," Vashevsky said. "How is it possible for the man to stay in office? He is a captive." The setting sun made his pale blue eyes shine. He shook his head. "There was Watergate and the President resigned. Hardly a terrible crime. Now this. Your system needs an overhaul." A deep chuckle rumbled in his throat.

"Polls show that the people overwhelmingly support him."

Vashevsky shook his head. "The General Secretary is not happy. All this instability is dangerous."

"You've put your people on alert," Foreman said, careful not to adopt an accusatory tone.

"There was no choice. It was not at all like the surgical bombing ploy of Reagan. Instability feeds the paranoia of our military. When in doubt, put the troops out."

"The President has refused to do this," Foreman said.

"Wise move on his part. Keeps our paranoids from acting hastily. But, Ned, there are problems. When you destabilize you set an uncontrollable course, especially among those fools in the Middle East."

"Can't you rein in your friends?" Foreman asked. "At least until we get things sorted out."

"Believe me, we are trying." Vashevsky sighed. "We are having our hands full just keeping some of them from massacring every American they can get their hands on. I think we can lean on the

Syrians and the Libyans. The Iranians are irascible. The Saudis are your problem." He lowered his voice. "The King must be really pissed off."

"He is. I've spoken to him."

"Your President can't keep denying his complicity, Ned. Our people know what is happening. It is ridiculous."

"I know."

"This Harkins." Vashevsky pointed to his temple and made a twirling motion. "He loves these macho games. Besides, we know where at least three of the people have been put."

Foreman's ears perked up. "Only three. You're slipping, Pete."

"We have to assume you know where the other two are. The Saudi boy and the Syrian girl."

"Wish we did," Foreman said sadly. "The FBI is on the case. But we're dealing with a clever bunch of bastards."

"The Mafiosa."

"It's as if we were all in on this great big secret. We are all winking at each other."

"Look, Ned, if it doesn't get out of hand, I know we can get the Syrian President to play ball. But if the girl is harmed, I assure you he will go crazy."

"You think our Mafiosa friend will sit still if they harm his daughter or his grandson?"

"It has troubled us, Ned," Vashevsky said. His knowledge of the American idiom was superb and his accent detectable only by the strange rhythm of his speech, not the pronunciation of his words. He hesitated for a moment, rare for him. Ned could see he was having trouble putting his thoughts in context. "There are those who believe that the President and Harkins staged these events to allow this action to proceed."

"And you, Pete? What do you believe?" Foreman asked.

"Ninety percent no."

"And the other ten percent?"

"This Harkins is a snake."

"Our snake." He looked pointedly at Vashevsky. "A requirement for the job."

"Nevertheless," Vashevsky said, scratching his chin. "He is capable of orchestrating the event."

"I'm sure of that. But I'm afraid it's out of character for the President," Foreman said. "No way. You're letting your penchant for concocting disinformation scenarios run away with you, Pete."

"All right, Ned," Vashevsky said. "Whatever the genesis of the act, the fact is inescapable. The President is colluding."

"There is a knife at his throat," Foreman said. "He's in a double bind. If he resigns, he's a dead man. If the man's daughter and grandson are not released unharmed, he's a dead man."

"It does limit his options," Vashevsky said. "It would certainly limit mine."

"I know the man. He can be manipulated only if he allows himself to be," Foreman said, bowing to loyalty. He owed the President a great deal. He also liked the man and respected his political instincts, the one indispensable ingredient for high office.

"You will never know what a man will do when his life is in danger."

"And the life of his wife," Foreman added.

"That," Vashevsky said, "is debatable."

Foreman blanched. The Soviets had a talent for heavy humor. Then he remembered that Vashevsky had at least two former wives.

Vashevsky smiled and shook his head. Despite his intriguing mind, he had a limited sense of subtlety. He took a package of chewing gum from his pocket and offered a stick to Foreman, who refused. Then he unwrapped a stick and popped it into his mouth, chewing contentedly.

"We must assume that he is acting according to the wishes of his captors." Vashevsky chomped on his gum. "It is possible, therefore, that he is a party to the idea, that he aids and abets and approves what is going on, whether out of fear or his own desires. It is not only a matter of life and death, Ned." He stretched out a pause with vigorous chewing. "Death is death. But life is the presidency. If he gets out of this alive, he would want to be whole. To continue in office."

Foreman studied the man. He had a benign look about him, kind and grandfatherly, hardly the demeanor for a tough KGB operative who had won his rank and privilege the hard way. Despite his more academic background, Foreman felt equal enough to match wits with Vashevsky. Neither felt threatened by the other. Each had learned to accept nothing at face value, to look behind the political masks and words, to distrust the apparent. And each enjoyed unraveling the puzzle of political motivation. Vashevsky, Foreman knew, was enjoying this episode immensely.

"You have a very hard view of human nature, Pete," Foreman said.

"Believe me, my friend, I long for innocence. But you must remember, your President is a man under our microscope. We must know him better than you, perhaps as well as you know our General Secretary. Your President, like all of them, is a man who does not wish to relinquish control. He must have calculated that it is safer for him and his wife if he continues to hold the reins of power. He is in a better position to know what this Padre will do if he opts out of governing. Our Mafia man wants his daughter and grandson back alive. He will do anything to save them. He is also not afraid to die which makes him, in a way, a fanatic and quite capable of killing the President and his wife if his daughter and grandson are harmed."

"Is that a revelation, Pete?"

"An introduction only. Frankly, I believe the President is playing the game on two tracks."

"Only two?"

"And it is dangerous on both counts. For himself and the country," Vashevsky said. "Yours and mine." He chewed heavily for a few moments. "Ned, the General Secretary would like to see this episode ended immediately. Indeed, the General Secretary has always been confused by your reaction to hostage-taking. Your President should have taken a page out of our book."

"Maybe he should enlist your services," Ned said, but only half-facetiously.

"The General Secretary offers it," Vashevsky said with unmistakable seriousness. "Ned, we can't allow this event to continue. One thing will lead to another. It will get out of hand."

"Why can't your own trusted people in Lebanon just go in and snatch them away from him? Your surrogate runs the show there."

"Our surrogates are idiots," Vashevsky said, "and this Safari is a clever son-of-a-bitch. Believe me, we are looking for him. If only he made a telephone call. We would trace him instantly."

Vashevsky spat out the chewed ball of gum. "However it is done, your President must be removed from office." He paused, then added: "One way or another."

Foreman turned his eyes from Vashevsky's. A sudden chill made him tremble.

"It is terrible, I agree," Vashevsky said. "There were tears in the General Secretary's voice. But I ask you, my friend, look at what we risk. Uncertainty is our mutual enemy. Better our stalemate than one or another of our surrogates acting alone. Our respective military people will get trigger-happy. This is the risk. I tell you there is no way to control these crazy people, Ned."

"You ought to know. Most of them are yours," Foreman replied. They had often traded barbs in the guise of banter. But neither of them ever became angry. They were too professional for that.

"We all agree. At least it has been illustrated that the tactic of terrorism and hostage-taking is too dangerous, too counterproductive," Vashevsky said with an air of contrition. "We have accepted it for too long among our friends."

Frankness was the treasure of their relationship. Often they were the first to admit when a favored tactic went awry. Both knew that the objective of the game was to control the balance between them, to keep the tension perfectly calibrated. At this moment it was out of control, the calibration terribly faulty.

Foreman was good at Machiavellian theory but bad at practicing it. Besides, as a man, he considered the President his friend and mentor. Although the idea that Vashevsky was imparting remained scrupulously unarticulated, it flew in the face of his value system. Did the President's life depend on the vehemence of his objection? Did ambition presume this kind of responsibility? He was merely an advisor, for chrissakes.

"I'm not comfortable with this idea," Foreman said.

"Nor are we."

"You've had more experience along these lines."

"I am sorry. I am only the messenger."

Foreman turned and walked up the path for a short distance. So they were scouring West Beirut looking for Safari. For them it would be easier to kill him, the woman, and the boy. It was certainly the road to stability. They've already made up their mind. Foreman was sure of that. Kill off the President by remote control. No one would know. He came back to where Vashevsky still stood.

"Just don't tell me it's because you want to save the world."

"I won't say it then, my friend."

"We've gone over that option as well and come up with the same conclusion. We'll never get them out alive. Besides, we can't stop you."

"Not really," Vashevsky said.

"Dead or alive, it won't matter to you," Foreman sighed.

"It does matter," Vashevsky said. "We would prefer to get them alive. Surely, as in your own scenario, it is most unlikely. Unless . . ."

Foreman felt that Vashevsky was sincerely disturbed by the news he was imparting. "We did consider another aspect," Vashevsky continued. "If our people were lucky enough to rescue the woman and her child, then we would have saved the life of your President."

Foreman felt a sudden burst of elation and optimism. Indeed, for the Soviets it would be the public relations coup of the century.

Vashevsky put out his hand.

"Some day as old men we will enjoy our nostalgia over a few vodkas," Vashevsky said.

"If we ever get to be old men," Foreman said. Considering this new-found knowledge, it seemed to be an unlikely possibility.

"You and I. No question about it."

Foreman took Vashevsky's hand.

"This Chalmers . . ." he began.

But Foreman had already turned and started back up the path.

## ✴ 33 ✴

IN THE DINING ROOM, THE PADRE SAT IN HIS CREASED AND NOW spotted waiter's uniform, his back to the draperies. His features were immobile. His beard had become sprouts of gray patches. Sacks of mottled chicken skin hung below his eyes. He had not slept. The television set was on, but playing only silent images. The antique clock on the buffet registered the time. Ahmed Safari's deadline was now only three hours away.

"My wife?" the President asked.

"She is comfortable," the Padre said. "Carmine has given me reports. She is resting in her dressing room."

The President nodded, annoyed at his sudden feeling of gratitude. Harkins was still seated in front of his computer terminal. He was animated now, still plugged into his covert jungle. When the President had come into the room, he and the Padre had exchanged their usual conspiratorial glances. Private transactions that did not include him seemed to pass between them.

The telephone console on the table had a shut-off switch for all incoming calls, with the exception of the so-called hot line. Throughout the crisis it had remained remarkably silent. The Soviets, he knew through his brief discussions with Foreman, were exceedingly edgy, but apparently not anxious enough to communicate with him directly. A wise course for them, he knew. They would not wish to be overtly involved.

He flicked the switch and the incoming buttons lit up immediately. He looked at the buttons with disinterest. He had no stomach to talk to anyone. Another fraudulent feather to put in his hat. He no longer governed. The country was spinning on its own.

He studied the faces of Harkins and the Padre. Lie down with dogs, he sighed, too filled with self-disgust to finish the homily. Inserting his hand in his pocket, he felt the thin blade, oddly cold to the touch. He drew his hand out of his pocket.

"Anything I should know?" he asked.

"Can't find Safari's hideout," Harkins said with obvious reluctance. "Clever bastard. He knows how to use the rabbit warrens of West Beirut. Our people are searching for him." He paused. "So is everybody else."

"And our hostages?" the President asked.

Harkins looked toward the Padre for assistance.

"We have them," the Padre said hoarsely. It was obvious to him that they were holding something back.

"The Saudis." Harkins coughed, clearing his throat. It was a blatant attempt to sidetrack the conversation. The President said nothing, knowing the value of measured silences. He must gather his concentration.

"They've threatened to pull out all their dollars from the States, our people in Riyadh have confirmed." Harkins looked toward the flashing lights of the telephone console. "I expect one of those calls to be the bearer of the news."

"Can't blame them," the President said pointedly to the Padre, who remained impassive. "There's a lot more to this than your own interests, Padre."

"Not for me," the Padre said.

"That's because you're not responsible for the general welfare and protection of anyone outside your group. The Saudi King has his own people to worry about, and I've got to think about two hundred and thirty million Americans," the President said.

"The Syrians are massing in front of the Golan Heights," Harkins interjected without looking up from his screen.

"Hear that Padre?" the President said. "What about the Iranians?"

"All they can mount are hit teams. No big military or economic threat. They're all tied up with Iraq."

"And the Libyans?"

"They've got planes, guns, and bombs. Not overly efficient, but from their perspective they might see this action as the straw that broke their camel's back."

The President looked at the Padre. "You know," he said, clearing his throat, "you reach a point when your own life means shit to you."

"I know."

At that moment Amy came into the room, followed by Benjy. He looked at her and shook his head.

"So you see," the old man said, "everything one does is in relationship to one's fear of death." The Padre got up from his chair. He was surprisingly agile for a man who had hardly moved a muscle for some time. He began pacing the room, then he stopped and looked at Harkins. "Tell him."

Harkins seemed to tremble. His eyes blinked nervously.

"He's got Safari's son," he said to the President.

"You let him?"

"I suppose I did," Harkins said. For the first time since he had met the man Harkins looked shaken.

"How?"

"Friends in Italy."

"That's why you had him delivered there," the President said.

"I didn't know the boy was that sick," Harkins protested. "My people were very careful. When they saw he was having an attack they took him to a hospital in Rome. That's why it took so long for them to report in. They had a safe house prepared, but they wouldn't chance it. I"—he looked helplessly at the Padre—"I sent word to his people where he was."

"Why?"

"He asked me to."

"Gave you an order you couldn't refuse?"

"Sometimes you have to cast your bread upon the waters."

"You gave no orders, Mr. President. Nor did I," Harkins said. So the pattern was revealed. Once again, he had reacted to future accountability. The President let it pass.

"These postmortems are not important, Mr. President," the Padre said. "It is out of your hands. This man Safari must know that we have his son. He must know that we will kill the boy if he harms my daughter or my grandson."

"Only the boy?" the President asked.

The Padre lowered his eyes but said nothing. He did not have to.

"It is a devil's bargain," the President said.

"A father's bargain," the Padre whispered.

The President looked at the console's flashing buttons, then at the television set showing images without sound. He glanced at Amy who stared uncomprehendingly. As if in self-defense, he picked up the phone and punched in a button.

"A moment please, Mr. President," an operator's voice said. He listened briefly to the statical sounds of an empty line.

"Go ahead please, Mr. Halloran."

Halloran! The President was confused. He had expected Chalmers. Not the head of the FBI.

"Mr. President."

"Yes, Halloran."

The Padre had moved back to the table and sat down. The

telephone conversation echoed over the speaker phone.

"Are you all right?" Halloran asked, his voice strained and hoarse.

"Yes," the President answered.

"We have a problem." His voice fell to a whisper. "I know we're being taped and the speaker-phone is on. But this one is the hottest potato of all, and frankly I need some direction on this. No one knows yet. Of course, after this conversation, they'll all know." The man sighed. "I'm not suggesting a cover-up."

"What the hell are you talking about, Halloran?"

"We think we found the Saudi boy," he blurted.

The President felt a freezing sensation in his stomach. The implication of Halloran's tone was quite clear. He looked swiftly at the Padre, who was impassive.

"Where?" the President asked.

"In the front seat of a car in the middle of Union Square in San Francisco. Body is badly riddled with bullets, barely recognizable. We have his wallet, all his credit cards, and wads of dough from the pockets. Nothing was touched. The message seems clear as hell. Just in case, we've sent for dental records and rushed the body to autopsy." Halloran had talked fast. Now he hesitated, then spoke again, more slowly. "Point is, Mr. President, I could try to stonewall it."

The President held down a wave of nausea.

"Stonewall it," the President said vaguely, as if his mind had not fully absorbed the information. Again he looked at the Padre. So this was what they had kept hidden. This was the message. Ruthless, devious, cold-blooded bastards. He sucked in deep breaths. Hold on, he urged himself.

"I could try, Mr. President," Halloran said tentatively. "After all, the ID is not totally confirmed. And the MO, well it's not ritual gangland. Usually one bullet in the back of the head. Might use that as a hook. Flimsy, though. The facts are too obvious. And the damned news people are crawling all over us. These local cops leak like hell. Mostly, I'm worried about all the Americans at risk in Saudi Arabia. I thought, even if this is not in my jurisdiction, I did not want to make the situation worse."

The President did not respond. He looked at the Padre, then at Harkins. Both showed no expression.

"No cover-ups, Halloran," the President said, clearing his throat.

"I just thought—"

"The buck stops here," the President said.

# ✷ 34 ✷

"YOU DON'T EAT, YOU GET WEAK," MRS. SANTORELLI SCOLDED. YET another bowl of pasta had gotten cold on the table in front of him.

"I'm sorry," Robert said, his attention riveted to the television set.

"You watch too much TV. Like my Giovanni."

It was incredible how little these momentous events interested her. He was sure she would simply dismiss what was happening as "man's work." The fact was that this "man's work" was going on directly under her nose. Over her telephone lines orders were given that had a direct impact on the lives of millions of people. It was all so banal. A little man sitting at an ancient table, using an old-fashioned black dial telephone to set in motion brutal and illegal activities.

The man who had arrived with a letter earlier that day had come again late in the evening and given the Pencil another letter. This time Robert did not press his interest. There was no point in getting information that would upset him. He would know soon enough.

The television news was nonstop, the speculation endless and repetitive. But the announcement of the death of the Saudi brought him out of his chair.

"You've murdered him," Robert shouted at the Pencil, who was on the phone at the time. The Pencil waved him quiet. He pictured Maria and Joey meeting the same fate, riddled with bullet holes, dumped by the roadside like garbage.

"You must calm down, Robert," the Pencil said gently.

Not a word came out of the White House, except that the President continued to deny to his top officials that he had anything to do with these events. More lies. He was on the point of shutting off the set when another bulletin stopped him.

He turned up the volume. The commentator, with great excitement, announced that the Syrian, Libyan, and Iranian leaders had jointly and unilaterally forced the release of all hostages being held with groups with whom they could hold a dialogue. The language was stilted but the meaning unmistakable. They had buckled. His heart pounded with joy.

"He's done it," he shouted.

The Pencil, too, showed rare emotion. He rose and came into the kitchen to watch the television. But the events still did not lure

Mrs. Santorelli, who remained at her stove stirring a pot with a wooden spoon.

The coverage centered now on scenes of hostages being bused to airports, giving thanks for their release. There was even coverage of men identified as terrorists shooting their guns in the air. It was bizarre. As a gesture of acknowledgment, world leaders were now calling for a release of the new hostages by "whoever was responsible."

Robert let the images flow over his consciousness. His elation had quickly subsided. He waited for word of Maria and Joey. The commentators speculated, but no word was forthcoming. Time passed and still no word came. The waiting was torture. The Pencil went back to his telephone.

"Maybe it wasn't enough," Robert said to the Pencil.

The Pencil understood, looked at Robert, and nodded.

"We still have the Syrian girl," Robert said. He was surprised, for he felt no shame.


# ★ 35 ★


ABOVE ALL, MARIA TRIED TO PRESERVE HER SENSE OF TIME. SHE forced herself to note outside noises, lengthening shadows, cooking smells, even the biological clock of her own body. She was in a dank basement, locked in a small room with walls of cinder block and a metal door. It was, she knew, an unfinished building, one of the many in West Beirut, its construction long ago abandoned.

She pressed her body against Joey. He slept, but it was a troubled dream-filled sleep. Occasionally he cried out, "Mama," and she kissed him on the head. "It's all right, sweets. Mama is here."

They had moved three times since yesterday. Or was it yesterday? Except for the blond boy, the others had vanished. It was her own euphemism. She had no doubts that Ahmed had killed them. It was only a matter of time before the blond boy met the same fate. Then her. They had dispensed with chains.

For food, they had given her stale bread loaves, chocolate bars, and a canteen of water. At first, in this new place, she had assumed that they had left her alone and she had pounded on the metal door. It had been opened by the blond boy, who had put the muzzle of his gun to Joey's head.

The knowledge that Ahmed's boy had been taken from his home

in Jordan had been a surprise. It was impossible to believe that this man, a killer, had fathered a son. That possibility granted, it was still impossible to believe that he could be so emotionally moved.

After he had absorbed the shock, he had gone on a rampage, breaking the television set, pounding the walls with his fist, shouting, and cursing. Oddly, he had refrained from any violent action against her or Joey. This omission was a source of hope.

Weeks before, in the comfort of her home, her son playing on the rug before the television set, her husband sitting in his favorite chair reading a book, she might have characterized these acts as despicable. Violence begets violence, she might have said, turning off the set.

Suddenly the metal door opened. Ahmed's figure was silhouetted against the light from a flickering bulb jerry-rigged on a strand of wire. Beside him she could make out the outlines of the blond boy. They walked into the room. She sat up quickly, releasing the boy, who continued to sleep.

"Again?" she asked.

"Yes," he said.

She could not make out his features, but his tone was flat, tired. She rose from the bare mattress and straightened her clothes. They had given her a pair of men's jeans, a denim shirt, and a wool sweater. He handed her a package of material held together by string.

"Put this on," he said.

She looked at it.

"Disguise?"

"Galabia."

He stood over her as she rose. The blond boy next to him moved. She could hear the click of metal, perhaps the sound of his gun clashing against the cartridge case around his shoulder. For the first time since her captivity, she felt, somehow, less intimidated. They needed her to be obedient, to play her role.

Up to then they had manipulated her by threatening her child. Above all, she decided, they needed him. Machismo, she decided. The male disease. Her father, too, would be its victim. She felt more trapped, more entangled in that idea than in this web of physical captivity.

"Who are we running from?" she asked.

She saw him look toward the boy.

"All sides," he said.

"Why don't you just exchange us for your boy?"

"I don't trust them," he said. His attitude alarmed her.

"Who is them?" she asked cautiously.

"Your father."

"But look at the lengths to which he has gone. He wants us back. What could be more obvious." She knew what he meant. Certain assumptions had already been accepted by both of them. Whatever was happening, both knew that it was her father's work.

"The Saudi boy is dead," Ahmed said suddenly.

"I'm very sorry about that."

"They are releasing all the others taken hostage by our people."

"So there it is. It's all over. Just release us and they'll release your boy."

"You don't understand," Ahmed sighed. He tapped his forehead. "The mentality."

"Considering my blood lines, I wouldn't be so sure."

"A man like your father will want to leave his mark. He will extract vengeance. It is his nature."

"Yours, too," she said.

"Everything must be paid for."

"What are you saying?"

"These Syrians and Libyans. They are demanding all hostages be released. But they are secretly promising that things will start again as soon as their people are sent home. Nothing will change with the others as well. They have offered me all kinds of money, all kinds of bribes."

"Well then, take them, for crying out loud, and let us go."

"First, I must get my boy." His voice quivered with emotion. "It is the only thing of real value I have."

"Put me in touch with my father. I'm sure it could be arranged. I will make him promise. He will also provide money, as much as you need for a lifetime."

"I won't believe him."

"I'm his daughter. He won't lie to me."

"I will not believe any promises made to women."

She turned away from him with disgust. She began, with slow deliberation, to put on the black galabia while her mind groped back and forth in time, searching for a way out.

"The veil, too," he said, watching her.

"Ridiculous," she said, holding the veil in front of her, trying to make sense of how it was to be worn. By then Joey had awakened and stood up. He was watching them with fear and curiosity. However things turned out, his scars would be deep and lasting.

"We have a little costume for the boy as well," Ahmed said, signaling to his companion, who produced a small package from under his arm. Ahmed took off the wrappings. It was striped pajamas and a Kaffiyen, the Arab headdress. He started to reach out for the boy.

"No," she cried. "Don't touch him."

Ahmed hesitated, glared at her, then stepped back. He tossed the package on the floor. Something in his gesture suggested the thread of an idea. For the moment she put aside the veil and dressed the boy.

"Why do I have to wear this, Mommy?" Joey asked.

"It's a new kind of game," she said. "A masquerade."

"I don't want to play." Joey pouted.

"Neither do I, sweets," Maria said. She stopped dressing him and gripped him by his thin, bony shoulders. "You've been the bravest most wonderful boy a mother could ask for." Her eyes misted and she made no effort to hide them from her son. A tear rolled over her eyelid. His little hand reached out and touched it.

"You mustn't cry, Mommy," Joey said. "Remember what you said."

"Not to cry," Maria said with effort. Her lip trembled. She nodded and tried to smile. "Damned right," she said, brushing away her tears. "We won't show them."

"No we won't, Mommy," the boy said emphatically, with a tone that belied his years. The experience had aged him. She gathered him in her arms and crushed him against her breast.

"I love you, my dear little boy."

"And I love you, Mommy."

"We must leave immediately," Ahmed said.

"It's gotten out of hand, hasn't it?" she asked, looking up at him. He did not answer.

She finished dressing him. "There," she said. "You look like a little Arab boy." Then she turned to her captor.

"Suppose I don't cooperate?" she asked cautiously. It was, she realized, a carefully measured speculation of defiance. He must know that she was testing the waters.

"Believe me . . ." he began, but he did not finish the sentence, leaving her to interpret. He glanced toward his blond boy, then back at her. "Death means nothing to me," he said. "I have lived with it all my life."

In the next moment time lost all meaning. A minisecond or a lifetime. It played out simultaneously before her eyes and in her mind in very slow motion. She saw the muzzle of the gun move, like the baton of an orchestra leader, pointing suddenly downward, then, like an unexpected drumroll, it tapped out a fiery message. Color and sound overwhelmed the semidarkness, a surreal sight as the blond boy's head disappeared in the sparkling shower of light.

# ✯ 36 ✯

SITTING AROUND THE DINING-ROOM TABLE, THEY CONTINUED TO watch the television monitor. The commentators were focusing now on the whereabouts of the Padre's daughter and grandson. They had finally gotten the message that what was happening, the release of the hostages and all the resultant hullabaloo, was peripheral to the real story. The President remained a hostage in his own White House and the Padre's daughter and grandson were not yet free.

The euphoria as reflected in the world of television was dying down. The talk turned more to deadlines and danger. And the atmosphere in the dining room grew increasingly downbeat.

The lights on the telephone console lit up. The President paid little attention. No point in doing anything until the woman and child were released. The Padre had stopped pacing and seated himself at the table. His three-day growth of beard made him look even older. Yet he seemed very much alert, waiting, watchful.

"How do you interpret this?" the President asked Harkins.

"He could be trying to strike a deal," Harkins answered. It seemed as good a stall as any.

"What kind of a deal?" the President asked.

"Perhaps the message wasn't loud enough," the Padre said, his face immobile.

"It got the point across to the Libyans, the Syrians, and the Iranians," Harkins said.

The capitulation of Syria, Libya, and Iran was, of course, a major geopolitical event. Whether these countries would permanently eschew terrorism in the future was debatable. At least the perpetrators would now understand that the tactic was a double-edged sword.

"There are limits," the President said, his voice barely a whisper. Harkins knew the mood. The President shook his head and rubbed his chin. Then he turned to Harkins.

"I want you to order your people to release the Libyan and the Iranian. Immediately. Do you understand that?"

Harkins nodded. He fought the desire to look toward the Padre for approval. The Padre said nothing and made no move to stop the order.

"And," the President said, addressing the Padre, "I would suggest you do the same to the people you hold. Perhaps the example will be enough for the man to act."

"I will order the boy released only after my daughter and grandson are safe," the Padre replied.

"You are an intelligent man," the President said. "Surely you have some sense of humanity. The fact is . . ." The President paused. Harkins knew he was digging deep inside himself, gathering all the residue of persuasive energy. "We've gone along." He looked at his wife. Acting or not, his expression conveyed a sense of futility, perhaps shame. He seemed to Harkins like a man throwing in his poker hand, faceup.

"You've had the benefit of . . ." His gaze met Harkins', then he pointed to the computer. "What more could possibly be done. You've even helped to accomplish something in the, forgive the political idiom, public good."

The Padre watched him impassively.

"What in the name of God will move you?"

He had scrupulously avoided the mention of pardon. Was it time now? He turned to Harkins. "Where are we heading?"

"He will release them," Harkins persisted.

"All right then," the President said to the Padre. "At the very least, there is no point in holding the Syrian girl."

"I will decide," the Padre said.

"Neither of us are God, Padre. You would be surprised how effective a gesture of goodwill can be."

"There is no goodwill for men like that. Only advantage."

Harkins watched the exchange for a moment, then turned toward the keyboard.

"Are you sure about this order, Mr. President?" he asked, knowing it was a message meant for the Padre. The Padre watched them without comment.

"Absolutely," the President said.

Harkins hesitated, his fingers poised on the keyboard. He wished he had more leeway to think it out.

"I can remove you instantly, Harkins," the President pressed. It seemed unrealistic. Without him, they would have no access to the computers.

Harkins had hardly finished tapping out the message when one of the networks announced yet another bulletin with the familiar words "This just in."

All eyes turned to the television set.

"Police in Amherst have found what appears to be the body of the twenty-one-year-old daughter of the Syrian President. The woman was apparently murdered by a burst of fire that has severely mutilated the body. Beside it police have found her pocketbook, which contained her license—"

"You bastards," the First Lady cried.

Her voice was shrill. When she stood up she toppled the chair. Harkins saw the object in her hand, a bit of flashing silver. She was holding a small pistol in firing position. She moved back a few steps, as if wishing to take in a wider range.

Benjy, who had been closest to her, started to move.

"No," the Padre barked. Benjy stopped in his tracks.

"Easy, Amy," the President said.

Although there was a slight tremor in her hand, she held the pistol firmly. Only her eyes betrayed her panic as she fought to keep herself under control. The men in the room froze, watching her.

"The choices are yours now, Mrs. Bernard," the Padre said.

"I'm not afraid," she said with effort.

"There's still time," Harkins said. He had not yet let go of the old assumptions. Perhaps now, with the Syrian's child gone, Safari would get the message. Odd, he thought, how he could not shut down his mind in the face of imminent death. He was, surprisingly, unafraid.

"You know it's wrong, Paul. These people are murderers. How can you deal with them?"

"Amy, please. Whatever happens, you have your own children to think about."

"These people are vermin, Paul."

"There were no clear choices, Amy. Please put that gun down."

"There were for me."

"Dying is not a choice," the President said.

She looked at the Padre. The panic was draining out of her eyes. She had obviously assessed her position. She was, very definitely, in control.

"None of you seem interested in that condition for yourselves," she mocked, looking at the Padre. "But you're quick to dispense it for others."

"I told you," the Padre said coolly. "Everything is in direct relation to the fear of death."

"Then you fear it as much as we do," she said, her voice stronger but still shaky. "I would say there were hot times ahead for you."

"Please, Amy."

The President stood up, took a cautious step forward. It did not deter her from pointing the gun in his direction.

"This is Paul, Amy," he said.

"Then act like Paul."

He stopped. In the long pause that followed, the commentator's voice seemed to fill the room. He was still talking about the young

Syrian girl. Then the scene shifted to the face of a man. He was the Syrian President. Tears were streaming down his cheeks. Although her attention, too, had been deflected to the screen, no one made a move to get to her.

"Was it really necessary?" she asked the Padre.

"The man is knee deep in other people's blood," the Padre responded. "He does not deserve your pity."

"And the girl?"

"Sins of the father." The Padre shrugged. "He does not cry for other people's losses."

"The girl was innocent."

She was becoming agitated again, losing control, waving the gun.

"Amy. One bullet in the wrong place will blow us all up."

"Paul," Amy said, the tremor returned to her voice. "You must resign. We can't have this on our consciences."

"You press that trigger, none of our consciences will exist," he said.

She was standing with her back to the closed draperies. She studied each of the men in the room. As she did so she pointed the gun at each of them in turn, as if making up her mind who should live and who should die.

When the blast came it startled no one. Barely a crackle. Then another. She continued to empty the magazine into the computer monitor until it was completely smashed. Then she calmly tossed the gun to the floor, where it fell with hardly a thud, muffled by the thick oriental carpet.

# ✷ 37 ✷

THEY HAD MOVED ON FOOT IN THE DUSK. MOST PEOPLE HAD AL-ready locked themselves into their shabby tenements in this part of West Beirut. A few could be seen sitting on windowsills silently watching the sparse traffic on the mean streets.

The night was thick with the smell of cooking oil and sesame. A cacophony of shouting children, the squawk of human anger, plaintive Arab music mixed with ear-splitting rock 'n' roll filled the air.

One gloomy street looked the same as any other. Maria held Joey's hand and Ahmed clutched her firmly under the arm. When people approached, Safari dragged them into an alley or into a doorway.

In the open streets she was more afraid than she had been in a closed room. Safari had about him an air of desperation that, she sensed, made him more dangerous, more savage. His grip hurt her arm but she said nothing, struggling to keep the pace. Only when they moved too fast did she resist.

"The boy. He can't keep up." He slowed down.

Earlier her mind had tried to contemplate avenues of escape. She was too tired to imagine them now. She felt like a bit of flotsam on a choppy river, at the mercy of the flow.

At one point he had stopped at the entrance of an apartment house. It was a broken-down tenement, but he was apparently familiar with it. He walked through the entrance. A pay phone hung from a cinder-block wall. He signaled her with the muzzle of his gun to squat on the floor against the opposite wall. She obeyed, welcoming the opportunity to rest, giving permission for Joey to urinate against the wall.

She barely listened as he whispered into the phone in Arabic. Although she did understand a few words, she could not put them in any logical context.

When he had finished he banged the receiver down and said in English, "They will know who they are dealing with now." He glared at her for a long moment, as if he expected some comment from her. She said nothing. It was safer, she decided, to be silent.

"You think all this is a pointless exercise?" he snapped.

Still she would not answer.

"He will negotiate with me directly."

"Who?" she asked timidly, as if it were a line in a play.

"The President of the United States."

She had been wrong to respond. He spoke between clenched teeth, his words hissing. "They will have to take notice. He will give me back my boy without conditions. Only then . . ." He reached out and roughly lifted Maria to her feet. She could smell his sour breath. Her eyes could barely focus. A frightened Joey buried his face in the folds of her galabia.

"I will make him do it," he said angrily. He was hurting her arm, but she would not acknowledge it.

Finally he dragged them outside the tenement and they walked a few more blocks. He ducked into another building, pushing her and the boy ahead of him. He led them through a darkened corridor to a door. Fishing a key out of his pocket, he opened it.

He flicked on the wall switch and the light revealed a reasonably comfortable basement studio apartment. There was a double bed, a television set, a desk on which was a telephone and framed photograph of a dark boy with sad eyes. To one side was a small pullman kitchen containing a sink. Of all the places she had been kept, this one seemed lived in. She suspected it was his own.

He rummaged in a cupboard and found a bottle of scotch. Opening it, he took a deep drag, then looked at his watch. Maria and Joey slowly sunk to the floor, their backs against a far wall. They were exhausted. The end of the line, she thought.

"Your son?" she whispered, tilting her chin toward the picture on the desk.

His response was to take another deep pull on the bottle. She looked up into his face. His eyes glared with intensity, his nostrils quivered.

"Soon," he said. Again he looked at his watch.

Turning, he switched on the television set. Light from the images on the screen flickered in the darkened room. She turned toward it, forcing her concentration.

The images seemed garbled, disconnected. Voices speaking different languages seemed to compete with each other for attention. Did these words and images concern her? she wondered. The voices spoke of death. The Saudi prince and the daughter of the Syrian President had been killed. Then a picture flashed on the screen of the same boy whose photograph rested on the desk. So it is, she thought. The voices droned on, speaking of anger and death.

Then came news of her father. He still held the President hostage in the White House. "Daddy, hurry," she whispered, tightening her hold on the boy.

Suddenly she saw smiling faces. Hostages released. Tears of joy and reunion.

"Filthy cowards," Safari cried. "Death to you all." He pointed the gun in the direction of the screen but did not pull the trigger.

She heard her own name being spoken and saw her picture again. The commentator spoke in Arabic. She could catch only bits and pieces. Then her image was gone, replaced by moving pictures of the President and his wife. They were laughing, holding hands. She heard the commentator mention Ahmed Safari. Then she saw his photograph.

Finally, she pieced it together. Safari was going to make the President negotiate for her life. By doing so, the President would admit his participation, his collusion. Moreover, he would be acknowledging their existence, their struggle. The commentator was highly biased. He reveled in the possibility.

Safari had given the President a deadline. If the President did not consent to this plan, he would kill her. Despite the sudden stab of fear, she thought only of her son. She crushed him to her. He started to whimper and she kissed away his tears.

She tried to force her optimism, but the fear continued. No President had ever agreed to negotiate with any terrorist. Was it possible that her father's bold act could actually change the unalterable policy of the United States?

And yet, if he failed to do so, she and her son would die.

# ⋆ 38 ⋆

THEY SAT AROUND THE TABLE CLUTTERED WITH THE REMAINS OF the computer monitor. The President's wife, her energies spent, brooded with bowed head as she sat. The Padre had no stomach to punish her. Besides, his concentration was elsewhere.

He glanced at the clock on the buffet and, as before, checked it against his own watch. The message of the Saudi and Syrian youngsters had its work. Angelo was crafty and clever. An image of him loomed in his mind. The pale face and sliver of black mustache. His face would be offering a rare smile. Once again he had shown his talent as an impresario.

Of all his men, the little Pencil and he were the most simpatico. He had achieved everything, including the transmission of his own private signals to the Padre. It had been a brilliant idea to change the signature of death. In his mind, the Padre embraced him.

They still had the sick Arab youngster as a bargaining chip. For their cooperation the Sicilian boys would demand their pound of flesh. They were entitled. Angelo would have made whatever deals were necessary. The crucial question now: Would the Arab's feelings of fatherhood prevail? He did not like to be at the mercy of another man's private sense of ritual.

If the Arab hurt Maria in any way, then his own boy would die. Indeed, he contemplated ordering the boy killed whatever the deal, as a message to others. And if his grandson were killed—again he faltered at imagining such a fate for this child—then, as he had promised, the President and his wife would be blown up. Himself included. The others as well. They, too, had given their word.

Suddenly their attention was arrested by the television. They watched as the commentator looked at the bulletin before him. "A

Beirut newspaper has reported it has just received a telephone call from the man still holding Maria and Joseph Michaels." The Padre sucked in a deep breath. Everyone in the room was instantly alert.

The commentator continued, "This man, Ahmed Safari, has indicated that he will adhere to the deadline previously given if his son is not immediately released unharmed. He has, however, agreed to negotiate that deadline, providing this negotiation is carried out directly with the President of the United States. Further, the President must be visible on television during the negotiation."

There it was, the ritual. The Padre took no satisfaction in his own prediction, although he saw it as a hopeful sign. It will seal the bargain, he thought. Harkins, too, let out an unmistakable sigh of relief.

"I told you. All bluff. All we have to do is figure out the mechanics of it. That's merely a technical detail." He looked at his watch.

The Padre distrusted Harkins' self-congratulatory note. He did not traffic in victories, only in necessities. He dared not allow himself to think that his daughter and grandson's freedom was imminent. He looked toward the President and, for some reason, did not find the assurance he needed.

"Shall I get cracking?" Harkins asked. "One phone call will do it. We'll need a minicam sent up and we can easily clear the satellite time. Our net will pick up the call and switch it right into that phone."

"Not yet," the President said.

"All the man wants is this last show," Harkins said. "They don't like to walk away when they have everybody's attention. He'll capitulate. No question about it."

"I have conditions," the President said calmly. The Padre saw his eyes. There was no mistaking his resolve.

"You must untie me and remove the liquid explosives from this room," the President said after a brief pause.

The Padre looked at the clock and nodded at his men. As one, they began to unbutton their clothes as they left the room.

"At least let me send for the minicam and make arrangements," Harkins pleaded.

The President ignored him. He looked directly into the Padre's eyes.

"You as well," the President said.

There was a long silence between them.

"I am sorry, Mr. President. I cannot do that."

"You've come all this way . . ." the President began. "If I don't answer that phone, he will kill your daughter."

"If you don't answer that phone, none of us will live, Mr. President," the Padre said. The President looked toward his wife. For the Padre it was impossible to know what passed between them.

"All right," the President said, turning to Harkins.

Harkins spoke hurriedly into the phone. In a matter of minutes the minicam was at the door of the sitting room. Harkins brought it into the dining room. He plugged it in and focused the lens on the President. The President sat at the head of the table in front of the console.

The men had filed back into the dining room and stood near the doorway. The Padre moved closer to the President, just out of range of the camera. They had shut off the television monitor.

For the first time since they had come into this room, there was complete silence. The Padre continued to watch the President. In a moment the President would be beyond his control. If the President betrayed him, the Padre vowed to himself, he would act.

At precisely the time arranged, a single blinking light went on in the console. The President hesitated, waited. The Padre watched him. Their eyes met. The President nodded. A red light began to blink below the lens of the minicam.

"Is this the President of the United States?" a voice said over the speaker-phone.

"It is," the President said. He lifted his eyes and looked around the room. One hand slipped into his pocket.

The President, his voice calm and firm, began, "Under no circumstances, whatever the consequences, will the President of United States ever negotiate with terrorists."

Then an arm shot out toward the Padre. He saw it coming, tried to deflect it. He was surprised it made no impact, no sound.

His body felt suddenly moist. Instead of moving toward the President, he forced himself to rise, then ran toward the wall, hitting it directly with the full impact of his body.

He fell to the floor, stunned, fighting for breath. Suddenly he heard a vaguely familiar sound, a staccato thudding. Despite the filter of distance, and the muffling effect of the speaker-phone, he recognized it. Machine guns. My Maria, he cried within himself. A sob bubbled up from his chest.

# ★ 39 ★

HE HAD TIED THEM BOTH TO PIPES IN THE PULLMAN KITCHEN. THIS time he had put gags in their mouths. Thankfully, he did not blindfold them. Maria suspected what he had meant by that. He could not resist having them watch his performance. The television set was on. A commentator was making remarks in Arabic. From his tone, she knew he was preparing his audience for something momentous.

Yet there was an air of uncertainty in the commentator's voice, as if he, too, were not completely convinced that the President had agreed to this so-called negotiation.

In her heart, as an American, she hoped he wouldn't. If Ahmed Safari got away with it, others would follow. She rebuked herself for having such thoughts. Above all, she wanted to live, although she felt fully prepared to die. After all, she told herself, one died only once.

But the sense of bravado was quickly drowned by a wave of uncontrollable panic. By straining at her bonds, she was able to touch Joey's shoulder with her hip.

"Don't be afraid, sweets," she whispered. But her fear for him was overwhelming, palpable. My baby, she cried to herself. You mustn't hurt my baby. Please Daddy. Save Joey. "Please," she said aloud.

"Quiet," Ahmed said urgently. Looking toward them, he pointed his gun. "Not a word. You understand."

She nodded, swallowing hard to keep down the backwash of salt tears. She was helpless, beyond despair, at the outer limits of hysteria. She pressed against her son, feeling the bonds cut into her wrists, ignoring the pain.

Safari picked up the phone. He held the instrument delicately, reverently. This was going to be his moment. Slowly, he put the instrument against his ear. As he waited, he turned toward her again and smiled. Look at me, his smile said. I have done it. She tried to close her eyes, but the effort eluded her. She was paralyzed, her body inert.

"Yes, it is I, Ahmed Safari. You say the connection is going through."

He glanced toward her again, smug, contemptuous, his eyes glistening with malevolent pride. She watched as he wet his lips and began to speak into the phone. Her eyes jumped to the television screen. She saw President Bernard. He was sitting at a table, a telephone console in front of him. He had not yet picked up the phone. She wondered, where is my father?

Apparently the connection had been made, but the President was refusing to pick up the telephone. Please, she begged him. She wanted to scream out her encouragement. She whipped her head from side to side in frustration.

"You must," she screamed.

He covered the receiver with the palm of the same hand in which he held the gun.

"I'll kill you now," he said.

"No," she whispered, straining to press against her son. "It's all right," she told Joey.

Safari turned away to watch the television. Still the President held back.

"His choice." Safari glanced toward her. His skin glistened with sweat. Again he pointed the gun directly at her. Its shaking belied his attempt to appear calm.

Then she saw the President reach out to grab at the phone. Her heart leapt with relief.

"Is this the President of the United States?" It was Safari's voice, unfamiliar in tone. She heard its echo on television. Then other words which seemed garbled, confused. She forced herself to concentrate, her eyes darting from the television set to Ahmed. She heard the President's voice.

"Under no circumstances," he began. Her comprehension seemed to dissolve. From somewhere deep inside herself she heard her cry of pain, as she struggled hopelessly against her bonds.

"You . . ." It was Safari's voice filling the room as his eyes sought hers. His stare was cruel as he leveled the muzzle of the gun directly at her forehead. Her own scream was drowned in the sounds of heavy footsteps and smashing wood. Then she saw bursts of flame and heard ear-splitting thumps of sound, like a hundred hammers at work simultaneously.

Is this how death comes? she wondered, on the cusp of sound and fury. Then she saw Safari jump in his chair like a puppet operated by a nervous hand. It took a moment for her to comprehend the situation. Safari slumped in his chair like a piece of bloody discarded meat. But her own fear for herself and her son made it impossible to dwell on Safari's fate. The men had turned their guns on her and Joey. There was no mistaking the intention in their eyes. She fought the urge to close her eyes.

The men were hesitating, looking toward another man who apparently was their leader. He barked at them in words she did not understand. He held up his hand, then concentrated on what was happening on the television. The men stood frozen in their poses, their guns continuing to point at her and Joey.

On the screen, she saw a close-up of her father's face. He looked old, defeated. The camera seemed to mock him, emphasize his frustration.

Suddenly, for a reason she could not immediately understand, her father flung himself against a wall, then slumped to the floor. She had closed her eyes briefly, expecting an explosion, or at the least a burst of gunfire. None came. The camera sought him out. He lay on the floor. His eyes were closed.

The leader, who had observed this event, picked up the telephone which dangled by its cord over the desk.

"I bring you greetings from the Soviet Union," the man said in accented English. He barked another order to his men. Slowly, they lowered their guns.

# ✯ 40 ✯

ROBERT HAD JUMPED FROM HIS CHAIR SCREAMING WITH JOY. HE EMbraced Mrs. Santorelli, hugged her, kissed her on her fat jowls.

"Thank God, thank God," he cried. Tears of joy streamed down his cheeks.

"We celebrate with my special pasta, yes?"

"Anything, Mrs. Santorelli."

Soon he would have them both in his arms. What did anything matter but that?

The Pencil stood to one side, impassively watching the monitor.

"Only a razor would have done it," he said, following the commentator's speculation of what had occurred. Apparently the authorities had crashed into the living quarters. Everyone had been taken away. As Robert's excitement cooled he joined the Pencil to watch the various live interviews.

Rocco, the Talker, came into the apartment and stood beside them.

"It is a propaganda field day for the Russians, of course," Ned Foreman, the President's National Security Advisor, was saying. "But then they deserve it. They saved the President's life. Perhaps we have here a new beginning on the road to world peace. Maybe, by a strange twist of fate, we have even broken the back of terrorism."

"Bullshit," Rocco sneered. "It is the Padre who made it possible." It was the longest sentence Robert had ever heard him utter.

Suddenly a wave of sadness washed over him. What would happen to his father-in-law now and the loyal men who accompanied him? How could he ever thank him? And yet, despite his happiness, something nagged at him. Surely the murders of the Saudi prince and the daughter of the Syrian President could not be excused.

Despite the happy outcome, he could not shake off the conflict in his heart and mind. After all, the freedom of Maria and Joey was paid for with their blood. Nor could he excuse himself. Hadn't he, in the end, stood on the sidelines and cheered them on? He looked at the Pencil.

"And the Arab boy?" Robert asked.

"He will go home to his mother. I have already made the arrangements," the Pencil said impassively.

"I feel very bad about the other two, Angelo," Robert said, compelled to express the thought.

"They will be going back to school."

Robert's heart lurched.

"They're alive?"

"We do not kill children for any government," Rocco said.

"Unfortunately, young people drive too fast," the Pencil said. He did not crack a smile. "It was no trouble finding bodies."

## ☆ 41 ☆

IN THE THIN LIGHT OF DAWN, SHE SAW THE BIRDS, FLYING HELTER skelter in their wallpaper cage. She imagined she heard wings flapping and strange eerie birdsongs.

"I heard your eyes blink," Paul whispered, reaching out to touch her hair.

"I have to change this wallpaper," she said. "This place should be an oasis of serenity. It's too noisy."

She laughed and cuddled close, cradling herself against Paul's shoulder. He felt good to be near and she reveled in the feel and smell of him. With remarkable efficiency, the staff had put things in order, scrubbed the place free of any traces of their ordeal.

The hullabaloo still lingered. The aftermath had been a media feast. He had addressed a joint session of Congress, told the story of his captivity, cited the evils of terrorism in any form. His bravery and courage were lauded. The Soviet Union, too, came in for plaudits. People were saying that their equally heroic gestures brought down the curtain on the cold war.

"So every cloud has a silver lining," she said.

"Or an Achilles' heel," he replied.

"You're mixing my metaphor."

Her effort to be cute won her a kiss on her head. She entwined her fingers in his and squeezed. He was silent for a long time. The light deepened, picking out shapes with greater clarity.

"Suppose they had blown us up? Would it have made any difference?" Paul whispered. Was this the first hint of what she had been waiting for? An explanation? Insight? She had not yet unraveled it for herself.

"It would to us," she said. "We'd both be dead." She wanted to say more, to offer contrition and apologies. She had been willful, impatient, romantically self-righteous. But it had taken him so long to get to the integrity part.

"There are times when the shortest distance between two points is not a straight line," he said. "The son of a bitch took us as far as we were willing to go."

Maybe even further, she decided. An honored homily bit the dust. Ends, on occasion, did justify means.

He turned his body and pressed himself against her.

She whispered, "A First Lady isn't even safe in her own bed anymore."

# ✯ 42 ✯

"HOW MUCH FURTHER, MOMMY?" JOEY ASKED, FOR THE TENTH TIME in the last half hour.

"A few miles more," Robert replied gently.

"About ten more minutes, sweets," Maria said.

She watched the rolling Pennsylvania countryside pass by. The brightness of the winter sun made her squint as its beams bounced off icy patches on the hard, fallow farmlands. The three of them sat up front, Joey between them, touching. These days they were always touching and embracing. She squeezed Joey's shoulder and kissed his cheek, then reached over and ruffled Robert's hair.

Six months ago he might have minded and fussily moved her hand away. Now he seemed to welcome the attention.

"Strange place for a birthday party," Robert said.

"Time marches on, even in the penitentiary," Maria replied. In front of Joey they used penitentiary instead of prison to describe his grandfather's residence.

"In thirty years, he'll be exactly one hundred," Robert said. "The judge had a sense of humor." He had sentenced the Padre and the others to from thirty to life. They had all pleaded guilty and been shipped off to Allenwood, which was only a couple of hours from Princeton where Robert had resumed his teaching.

"Away from his life in the Village, I just don't know how he'll take it," Maria said. It worried her deeply.

"Let's face it, Maria. Where he is will be better for a lot of people."

"I suppose," she mused.

It was a rare remark on his part.

Before sentencing, the Padre and his men had been held in a maximum-security cell on Riker's Island, less than a mile from the island of Manhattan. Visits there were severely restricted, but the authorities had relented for that first day when she and Joey had arrived home by plane. She hadn't seem him since, although she had talked to him on the phone.

They saw the sign, Allenwood Correctional Facility, and turned into a well-kept road. At least it was a minimum-security prison and the signs were clearly visible: manicured lawns, neat buildings, no fences, even a tennis court in the distance. The decision to send him there had surprised her. She had, considering who he was, expected worse. His lawyers had hinted about the influence of a person in a very high position of power. Neither of them had dared to question what that meant.

They parked the car in the parking lot, where they found Benjy waiting for them. He shook hands with Robert, kissed Maria's cheek, and patted Joey's head. She opened the trunk and took out a birthday cake.

"Is he all right?" she asked solemnly.

"You'll see."

"Thirty years is such a long time," she whispered.

They followed Benjy into a clean airy building, through a white-washed corridor, and into a large dining room, currently serving cafeteria style. Men sat around in groups eating lunch. Some lifted their eyes and looked at her briefly.

"I don't see him," she said after a cursory look around the large room.

"He's in there," Benjy said.

They followed him through another doorway to a small, neat room. There were photographs on the wall depicting scenes from New York and Italy.

He did not see her immediately. Joey and Robert stood beside her. She had stopped moving and she held them back.

She needed to freeze the moment in her mind. There he sat at a round table covered with a crisp, checkered tablecloth. On his face was a two- or three-day sprout of beard. He wore a frayed white-on-white shirt with the collar unbuttoned. Beside him sat Vinnie, the Prune. Benjy took his seat beside him at the table. He did not look up. He was busy concentrating on pouring Chianti into their glasses.

At that moment she saw the Canary, his bovine bulk swathed in an apron as he moved across the room precariously carrying a large platter of antipasto. The men looked up and watched him. He moved with great care. When he reached the table with the platter intact, her father patted him on the arm.

"You did good, Carmine," she heard her father say.

Across the table from the Padre sat little Angelo Petinno, the Pencil. There were scraps of paper in front of him and a pencil in his hand.